ALL THAT WAS

TANYA E WILLIAMS

RIPPLING EFFECTS

For Kari Leigh
"Click"

CHAPTER 1

*S*unday, February 8, 2015
Emily

The warm air of the home envelops Emily in a long overdue embrace as she and her boyfriend step inside. The appealing aromas coming from the kitchen lift the corners of her mouth as she slides her coat from her shoulders. Inhaling deeply, her stomach growls in anticipation. Anxious or hungry? Emily contemplates the question for a fleeting moment as she places a hand over her stomach to quell the gurgling sound. An unsettling feeling has followed her since she flipped the calendar to February eight days ago.

"We're here," Emily calls out, looping her purse strap over the bannister railing.

"In the kitchen," Veronica calls back over the hum of the oven fan. "Dinner is almost ready."

Ryan, Emily's boyfriend of two years, is a short step

TANYA E WILLIAMS

behind her as they enter the recently renovated, farmhouse-style kitchen. A knowing glance over her shoulder tussles her brunette waves while confirming Ryan's delight as the sight of Sunday dinner comes into view. He licks his lips as he watches Veronica pull an extra-large casserole dish of bubbling lasagna from the wall oven.

"Smells good." Ryan steps forward to close the oven door behind Veronica before placing a peck on her cheek.

"I know it is your favorite." Veronica beams at Ryan as she fans the air with her oven mitt then turns her attention toward Emily. "Hey, Em. It's good to see you."

Veronica steps forward and folds Emily into a warm embrace, both of them leaning into one another momentarily before Emily grabs the salad tongs and begins tossing the greens in Caesar dressing.

"Anything I can do?" Ryan asks, stepping out of the way. Veronica and Emily move about the kitchen, both of them in time with the familiar dance of preparing a meal together.

"Hey, Ryan." Colin enters the room, a bottle of red wine in one hand. Though his button-down collared shirt is missing its weekday jacket and tie tonight, Colin's erect posture oozes the confidence of a man at ease in front of a crowded courtroom. His athletic build tells tales about his age, and only his broad smile causing crinkles near the edges of his eyes gives away his fifty years of life experience.

Ryan extends his hand for a friendly shake before Colin crosses the hardwood floor, wrapping Emily in a fierce hug. "Hey, kiddo. How are you doing?"

Emily's face lights up as she returns his hug.

"Em, you've got the salad?" Veronica pivots, surveying the granite kitchen island. The shimmering silk of her navy blouse ripples as she moves, its hem tucked into her dark skinny jeans. "Okay, I think we are all set. Let's eat."

2

The four of them settle into the dining-room chairs. The new plush chairs add an elegant contrast to the antique dining table, Emily thinks as she takes her place beside Ryan. Veronica, with the seasoned hand of a woman who entertains frequently, dishes lasagna onto the men's plates while Emily reaches for a piece of crusty garlic bread before filling her own plate with the cheesy casserole.

Fork in hand, Emily chases a rogue noodle around her plate. She fills the air with chatter about her upcoming work project. "Mr. Holt says the archives haven't been touched in decades. He says he'd be amazed if I am able to make heads or tails of them by the end of the summer."

From across the table, Colin's gray eyes beam at Emily as she pauses to take a bite of bread. "I'm sure you are just the person for the job, Em."

"I hope so. I know it will be an insane amount of work, but I am really looking forward to the challenge. I've never worked with church records before, and I certainly don't have any experience with documents as old as these. I guess I always imagined records of this age would be displayed behind glass, safely under lock and key in a library or a museum. I definitely didn't think they would be sitting in a basement storage room, gathering dust." Emily's eyes search the ceiling as she thinks over the research projects she undertook as a law student at the University of Washington, trying to ascertain the most historical items she's studied.

Veronica, seizing the lull in the conversation, places her knife and fork on either side of her plate. She takes a deep breath as she sweeps her thick ebony hair over one shoulder, any silver strands covered by frequent salon visits. "Emily, I was thinking of heading over to the cemetery next week. Flowers are always a nice addition when the sky is so dreary, and with the anniversary coming up, I thought—"

Emily's shoulders stiffen slightly.

"I wondered." Veronica tries again, a hesitation in her delivery. "Well, I thought you might like to join me. I could pick you up, make a day of it. Grab some lunch in one of those trendy cafes." Veronica's eyes shift quickly toward Colin, who is seated beside her, before settling once more on Emily. "We can go whichever day fits best with your schedule. I know how busy you are. Maybe Ryan would like to join us. I don't think he has ever visited the grave sites. Have you, Ryan?" Veronica inclines her head toward Ryan as he looks up, a panicked expression settling over his boyish features.

Looking somewhere between a deer caught in the headlights and an unsuspecting party guest who has stumbled into the middle of an awkward conversation, a subtle shake of his head is Ryan's only response. Busying himself while dropping his eyes away from Veronica's, he scoops a heaping forkful of lasagna into his mouth and begins to chew slowly.

Clearing her throat, Emily buys herself some time to tuck her reaction safely beneath the surface, out of sight from those around her. Her mind whirs, desperate to switch gears in the conversation, and she kicks herself. She'd believed she could avoid this type of conversation tonight, but that had been wishful thinking. She considers the topic of the drab Seattle winter but shakes her head almost imperceptibly. The thought of such mundane conversation with those whose lives are deeply tangled with her own is disappointing at best. She hunts for words suitable to satisfy the questions behind the inquiring eyes of the couple across from her.

Colin bridges the gap with a disarming smile. "I can't believe how fast the time has gone. Seems like only yesterday we were celebrating you passing the bar exam."

Meeting his eyes, relief spreads across her face. Grateful for the life raft, Emily forces a smile. "The months are moving fast, but then again I don't mind if winter speeds by us." She cringes as the words leave her lips. *Couldn't leave the weather out of it*, she scolds herself. They deserve more from her, and her inability to give them more only adds to her discomfort.

Taking a bite of lasagna, Colin nods in agreement. The gray peppered about his temples shimmers in the light of the dining room as his head bobs up and down. "We are in the thick of it now. I've always found February challenges my love for this city. The rain and dark. The sleet and wind." He glances toward Veronica, an amused expression softening his features. "You'd think we would wise up and plan a sunny vacation for this time of year."

"Where would you go?" Emily jumps at the opportunity to steer the conversation away from the cemetery, herself, and Seattle in February.

"The white-sand beaches of the Caribbean seem to call out to me when the gray sky dips low enough to kiss the ground." Colin swirls his glass of red wine before taking a thoughtful sip.

"That sounds lovely." Emily stabs a piece of lasagna with her fork.

"I could certainly get on board with a trip to the Caribbean." Ryan adds, raising his own wine glass to Colin's in a toast.

"You should know." Veronica's words are soft, but her message is straight as an arrow. "We would never leave Seattle in February, Em. Just in case." The pause sends a shiver of nervousness down the length of Emily's spine. "Just in case you needed us. You know?"

Emily shifts in her seat. Sipping from her water glass, Emily averts her eyes. Unable to respond verbally, she only nods in acknowledgement of Veronica's concern.

"Your parents would be so proud of you." Colin's words,

though ushered in a demure and reminiscent tone, assault her as if they've been fired out of a cannon.

With another subtle movement of her head, Emily ignores the silence that has settled at the dinner table like an uninvited guest. She turns her attention back toward her dinner plate.

Emily's overwhelming work schedule has meant missing Sunday dinner with Colin and Veronica since Christmas. She hates that her absence may have made her appear unappreciative. Colin and Veronica became her legal guardians after her parents' accident left her orphaned and alone a decade ago. Guilt creeps up the back of Emily's neck, spreading like a heat rash, yet her need to remain stoic wins out over a polite response.

Ever since the ball dropped on 2015, though she has kept her disquiet to herself, Emily's trepidation over something she is unable to put her finger on has been nudging her from the furthest corner of her mind.

The tenth anniversary of her parents' death is like a beacon, blinking with more intensity as the calendar draws near to that fateful February day. Entirely ignoring the significance of the month seemed achievable, at least within the confines of her mind. But being here with Colin and Veronica, the thought of ignoring the anniversary feels inappropriate and nearly impossible.

Suspecting the root of her wariness has more to do with shadows from the past, Emily has done what she always has. She squared her shoulders and plowed ahead. Moving forward is the only path worthy of her time and attention. This mantra has guided her thoughts and her actions for years. But her mantra has been required more often these past few weeks, and the strength it so readily provided has waned.

Feeling Veronica's eyes watching her, Emily lifts her head,

pasting what she hopes is a pleasant and convincing smile upon her face. "Thanks again for having us. This is delicious." Scooping another forkful of lasagna into her mouth, Emily smiles again before reaching for her glass of water, shifting her gaze away from Veronica's penetrating brown eyes.

"We would love to see you more often, Em." Veronica pauses as her long lashes blink, matching the cadence of her words, handed out with cautious sincerity. "This is your home. You are always welcome here." Veronica's shoulders rise and fall in what Emily interprets as resignation. "You don't even need to call ahead. You can pop over anytime you like." Veronica smiles as Colin places his hand over hers and they exchange a look.

Perhaps sensing the rising tension, Colin clears his throat and returns his attention to his own plate. "So, Emily, back to your first research assignment as a lawyer."

The conversation shifts and Emily breathes a sigh of relief as the familiar smile plays about Colin's lips. "I remember those days." A soft chuckle vibrates deep within his throat. "First-year lawyers, us old servants of the court know all too well. The grunt workers of every firm, am I right?"

Emily inclines her head in agreement, but a soft shrug of her shoulders tells him she isn't worried about the workload.

"Anyway, which church basement will you be lurking in for the next several months?" Colin teases Emily about her upcoming project.

"First Church." Emily sips from her water glass, having nearly finished her lasagna. "On Marion and Fifth." Her tone is light and conversational once more, relieved to have found herself on safer ground with the return to work-related conversation.

Colin leans back against the solid frame of his dining

room chair with a light thud. "Really?" His smile broadens as his eyes squint, a question seemingly burning behind them. His fork hovers in midair, its trajectory lost between his mouth and the dinner plate. "Your parents married there. In June 1983. I was the best man. Did you remember that?"

Emily inhales sharply at the mention of her parents. She hadn't known about their connection to the church in which, until this moment, she was excited about beginning work. Colin's question sucks the air from the room like a high-powered vacuum. Her inability to speak of her parents or their deaths grips her. Emily's heart feels as if it has become lodged in her throat, blocking both her breathing and her voice. The realization of what this new information will mean for her shakes the resolve she barely had a grasp on. Out of reflex she stands, wrenching herself from the table. A glass topples, and cutlery clatters against a plate. Colin's and Veronica's faces deflate as Emily excuses herself to seek refuge in the bathroom down the hall.

"Em, please." Ryan's plea is laced in a whisper as she bolts from the room, determination to control her emotions fueling her steps.

Several minutes pass as Emily hides away from what is surely to be an uncomfortable conversation in the dining room. After pacing about the compact room, she turns on both the hot and cold taps, opening them to full force. The sound of the water drowns out the frantic whispers coming from the three remaining in the dining room in addition to the silent but distraught words pushing from inside her throbbing brain.

Splashing her face with water, Emily peers into the large oval mirror. Her cheeks are mottling pink and pale, though no tears have dared to disobey her and fall. "Crying is of little use," she reminds herself in a controlled whisper. She stares at her reflection, challenging her weakened state of mind with narrowed eyes and a determined expression. She will win this emotional battle, just as she has all the others.

Calming herself with a few deep breaths, Emily grasps for a shred of dignity. She pats her cheeks with both palms, encouraging her composure to reinstate itself. With a last look in the mirror, she tucks her hair neatly behind her ears, ready to face Colin, Veronica, and the rest of Sunday dinner. Unlocking the bathroom door, Emily steps into the hall to find Veronica leaning against the wall, an anxious expression painted across her face.

"Colin didn't mean to upset you. Neither did I for that matter." Veronica bursts forward. Her voice is quiet and soothing despite the nervous twitching of her arms. Emily assumes she wants nothing more than to reach out and embrace her in a firm hug.

"It's fine. I'm fine." Emily's voice, clipped and guarded, rushes from her lips.

"If you were fine, as you say you are, you wouldn't run out of the room every time someone mentions your mom and dad." Veronica takes a tentative step forward.

Emily stiffens, her feigned composure dissolving like sugar in water.

"The offer is still open." Veronica inclines her head, trying to draw Emily's eyes upward. "Colin and I are happy to cover the cost of counseling. It's been ten years, Emily. Don't you think it is time?"

"There is nothing I can do to bring them back." Emily's voice quavers, contradicting the strength of her words.

Veronica nods. "True. But does their death have to be a life sentence for you?" Veronica's words are gentle, but her point hits home. "Don't you think the time has come, Em? It's okay for you to be happy, you know." Veronica steps forward, her arms reaching to wrap Emily in an embrace.

Emily steps back, her movements stiff and controlled. "Happy?" She scoffs. "You can't possibly understand." Throwing her hands in the air, Emily moves past Veronica, brushing against her shoulders in the narrow hallway. Emily pivots in an abrupt movement. "Don't you get it? There is no happily ever after. Not for me at least. Not anymore."

"Em, please." Veronica's voice bounces off the walls, rising with her mounting frustration.

Colin and Ryan step into the hallway from the dining room. Seeing Ryan firmly holding his cloth napkin, Emily lets out a long sigh. "Let's just finish dinner. Okay?"

"We aren't done discussing this, Emily. You can't go through the rest of your life pretending everything is fine. You had parents, Em. And they loved you."

"Thank you for pointing out the obvious, Veronica." Emily's voice trembles, evidence of the thoughts held tightly in her clenched fists. "I am well aware of everything I had."

"I can only imagine how hard this is for you. But you are not alone, Em. You have us. You have Colin and me." Veronica looks past Emily with a weak smile. "And Ryan. We can help you. We want to help you. You just have to open the door a little and let us in."

Emily squares her shoulders and raises an eyebrow. A rare condescending demeanor takes over her usually polite features. "What exactly do you think I need help with? Haven't I gotten a degree? Haven't I managed to live on my own, afford my own life, start my own career?"

Not waiting for an answer, Emily tugs her winter coat from the hall closet before shooting Ryan a pointed time-to-go look. Shoving her feet into her low-heeled boots, Emily grabs her purse off the railing and opens the front door. "I think I am doing pretty well actually. I mean no disrespect, to either of you." Emily inclines her head in Veronica and then Colin's direction. "But, I think I've got it covered. Thank you for dinner." Emily steps out the door and walks away, leaving Ryan to utter a flurry of apologies as he hurries to slide on his own jacket and shoes before following her out the door.

CHAPTER 2

*S*unday, February 15, 2015
Emily

A week later, Emily is sitting in a cozy corner of Murph's bar and restaurant, still thinking about the disastrous dinner at Colin and Veronica's while she waits for Ryan to arrive. Though she spoke with Colin the following day, in an attempt to calm the air between them, she can't help but revisit his announcement about her parents. They married in the church where she is beginning work first thing tomorrow morning. Rattled by the revelation, Emily feels like she's lost at sea with the unforgiving rains of a hurricane tossing her about.

"Hey, you." Ryan's boundless energy and ever-present smile pulls her from her worrisome thoughts. He hangs his rain-soaked jacket on the hook beside the table and slides into the booth, beside her. Leaning over, he pecks her cheek and squeezes her hand before flipping through the bar's booklet-sized menu of drinks and appetizers.

"Are you eating?" A smile tugs on Emily's lips. "I thought you were going to your mom's for lunch."

Ryan shrugs, his eyes widening at a photo of a towering plate of onion rings. "I can always eat." Gesturing toward the photo, Ryan reads out loud. *"Famous onion rings.* Now who could pass those up?" He closes the menu, clearly pleased with his selection.

After ordering, they sip wine while waiting for the food to arrive. Cautiously, Ryan broaches the subject on Emily's mind. "Have you talked to Colin or Veronica today?"

"Was I supposed to?" Emily sips her wine and lets her eyes wander around the bar, purposely avoiding Ryan's gaze.

"Em, come on. You said you would call them later in the week. You can't get much later than Sunday afternoon. Avoiding them won't solve anything, you know."

Emily sighs. "I'd really rather not. I talked to Colin earlier in the week and he seemed fine. Besides, I have enough to think about. I'm starting the project at the church tomorrow."

The food arrives and Emily toys with her salad. Plucking a cherry tomato from beneath a layer of iceberg lettuce, she fiddles with the white cloth napkin as she pops the ripened morsel into her mouth and bites down. Her lips pucker, one hand going to her mouth, while the other presses against her stomach. Her body's response to the burst of acidity forced upon her already-churning digestive system lingers for a few moments before she pushes away the side plate. Emily grasps her glass of pinot gris with both hands, trying to hide the slight tremble in her fingers.

"It's okay to be nervous, Em. New projects can be exciting, but they also have a mountain of unknowns attached to them." Ryan grasps her hand and squeezes reassurance into her fingers.

While Ryan digs into his plate of perfectly browned onion

rings, Emily scrutinizes her emotions. Her nervousness about the church project was well under control until Colin shed light on her parents' connection to the place. The anxiety lying just beneath her ribcage has grown this week, transforming into something much more than first-day jitters. Colin didn't mean any harm, Emily is certain. The man is too good-hearted to consider hurting another, even by accident. With Emily, though, the little girl of his deceased best friend, Colin's desire to cause no ill is magnified by a thousand. She knows that he and Veronica love her like she is their own. After a torrential rainstorm caused an out of control vehicle to collide with her parents' car, sending them careening over an embankment, Colin and Veronica took her in without hesitation.

Emily watches Ryan lick his fingers as he finishes the last onion ring. She swirls the wine in her glass, deciding Colin likely intended his remark to be a jovial addition to the conversation. Perhaps he meant it as a nugget for her to treasure, a fond memory of her parents' lives.

Wiping his hands on a napkin before draining the wine from his glass, Ryan tugs on Emily's sleeve and pulls her from her thoughts. "I better get going." He slides out from the plush booth and stands. "I still think you should call Colin tonight. Like I told you on the way home last week, we should have stayed and finished the conversation. Running away seldom solves anything, Em."

"And like I told you, I'm not running away. I am simply tired of rehashing the same things we've been talking about for ten years." Emily's posture straightens as she makes her point.

"Well, I guess that is where you and Colin differ. According to him, you haven't been talking about anything. It has been a one-sided conversation, Em, and they are worried about you."

Emily checks the time on her phone. "Don't you have to go? You know how hard your mom works to get lunch on the table for everyone."

Ryan leans across the table and brushes Emily's lips with his own. "Don't think I didn't notice how you changed the subject." He shakes his head lightly. "See you tomorrow night?"

"See you tomorrow night."

Emily offers him a little wave when he smiles back at her from the restaurant's door. She shakes away the memory of their hasty departure and Ryan's disgruntled words last Sunday.

Spreading *The Seattle Times* across the table, Emily slides her wineglass to the side. She turns pages, making her way to the middle of the paper.

While she is scanning the pages, activity beyond the window of Murph's draws Emily's attention. Aware of her own still slightly damp skin, she watches the downpour sloshing beyond the pane. All week, her thoughts have been repeatedly tugged back to her parents' connection to the church, and Emily feels far from settled.

A nervous hand runs through her rain-misted brunette waves as she attempts to pull herself together. Returning her grasp to the glass, she takes a gulp of wine and feels it rush down her throat. The chilled liquid elicits a full-body shiver. Setting the wineglass on the polished mahogany table, Emily glances up as a waitress hurries by. She considers asking for something warmer than her wine, perhaps something stronger. Before Emily can utter her request, the waitress disappears into the hall and behind the swinging doors that lead to the kitchen.

Less than an hour ago, Emily sequestered herself into the plush, velvety green corner booth at the back of Murph's. With another glance out the window, she contemplates the drab weather and how it mirrors her own unsettled mood. She distracts her thoughts by watching the wet feet of hurried Seattleites as they rush by the half window, dodging raindrops and each other this dark, drizzling, and altogether unpleasant afternoon.

The unusual vantage point from the almost below-ground restaurant windows is prevalent throughout Seattle's downtown historic buildings. Given the city's steeply sloped streets and the decision to build on top of the existing footprint after the Great Fire of 1889, what began as the city's original street-level business district now sits several feet below the modern sidewalks. Thus, only feet and the occasional glimpse of a passing canine nose are visible beyond the windows of Emily's secluded table in the farthest reaches of the historic and landmark-protected building.

The reserved table, along with any tab accumulated at it, belongs to Patterson and Holt, a large but family-friendly law firm. Emily signed on as a result of the firm's persistent headhunting during her final semester of law school last year. The table at Murph's is a company perk that, given the restaurant's proximity to the church, Emily is likely to use often.

Glancing around the bar, Emily takes in the upscale décor that perfectly matches the above-average address. With a secluded restaurant on one side and the bar situated street side, Murph's bustles with activity on this rainy Sunday afternoon. An upgrade from her usual burger and beer joint during law school, Murph's is refined, Emily decides as her eyes wash over the dark wood tables, the early 1900s banker-style lighting, and the glass shelves of liquor with labels a first-year lawyer wouldn't consider ordering due to the price tag that accompanies them.

Emily came to Murph's hoping to calm her nerves before she begins her position at the church tomorrow. So far, a sense of calm has been elusive. All she has to show for an afternoon spent sipping wine in a corner booth is a dull ache in her overthinking brain.

"It's Emily, isn't it?" A tall, slender, blond server brushes up beside the booth. "Your server is on her break. I can help you with anything you need."

"Hi, yes. I'm Emily. I'm sorry, do we know each other?"

"We haven't met before, but I added your name to the table last week. Between you and me, yours and Mr. Holt's are the only names on the list. I was eager to meet the mysterious Emily who is worthy of such an honor." The waitress hides a giggle behind her hand. "Mr. Holt mentioned I could expect to see you soon. I'm Allison, and I hear we will be seeing a lot of each other. Mr. Holt tells me you are working on the case for the church. Starting tomorrow, I think he said."

Emily places both palms against her swirling midsection. "Yes. They have tasked me with archiving their collection."

"No Supreme Court appearances for you, then?" Allison shifts a tray in her hands and leans over the table toward the open newspaper. "I read the article on my break. Tough spot for sure. I imagine you aren't allowed to have an opinion on the matter, but it would be hard to see that beautiful building torn down."

"Well in all honesty, my opinion is the same as our client's. They own the land and building after all." Emily pauses a moment to measure her thoughts. "Beautiful or not, I do not believe the city is in the right to force an owner of a privately owned property into the regulations of a landmark building. Especially given that the designation comes with a hefty price tag for historical upkeep, not to mention the limitations that landmark status places on renovations. The church might not be able to serve the changing needs of its congregation if they are forced into the historic status." As the words leave Emily's lips, it occurs to her that if not for this lawsuit, she would never have known about her parents' ties to the church. If only she could go back in time and choose a different law firm to sign on with, a firm with no connection to the case currently sitting with the Supreme Court of Washington State. *If only.*

"I can see that side too." Allison lowers her voice another octave. "Is the salad okay, Emily? It doesn't look like you've touched it."

Emily offers a polite smile. Politeness was the cornerstone of her upbringing, and some habits stay with you, even after the teachers have departed. "I'm just not hungry, I guess."

"Rainy weather makes me think soup is an excellent idea." Allison nods toward the rain-soaked windowpane. Her blond ponytail swings side to side. It's tied back with a thin black ribbon matching her formal black-and-white uniform, crisp apron, and starched bow tie. "Roasted tomato with parmesan croutons is on the menu. Are you sure you don't want to try it?"

Emily shakes her head swiftly and decisively, feeling the bile from the recently consumed tomato racing to rise. "Another glass of wine though. That would be great." A tight-lipped smile stretches across her lips before she drains the glass, begging the churning in her stomach to release its grip.

"Look at you. You certainly know how to spend a rainy Sunday afternoon." Allison winks with a playful smile before clearing Emily's salad plate and turning on her heel toward the kitchen. Glancing back over her shoulder, she gives Emily a knowing look. "How about some soda crackers to go with that wine?" Emily nods, feeling a tinge of embarrassment at being found out by the friendly waitress, who seems to recognize nervous energy. With a swing in her step, Allison disappears into the hallway that leads toward the kitchen doors.

Emily turns her attention back to the newspaper, reading one reporter's opinion on the case that has spanned the better part of two decades and now resides on the docket of the Supreme Court of Washington State. With Emily having read the case's brief several times over, the article offers no new information, save for the reporter's opinion of the Friends of the First Church. The community organization has come together to persuade city hall that the church must remain, not always considering what the owners of the church can afford.

Emily's gaze settles on the rain-beaten window. The smooth jazz playing in the background soothes the sharp corners of her analytical mind, and her vision softens, blurring the raindrops on the glass. The wine works its magic, warming her through. She reclines deeper into the plush green cushion with a soft sigh. The hushed environment of Murph's takes the edge off the day, along with her worries about what tomorrow may hold.

Emily is sinking further into a state of relaxation when the connection between her parents and the church sneaks into her periphery. Without warning, a tear escapes and trickles down her cheek. She has allowed herself to be lulled across a dangerous line. Letting her guard down is far from acceptable. Blinking her eyes in frustration, she attempts to hold back the waterfall that, after years of being dammed up, is determined to escape. Emily curses under her breath at this sudden lack of control. Not a single emotionally charged tear has left her eyes in years, a feat Emily remains intent to uphold. *How could I have let myself be blindsided by these emotions?* Arguments filter through her mind. She takes a deep breath and tries to allow space for a sliver of grace to find her. But disdain pushes past, an overbearing warden that refuses to back down.

Grabbing her rain jacket strewn across the curved seat, Emily searches for the opening to her jacket pocket and pulls out her phone. Turning over the phone to illuminate the screen, she places it on the table, willing a message from Ryan to appear. No message, no voicemail. Shaking her head, Emily realizes too late that she should have gone with Ryan to his family gathering, rather than feigning a desire to prepare for the week ahead. He may not be aware, given Emily's strong silence on all things emotional, but Ryan is the grounding force that keeps her distracted and happy. She doesn't let herself dwell too long on whether the distraction or the happiness is her true saving grace.

"Haven't enough years passed yet?" Emily asks herself, in a whisper fit for a frightened child. Until learning of the church and its significance in her parents' lives, she had succeeded in keeping her emotions in check. She certainly hasn't spent the past ten years distraught and wrung out by emotion, like she has been since learning where her parents were married.

A muffled squeak passes through her closed lips as a memory flits across her mind. She was sixteen years old. She was curled up on the sofa, reading a book for English class, when the doorbell rang. Emily drops her head into her hands as she remembers the two uniformed police officers standing in the entryway of their family home. "They only went out for dinner." She pleaded with the officers to understand, her ears and heart unwilling to comprehend the devastating news. Her parents were gone. Just like that. A car crash had, in an instant, turned her life upside down.

Everything Emily knew was wiped out, leaving nothing but barren landscape. Looking up, she glances around the crowded restaurant before wrapping her arms around herself, trying to still the trembling inside her. She yearns for her mother's hug with a desire so deep it could swallow her from the inside out. If only she had known that day would be the last, she would have held her mother tighter. She would have insisted her parents order dinner in. She would have tossed her book report aside and joined them for dinner out instead. So many ways she could have changed the outcome. Even after all these years, the things she should have done haunt her the most.

Wrapping her jacket around her shoulders, determined to pull together her unwilling emotions, Emily thinks about how things used to be. Even before that fateful day, she couldn't wait to grow up and be just like them, lawyers with a homey family law practice and lives full of grand adventures. Emily swipes at the tears now streaming down her cheeks as her mom's smile flashes through her memory. Her radiant smile could coax Emily into being brave if she was nervous, happy if she was feeling sad. Her smile was even strong enough to tease out a laugh at the corny jokes that only her mom thought were funny.

Until the nightmare of that dark evening, Emily believed there was good in the world around her. She believed all things were possible. After a childhood filled with princess films and fairy tales, believing wholeheartedly that dreams really did come true was natural. She had faith as big as mountains and enough love in her heart to power the entire downtown core of Seattle. But none of it was enough to bring them back.

On that fateful night, she lost not only her family, but the innocence of believing in happily ever after. That was the first time she became aware that nothing lasts forever.

Placing a wineglass on the table, Allison startles Emily from her thoughts. Allison's concerned eyes take in Emily's grief-stricken expression. "You okay, love?"

The sharp awareness of her surroundings snaps her back to the present. "Fine. Thank you." She whispers the words as she shoves her phone into her jacket pocket. "I'm not going to need that. Sorry for the trouble." Emily attempts to shuffle her body out of the booth, her eyes narrowed toward the door. The velvet cushion tugs at Emily's skirt, holding it hostage as she tries to break free. Wrapping her raincoat around her with flailing arms, Emily offers another feeble apology and dashes out the door, under the darkened and rain-heavy sky.

CHAPTER 3

M onday, February 16, 2015
Emily

With a stoic expression, Emily climbs the steps toward the church's oversized wooden front door. Pulling on the handle, she glances behind her, taking in the tall, glass-faced office towers erected all around the stately historic church building. The Rainier Club, positioned behind the church's domed sanctuary, is the only building of similar height and age remaining in the few blocks that surround the church.

A hush greets Emily as she steps into the church's front lobby, the narthex, she's been told in the briefing notes that accompanied an interior map of the building, provided by Mr. Holt. The scent of old books mixed with long-extinguished candles descends upon her. The familiar aroma is a comfort to her. She could spend countless hours in a library, museum, or antique bookstore. Her love of history and of books in general is the reason she was excited to learn about the archival project.

A sigh leaves her pursed lips. Now, though, she can't seem to separate the task before her from the awareness that her parents, too, had a place in this building. Perhaps it would be easier for her if the building's fate were already decided and the need to organize the archives didn't exist. Emily pushes down the weight of the troublesome thought, feeling her worry drop like a stone into her abdomen. She busies her mind by letting her eyes roam the walls, the ceiling, and the polished wood banister that encases the wide and intricately crafted staircase to the upper floors.

"Ah, Ms. Reed. There you are," says Mrs. Peters, the church administrator Emily met a few weeks back at the downtown offices of Patterson and Holt. Mrs. Peters, dressed in a matching plaid patterned tweed skirt and jacket reminiscent of the 1950s era, toddles down the stairs, a square purse with a short stiff strap tucked into the crook of her left elbow. Her right hand caresses the banister, guiding and supporting her steps.

"Hello, Mrs. Peters. It is nice to see you again." Emily steps forward to shake the woman's hand as she reaches the bottom of the staircase.

"Are you ready to get started, dear?" Mrs. Peters' artificially colored pink lips smile back at her with encouragement.

"Absolutely." Emily nods convincingly, dispelling any indication that she is anything but ready. Then she steps aside so the church woman can show her the way.

Mrs. Peters rattles on about the state of the archives as the two women locate a far less opulent set of stairs and begin the downward path toward the storage room. The temperature drops with each step, and Emily contemplates whether she has worn a warm enough sweater under her winter jacket.

"Well, this is it." Mrs. Peters' smile fades and a nervous expression takes its place. The women stand on a small patch of aging linoleum before a closed door. "They told you. The room isn't . . ." Mrs. Peters' words fall short of making a complete sentence. She shrugs and says, "Well, I suppose you should see it for yourself." She pushes open the storage room door with a nudge of her hip and reaches for the light switch. A cool whoosh of air rushes toward them, accompanied by the dank smell of a musty and earthen basement room.

Emily's eyes roam over the debris as the dim light shudders to life. Boxes upon boxes, some in varying stages of disintegration and decay, lay scattered about the room, held hostage by pieces of old furniture and office cabinets.

"It is indeed a mess, Ms. Reed." Mrs. Peters apologetically places a hand on Emily's arm. "I am sorry to say so."

Emily steps farther into the room, her eyes adjusting to the muted light. "Well, you did say they have used it as a storage room." With little space to move about, she considers where she might begin the task. "What would you like me to do with the items that are not being archived?" Emily glances at a row of dated and somewhat beaten up filing cabinets.

"We have decided to remove everything that no longer serves the space. I've spoken to our janitor, and he has suggested you pile the unnecessary items by the door. He will take care of removing them." Mrs. Peters looks behind her, surveying the limited space near the door. "I imagine this will take some time." The church lady sighs before adding, "Perhaps you could make a separate pile of any items you are unsure of? That way we can go through them before they are tossed."

"Of course. I would hate to see something of value

discarded." Emily gently drops her shoulder bag to the concrete floor and rests her hands on her hips. "Well, I have my work cut out for me. I suppose I had better get started."

"Then I will leave you be, dear." Mrs. Peters turns back toward the door. "If you have any questions at all, don't hesitate to let me know. My office is on the top floor. There is a water cooler in the hall on the floor above the main entrance, if you need it."

"Thank you." Emily offers a sincere smile intended to hide her bubbling nerves. A step creaks slightly beneath the old lady's weight as she heads back up the stairs to a warmer and certainly more hospitable room in the old building.

Emily scans the room, a sense of dread filling the space. The earthy smell of the basement room, along with the clutter held captive within its walls, reminds her of a weekend clean-up project initiated by her dad when she was ten years old. The garage attached to her childhood home was, as far she could tell, used as a great big box for things without permanent homes. Emily recalls how the garage and its cast-aside contents intimidated her. Her infrequent trips to the musty space were lightning quick and riddled with goosebumps, as imagined threats lurked in every shadowy corner. Even after the garage had been organized and Dad had paid her the two dollars he'd promised, Emily continued to avoid the space for the remaining six years she lived in the house.

The memory does little to spur her on, and an hour later, Emily finds herself standing near the middle of the overwhelming room, not a single item sorted or relocated. She wiggled her way through small gaps in the clutter, surveying the room and its hidden treasures with a wary eye as she moved. From her new vantage point, she examines the chaos, determined to locate the best place to begin.

"When in doubt, start at the beginning." An older gentleman stands in the doorway of the dusty basement room, startling her with his words. He is dressed in a crisp white clergy collar, a dark blue suit jacket, and dress pants.

"If I didn't know better, I'd say a bomb went off in here," Emily replies concealing her disquiet as she turns to greet the friendly face. The man appears jubilant yet reserved.

"Well, there was the earthquake of 2001. Closed the building down for six months, it did." He moves toward a pile of beams stacked in disarray on the floor. Emily follows him with her eyes before grabbing her phone from her jeans pocket and snapping a few photos of the clutter from her new vantage point. She kneels down for a better angle of the room's chaos.

"It is very nice to meet you, Emily. I am Pastor Michael."

Emily stands from her crouched position. "It is nice to meet you, Pastor Michael."

Pastor Michael stands with his hands clasped behind his back, his expression thoughtful. "Ah, it will be a sad day when this building is no more. I suppose change is one of the constants and time does go by." Catching Emily's eye, he continues, "Be sure to visit the sanctuary while you are here, Emily. This building has stories to share and becoming familiar with the sanctuary will give you a broader view of what you find within these boxes." Pastor Michael nods with certainty. "I won't keep you. I only wished to introduce myself and make myself available to you should you need anything at all."

"Thank you. That is very kind." Emily looks over the room once more while Pastor Michael strolls leisurely toward the door. "I suppose there is no time like the present." Emily glances over her shoulder while pushing up her sleeves, bolstered by the visit of the kind gentleman. She casts him a save-me-if-I-fall-in kind of look as Pastor Michael reaches the door's threshold. Emily balances on one foot and steps carefully into a small space surrounded by broken furniture, boxes, and desk lamps with tangled cords.

Turning in a complete circle from her new location, Emily shakes her head at the piles of disorganized debris, but she is grateful for the distraction the mess provides from her mind's whirring. She is even more thankful that her boss, Mr. Holt, suggested she wear jeans and a sweatshirt. Mounds of papers lay scattered on tabletops, chairs, and even the unfinished cement floor. A bookshelf, overflowing with photo albums and registries, leans at a precarious angle against a cement brick wall. At first glance, the room appears to be for anything that is no longer of use. *Junk* is Emily's first impression as her eye darts about the room, with each pile competing for attention.

Spotting a well-worn but solid-looking desk among the discarded furniture, Emily sets her sights on the useful piece of furniture. She busies herself with the all-consuming, physically demanding task as she digs in, knowing she will need a flat surface to examine each artifact. Nudging all memories of her parents to the back corner of her mind, she launches into action, dragging and pushing boxes out of the way, creating a path to the desk. Emily is spurred on a few hours later when she comes across a 1920s office chair, its wheels still in working order. Loading the chair with anything irrelevant to her archiving quest, she repeatedly rolls it as far out of her way and closest to the door as possible, creating a fresh pile of what she considers rubbish for the janitor to remove.

At half past one, Emily stands to stretch her back and examines her progress. A path wide enough for a quick escape, should she need one, reaches from the back concrete wall all the way to the door. Once the janitor has taken the rubbish, she will be able to move about the room without fear of inadvertently knocking something over. Rolling her newly ordained transport chair into the center of the cleared path, Emily grabs her sandwich and apple from her bag by the door and sits with a thud onto the hard wooden seat. She is covered in dust, with wisps of hair that escaped her ponytail sticking up at odd angles around her face. Emily wipes her hands on her jeans before biting into her sandwich with a sigh.

After a well-deserved break and a trip to the water cooler to refill her bottle, Emily is back in the basement, ready to dive past the debris and into the records she came here to organize. A shiver runs the length of her spine as she reenters the chilly room. Clearing off the top of the neglected desk, Emily discovers the wobble that surely caused the desk's relocation to the bowels of the building. She retrieves a pad of yellow sticky notes from the few supplies she brought from the office. Placing the pad under one of the desk's legs steadies the beast, much to her delight.

Several hours later, with the desk relocated to a better position within the room, Emily hoists her first box onto the wooden office chair and rolls it down the path, toward her new work space. Pleased with her ingenuity and the innovative mode of box transportation, she grabs a notebook and pen from her bag and prepares to make notes of her research findings.

Pushing aside the daunting task of having to transcribe all of her notes from paper into an organized electronic format for the church's final records, Emily lifts the lid off the box. Peering inside, she takes a deep breath before pulling free an upside-down wooden picture frame. Turning the frame right side up, she expects to see a photograph. Instead, in the center of the matting, secured to the wooden backing of the delicately carved frame, is an American dime.

Emily squints at the framed dime. The 1907 date and

inscribed *UNITED STATES OF AMERICA* are visible, despite the insufficient overhead lighting of what may be the darkest room in the church. Rotating the frame in her hands, Emily searches for a stronger beam of light, while making a mental note to bring a better light source tomorrow.

Peering into the box again, Emily searches for information that might explain the dime. She reaches for a bundle of papers tied together with what appears to be decades old kitchen string. She unties the string and the papers come away, wrinkled, aged, and obviously well used. With care, Emily turns one page after another, by the third page realizing she is holding the building plans for a small home or some sort of multi-roomed structure. An hour or more passes as she immerses herself in the building's layout. Out loud, Emily counts twelve rooms lining a long hallway, all mirror images of one another and the approximate size of bedrooms. She imagines herself walking the floor plan. She flips pages back and forth, starting at the front door each time while walking her fingers around the building.

The plans show a large entryway that opens into an oversized sitting room with an equally oversized hearth, which for the era, would have been the space's primary heating source. The 1907 date is handwritten in the corner of each page, along with the name of the project. A kitchen is tucked behind a wall, with only a single door allowing access. The kitchen plans indicate two wood-burning stoves and an extensive open area, where Emily assumes one would place a large table.

The Cottage, printed with neat, slanted handwriting in the bottom right corner of each page, leads Emily to believe the drawings are not for a home. The building must have been intended to have guests, she speculates. And at least twelve at a time. Though interesting, the building plans show no connection to the framed ten-cent piece. Digging farther into the box, Emily lets out a slow breath while she contemplates whether she is on a wild goose chase. Perhaps only scraps of unrelated information fill the immense number of boxes yet to be examined. A shudder runs through her at the thought as an imagined picture of herself ten years from now still immersed in the ramshackle disorganization of the basement, drifts across her mind.

A leather-bound notebook rests on top of a handful of black-and-white photographs. Setting the notebook on the desk, Emily leafs through the photos. The first photograph shows about twenty-five women standing in front of a low-roofed building, the building barely visible behind them. On instinct, Emily flips the photograph over. Scrawled on the back in slanted handwriting is *The Fresh Air Cottage*. "So they are connected," Emily says to the empty room as she continues to examine each photograph one by one. One picture includes a small child leaning on a pair of old-fashioned crutches. Though his legs splay in unnatural directions, his face is lit up with a wide smile. His smile traverses the years between the past and the present, bringing a smile to Emily's own lips. Running her thumb across the boy's legs, a pang of sadness leaps from her heart. He was so young, the life ahead of him filled with challenges.

Placing the photographs on top of the drawings, Emily opens the notebook. Neatly printed on the lined paper is an itemized list of building supplies and a hand-drawn column to the right. Beside each nail, board, and can of paint is an amount, with a double-underlined running tally at the bottom of each page.

"I see you've found the box from the Children's Orthopedic Hospital." Pastor Michael's voice cuts across the room with a slight echo.

"Is that what this is? I wasn't sure." Emily holds up the notebook to show him her discovery.

"The story goes . . ." Pastor Michael takes a few steps into the room. "A woman named Mrs. Clise had watched a neighbor's child struggle with a debilitating condition that prevented him from joining in with the other children's play. Mrs. Clise was moved to improve the boy's life. She pledged to find and pay for a doctor to help the boy. However, she learned that although a procedure to correct the boy's condition existed, there was no facility or doctor in all the Pacific Northwest who could help the child."

With Emily's full attention on his story, Pastor Michael continues. "A determined woman she was. Mrs. Clise thought on the situation and then adjusted her vision. She called a gathering of influential ladies in the community, intending to convince them of the need for a children's hospital that could issue such healing treatments."

"So, they built a hospital? How wonderful of them to be so industrious and in an age when women didn't have the right to vote, much less to pursue such a large undertaking." Emily's female pride bursts through as she considers the challenges those women must have faced in bringing such a plan to their husbands. The husbands were surely the ones who decided where their money was spent in 1907.

"Ah, the right to vote. Well, that is a topic for another day, but you should know that Seattle women are strong and resourceful, not unlike you, my dear. They were voting all the way back in the late 1800s." Pastor Michael's impish smile fuels the questions flying about Emily's brain. But his hands, held out at waist height, bide her to hold her tongue.

"The first hospital was a few beds within the day's current Seattle General Hospital. The women of Seattle knitted and sewed, rummaged through their closets, and organized bake sales to raise funds for the children's orthopedic program. The program was a tremendous success. So much so that demand soon exceeded the allotted space at the general hospital. The women then set out with an alternative plan. They would build a twelve-bed cottage to service the needs of children both within and outside of Seattle."

"The Fresh Air Cottage." Emily nods in understanding.

"Yes. The Fresh Air Cottage. The guild of women raised two thousand, five hundred dollars and set plans for the new building. They encountered a problem though. No builder in the vicinity would build their dream cottage for the price they were prepared to pay."

Engrossed in Pastor Michael's story, Emily moves the box's lid from the chair and sits to listen with full concentration. "What did they do?"

"The women were coming to terms with making concessions on their design. Losing a hallway from the cottage wasn't the worst that could happen as long as the building could still do good in the community. However, Mrs. Maude B. Parsons would hear nothing of the sort. The women had raised the funds all on their own. They had decided on a building plan. They had acquired the land necessary to build the cottage. No, Mrs. Parsons would not allow any concession on the design of the cottage."

Emily leans forward, eager to hear the story unfold.

"Instead, Mrs. Parsons, who knew nothing of building herself, told the guild that she would build the cottage for the allotted funds and that, should the cost exceed the two thousand and five hundred dollars, she would personally make up the difference."

"She did?" Emily's eyes widen in response. She is both impressed and stunned by the tenacity of Seattle women in 1907.

"She did." Pastor Michael smiles mischievously. "They built the cottage precisely to the agreed upon design plans, with Mrs. Parsons at the helm as superintendent. Mrs. Parsons purchased every board and nail, and when she was done, the Fresh Air Cottage was complete, and she had ten cents left over."

Emily reaches excitedly for the frame sitting on the desk. "The dime. The framed dime." Laughing out loud, Emily clutches the frame to her chest. "That is amazing. She really did that?"

"They really did that," Pastor Michael says with a grin. "All things are possible if you are willing to alter your perception of a situation."

Emily admires the framed dime with fresh eyes. With a nod of his head, Pastor Michael turns to leave the room. Over his shoulder he says, "Take your time in here. There is much to discover. Never hurry, Emily. Never worry. All things in life work out how they are supposed to in the end."

Emily's head snaps up in recognition of the verse, a bite of nostalgia reverberates through her body like a lightning bolt straight to her heart. She is about to tell him that *Charlotte's Web* is one of her favorite childhood stories. Her mother used to read it to her whenever Emily was feeling overwhelmed by something, always quoting the well-known line, *Never hurry. Never worry.* But by the time she looks up, Pastor Michael has already left the room.

CHAPTER 4

*M*onday, February 16, 2015
Elizabet

The girl they call Emily arrived today, spending the entirety of an overly long day in the basement storage room. If I am being honest, I was a little put out by the activity taking place in the storage room. All these years, I have had the freedom to roam, tucking myself into corners only when necessary. But the storage room has been my haven, save for the sanctuary of course. The shadowy basement room is uninviting to most, which makes it a perfect place for me to visit my memories.

At first glance, I must admit the girl's tenacity did remind me a little of myself at her age. She is intelligent for sure, but also a little wary of the world around her. I could tell by the way her eyes moved around the room, inquisitively, taking in everything at once. I initially considered her wariness might be due to the less than welcoming quarters of that dingy old room. The mess took decades to acquire, after all. Curiosity about our new guest aside, I did enjoy watching her work. Perhaps observing her will become a new favorite pastime. Lord knows I have plenty of time to pass.

She couldn't help but stir up dust as she set about to right the room, and I surely can't blame her for that. But the memories she stirred up along with all the dust—those are a different matter altogether. The basement storage room has been the perfect spot for me to think during these past eighty years, not to mention the lifetime I enjoyed before them. It is quiet and seldom visited. And it is full of objects from years past, which bring me contentment and put me at ease. Being close to the past, lingering around our triumphs and even some of our challenges, brings me comfort when nothing else will.

She is an efficient taskmaster, that is for certain. She appeared to decide on a course of action and then began ticking things off an imaginary list. We could have used a girl like her back when Seattle was coming into its own. A girl with gumption, a hardy work ethic, and a desire to do good. Someone who isn't afraid to get her hands dirty.

I cast another glance around the large oval room, the pews lining up in rows offer the fluidity of the rounded walls a sense of order and stability. Having spent significant time concerning myself with Emily and the storage room, my patience is beginning to wear thin. I wait near the front corner of the sanctuary, the smooth curve of the walls wrapping around me like the wool suit jacket I wear buttoned high around my waist. "Where is Dorothea, anyway? She said she would meet me here. Said she had news of our dear sanctuary." In moments such as these, when the differences between us are as stark as black ink on white paper, I wonder how we became so dear to each other.

Shaking my head in disapproval of my friend's tardiness, I contemplate our opposing natures. Where she is voluptuous and round, I am narrow waisted with an erect spine and perfectly squared shoulders. Dorothea has a flamboyant style, with large, plumed hats, clattering costume jewelry, and dress lengths revealing her feet and ankles. I, on the other hand, wear a long dark skirt and suit jacket. My tall black boots and white lace gloves finish my ensemble, covering me almost entirely from head to toe. The flimsy, shimmering fabrics around Dorothea gather and float with each step, commanding the eye's attention, regardless of whether she intends to make a grand entrance.

My sturdy wool suit, complemented by a silk braid at its edges and a contrasting high-necked white silk blouse, is a sensible choice. Still, I am aware of my somewhat dowdy appearance whenever Dorothea is nearby. Our chosen clothing selections aside, a friendship such as ours is not what I would call naturally occurring. Really, our paths should never have crossed. We hail from two opposing circles of society. I daresay no one could have guessed we would become even remotely acquainted, much less lifelong friends. Dorothea's profession as the madame of Seattle's largest brothel simply did not fit with my life of social gatherings, gala events, and the goings on of the elite upper class.

Movement always helps to pass the time, so I begin to pace from one side of the sanctuary to the other. As I wait for my belated friend, I imagine the pipe organ a few feet in front of me is playing my favorite hymn. As I hear the imaginary music, I think back to my forty-sixth year. Forty-six wasn't my best year, but forty-seven was undeniably my most dreadful one.

If it were up to me, I would be forty-six forever. The memories of living without my dear Rupert resemble nightmares more than anything else. I was a fool for that man, and after he departed this world, I lost all hope, all happiness. Yes, forty-six was a much more pleasant year in my life.

I have no idea where Rupert has gone, and this troubles me greatly. In the years after his death, this is the place I felt his presence the strongest. In the sanctuary, with its rich colors and stained-glass windows, I was certain I could hear my Rupert speak to me. The space was the provider of comfort, the stiller of trembling hearts. Given that Rupert never resided in the mansion he built for us, I didn't expect to find him there at all. So it became routine to visit him here at the church instead. We said our vows here in 1910, the year the church was dedicated, and we bowed our heads together as a married couple each Sunday morning after that. That is why I remain here, I suppose. I wait, sometimes with patience and other times with such longing my heart feels as if it will break in two all over again.

Every Wednesday after Rupert's passing, my driver would hitch up the wagon and we would plod into town. Down the steep descent of Capitol Hill and around the plentiful and new-fashioned automobiles and their pesky traffic lights. Perhaps we were an eyesore to those who were so easily lured into the metal boxes with wheels, so-called progress at the heart of their desires. But for me, traveling in anything but a horse-drawn carriage was out of the question. The gentlemen folk at the city offices were kind enough to grant me this small indulgence. Given Rupert's many years of service and financial support to the city, it was indeed the least they could do for the grieving widow of one of Seattle's finest residents. So, our weekly pilgrimage to the church took place every Wednesday morning from 1922 all the way through to 1935, when my own lifeless body was brought through Seattle one final time, en route first to my church and then to the cemetery to lie beside Rupert.

Before any further melancholy can take hold of me, I give up waiting for Dorothea and instead venture down to the basement for another peek at the blossoming tidiness. Gliding into the storage room, my presence chills the air about me. I am alone, and that is precisely how I like it, for now anyway. I make my way past the rubbish pile and down the newly created aisle, free from boxes and debris. I twirl around the desk Emily heaved into the center of the room. I was desperate to help her as she pushed and pulled the sturdy, almost immovable office desk, but aside from cheering her on from the shadows, I was unable to offer any physical assistance. That was one of the few times I have felt the limitations of my existence here.

My twirl turns into another, and soon I am rushing about the room. I dodge piles of items, in the beginning stages of organization, while dancing to the music I hear inside my head. I spin as if Rupert's strong frame is guiding me through a rousing waltz. Oh, how I loved to dance. In Rupert's arms I felt like a princess, full of grace and poise. Dancing was the only time I truly felt like the woman he thought I was. Most suitors, in my young adult years, could hardly wait to return me to my parents' home, often cutting the evening short if I happened to voice my opinion on some matter of politics or worldly events. Their evenings out with me were often a favor to my father, payment for helpful advice my father had provided.

I had given up entirely on the hope of marriage or children. I wasn't undesirable, at least not according to my mother, but I was apparently too outspoken for my own good. I bit my tongue in response to such admonishments from my mother, desperately wanting to point out the obvious. She too was a woman of great opinions, and father didn't seem to take issue with her sharing her own thoughts. I had been raised to think for myself. I wasn't inclined to hide my opinions away for fear of a man feeling, well, less than a man, I suppose.

I am pulled from my reverie by a squeak in the stairwell. I cloak myself in the shadows of the corner and reprimand myself for my lack of self-control. The door opens swiftly, and the girl turns on the light. She stands still in the doorway as the beam slowly shudders to life before bathing the room in a muted yellow hue.

She glances around the room, wearing a perplexed expression for a moment so fleeting I can't be certain it was even there. Emily steps past the pile of rubbish with hurried steps, walking along the cleared path toward the desk. She grabs a rectangular object from the desk's surface, one I hadn't even noticed.

Tapping the object, it illuminates her face. I realize she has come to collect a telephone. I don't quite understand how such things operate without a wall and wires or an operator to connect a call through. But I do recognize the object, having watched them become popular around the church in recent years. Dorothea and I have been known to have lengthy discussions on the benefits of such inventions. Dorothea is always the one in favor of such items, deeming them signs of progress.

Emily looks up from her telephone and casts a curious glance over her shoulder, toward my darkened corner. In seeing her eyes sparkle in the muted light, I realize the song I was dancing to is still playing in the back of my mind, like a record playing in the background of a social gathering, enjoyed over aperitifs and hors d'oeuvres.

The look on her face is inquisitive, and worry washes over me at the thought of having misjudged the girl. Perhaps she is more aware than I realized. My mind runs wild with fear of being discovered. But after a moment's pause, she slips the phone into her jacket pocket, and walks toward the door. Emily glances once more around the room as she flips off the light and closes the door slowly behind her.

CHAPTER 5

*M*onday, February 16, 2015
Emily

Arriving home after an exhausting first day in the church archives, Emily runs a hot shower. She isn't certain whether her fatigue is due to the physical nature of the day or the emotional toll of keeping memories of her parents at bay. Climbing under the steam, she attempts to wash away the tears that threaten to fall. Desperately, she tries to eradicate the chill still rippling through her.

After thirty minutes, with the water sometimes hot enough to scald, Emily expects to feel renewed. She discovered within months of her parents' passing that a hot shower affords her the necessary time to regroup and tuck her emotions away before entering the world again. Though she didn't like to admit it to herself, Emily has spent more time over the past ten years under the spout of a hot shower than she has talking about her loss.

Emily sighs, lost in thought, with Pastor Michael's parting words rattling around her brain. Her mom would impart those same words to her whenever she was feeling anxious about something. *Never hurry, never worry* echoes through her mind like a faint memory as she towel dries her hair with a forceful back-and-forth motion. The brisk movement relaxes her as she massages the dull ache from her head.

All these years, Emily has purposely raced against the calendar, checking everything off her list as quickly as possible. She is wary of the niggling suspicion that despite having finally reached the pinnacle of her goals, she is still trying to outrun all that haunts her. Despite this growing awareness, she remains determined to live a life full enough for three.

Emily's dedication to her life's path has allowed little room for anything else. She designed her plan with the sheer will of a devastated teenager and promised to live as they would have. There wasn't time to wallow or grieve, or to let emotions get the better of her. There was only time for action, and to Emily, action meant moving forward in life.

The plan seemed simple enough. Graduate with honors from high school. Get her law degree and be sought after by firms. The reality, though, hasn't felt like Emily thought it would. She went through the paces and ticked all the boxes. She was eagerly pursued by several Seattle law firms. For the past several months, she has been waiting with bated breath for the pressure to release. She expected the successes she spent years striving toward to fill her up and make her whole again.

Emily's first thought when elation didn't immediately course through her veins was to blame her financial burden. Law school wasn't cheap, and despite earning a good salary for a first-year associate, Emily will need years to pay off the debt from supporting herself through school.

Emily's parents were forward thinkers, even in death. Having put their own selves through school, they felt it was their duty to teach their only daughter the value of earning one's education. An inheritance is waiting for her, but not until she turns twenty-nine years old. Until then, Emily lives as if there is no inheritance at all. This is the reality of her day-to-day life, but it is also a convenient method for pushing aside thoughts of the past.

Emily's phone buzzes along the surface of the old army trunk she uses as a makeshift coffee table and storage unit. Ryan's name scrolls across the phone's display. Butterflies take flight in her stomach as she swipes right to answer.

"Hey there," Emily says, stifling her anxious energy and pasting a smile on her lips, a trick she uses to round out her voice.

"Hey, beautiful. Didn't think I'd get the real you." Ryan's childlike chuckle permeates the distance between them. "I thought I'd be sent straight to voicemail. I thought you'd be deep in concentration, poring over the case files again like you've been doing for days now. Ignoring the love of your life in the meantime, I might add." Ryan chuckles again.

"I'm home, and to be honest, I'm beat. I would be happy to stay put. Any chance you want to come here instead of dinner out?

"Bottle of wine and Chinese takeout?"

"You know me so well." Emily smiles, giving in and believing her own words, if only for a moment.

"See you in twenty."

"See you soon." Emily hangs up the phone and surveys the mess that is her apartment.

Fifteen minutes later, she has loaded the dishwasher and

run the vacuum in a haphazard frenzy. She's dressed in yoga pants, reading socks, and her favorite purple University of Washington sweatshirt. The door buzzer rings as she's tucking a few straggling locks into a messy bun at the nape of her neck.

Settled on cushions pulled from the sofa, Ryan and Emily lounge on the floor, chopsticks hovering over open boxes of beef and broccoli, chow mein, and lemon chicken.

"This is so good. Just what I needed." Emily winks before sipping wine from her plastic wineglass. "So, how is everybody at your mom's place?"

"Ah! You should have been there, Em. The nephews were running amok yesterday, wired on something sweet Dad probably snuck their way without my brother noticing." Ryan pauses, stabbing at a piece of beef that is eluding his less than stellar chopstick skills. "You know me. It's always enjoyable when the entire family is together."

"Yeah, I know you." Emily smiles, trying to hide that the mention of an intact, happy family makes her feel like a knife is slicing through her. "The quintessential family guy."

"It's not a terrible thing, you know." Ryan abandons his chopsticks and spears his chow mein with a fork. "Wanting to settle down, have a family, a career. You to wake up to every morning." Leaning over, Ryan kisses Emily with an intensity that, without fail, makes her forget everything that is wrong in her life. His kiss lingers, drawing her in before he pulls away and searches her eyes, a devilish expression written across his face. "Just think of the benefits," he whispers as he plays with her hair.

"Just think." Emily returns his smile before breaking the spell by sneaking a piece of lemon chicken from under his outstretched arm.

"So, big week, Em?" Ryan leans back and digs into his chow mein.

Emily lets the question hang between them, scooping another mouthful as she contemplates the intended direction of Ryan's comment.

"How did things look at the church?" Ryan continues. "Is it organized chaos or just chaos?"

Relief floods Emily as Ryan's topic of conversation becomes clear. Work. *He means work,* she thinks. The tension in her shoulders relaxes the instant she comprehends that the conversation will not revolve around her parents, their deaths, a visit to the cemetery, or their connection to the church. "It's pretty much chaos." She shrugs and sips her wine. "I might have wasted a little too much time just staring at the mess. It's like a junk store met a tornado and then a volcano erupted, coating everything in the room with a fine filthy dust."

"New projects are always fun." Ryan leans against the sofa, holding his plastic wineglass gingerly so as not to crush the flimsy plastic. "I'm starting a new project tomorrow too."

"You are? Why haven't I heard about this until now? Are you keeping secrets from me?" Emily teases. With her container empty, she sets down her chopsticks and leans back to join Ryan against the sofa.

"I am heading up a team to design a new multi-use building downtown. The client has asked three architect firms to submit drawings and proposals, including us." Ryan slides his arm around Emily's shoulders.

"That is great. Where is the building?" Emily moves closer to Ryan, leaning into his embrace.

"They have sworn me to secrecy. Sorry, Em." Ryan shrugs, a mischievous smile creeping onto his lips.

Emily pulls away, positioning herself in front of Ryan.

"You mean to tell me they have given you an amazing opportunity at work and you can't say what it is?"

"Yep. That about sums it up." Ryan laughs at Emily's furrowed brow. "It is a cool opportunity, but that is about all I can tell you. Come here. I promise to divulge everything just as soon as I am able." Emily leans forward as Ryan wraps both arms around her, nuzzling the top of her head with kisses. "Besides," Ryan breathes, his lips brushing close to Emily's ear, "let's not pretend you tell me everything. Okay, Em?"

Emily pushes off from Ryan's chest and sits up straight, folding her knees to sit cross-legged. "What exactly are you referring to?"

"I overheard you talking to Veronica last week, before we made our quick getaway." Ryan rolls his eyes at the words *quick getaway*.

Emily sucks in a breath of air and holds it, waiting for the other shoe to drop.

"It isn't like you to be rude. And to Veronica, no less. She and Colin have done so much for you. I just don't understand why you push her away. Why you push them away." Ryan reaches for Emily's hand, cradling it in his own.

Emily pulls her hand free from Ryan's and pretends to pick at a fingernail. "You wouldn't understand. She's always pushing me to be someone I'm not. She thought that by now . . ." Tears brim in Emily's eyes. "She thought that by now I'd be open to seeing someone, to talk about things."

"Maybe she's right. Maybe it is time to move forward and work through all that you lost. You have to admit, it is a long time to hold it all in." Ryan scans the ceiling. "If you won't talk to a professional, you know you can always talk to me."

"Thanks, but I'm good." Shoving the tears back down where they belong, Emily continues. "And in case nobody has noticed, I have moved forward. That is the only direction I've been moving." Emily pushes herself up from the floor and begins clearing containers from the coffee table.

Ryan lets out an exasperated breath and nods repeatedly as Emily heads for the kitchen. "Yep, you're good all right. Good at building walls."

"I heard that." Emily calls to him as the garbage lid slams shut.

"I know you've got a lot on your plate with work this week, so I'll let it go, for now. But Em, you will have to open up to me at some point if we are going to have a future together."

Emily walks back into the living room, her arms folded across her chest.

Ryan lifts himself from the floor and meets her where she stands. He pulls her into a warm embrace. "I want to marry you, Emily Reed. But I won't. Not until you can open up to me. Not until you can be honest with yourself."

Emily remains silent in Ryan's arms, her head swirling with words left unspoken.

Ryan pulls back, dipping his head to meet her eyes. "Maybe you should have been the architect and I should have been the lawyer." Emily's puzzled face encourages him. "You know, with your wall-building expertise and my powers of persuasion. If we just swap careers, we'd be all set."

"Ha ha, you're hilarious." Emily swats Ryan's arm lightheartedly. He wraps her in another embrace before closing the distance between his lips and hers.

Walking toward the door, Ryan pauses and turns to face Emily. As he inclines his head, a serious expression replaces his amused one. "Good luck with the dungeon, Em. I'll be thinking of you. If you need me for anything at all, I'm just a phone call away." Ryan slips on his jacket, kisses her one more time, and walks out the door.

She waits for the click of the latch before releasing her breath. Tugging the elastic free from her hair, Emily curses, uneasiness once more nibbling at the edges of her mind.

She tries to distract herself by puttering back and forth, cleaning up between the kitchen and the living room. Emily pours herself another glass of wine and cozies into the deepest part of the sofa cushions, tucking a blanket around her lap. Beaten down by the stress of the week, with little resolve remaining within her, Emily gives in to the moment. She taps her phone until the smooth vocals of Frank Sinatra fill the room from the wireless speaker.

"Here's to you, Frank." Emily raises her glass in a toast, as the sound of her dad's favorite artist mists her eyes with tears. She remembers her dad's waltz lessons as he helped her prepare for a high school dance. Despite knowing there would not be any kind of waltzing at the school function, she hadn't been willing to give up an evening with her dad, even at the age of fourteen. They danced almost all the way through a Sinatra album, with her mom watching from her favorite chair, a wide smile spread across her lips.

As the final song on the album began to play, Dad bowed slightly and thanked Emily for the dances. He stepped toward Mom and explained that this particular song was forever reserved for the love of his life. But not to worry, if Emily ever needed him for anything, he was only a phone call away. Ryan's words flash through Emily's mind. *He is only a phone call away.* She smiles at the similarity between Ryan and her dad.

Dad took Mom's hand and guided her to the center of the room, where they gazed into each other's eyes. Emily moved to a shadowy corner of the room and watched as Dad sang Mom Frank's musical love letter. Mesmerized by the music and the love between them, Emily found herself wishing that one day she would be loved with such honesty and intensity.

The memory plays across Emily's mind, rich in color and brimming with emotion. After connecting Ryan's words to the memory, she struggles to think of anything else. *He is just a phone call away*. Ryan definitely possesses the ability to calm her with his words and with his presence, but also with the honest and intense way he loves her every day. *That is something to be thankful for*, she thinks as she switches off the lights and calls it a night.

CHAPTER 6

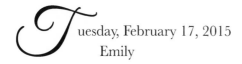 uesday, February 17, 2015
Emily

The morning light filters through the closed slats in the apartment's white metal blinds. Emily rolls away from the brightness, sinking into the warmth and coziness of her childhood bedspread. She seldom sleeps late anymore. She is simply too busy cramming everything into each day.

If she were being honest with herself though, refusing to linger among the comfort of her bed with a good book is just another way for her push back the memory of lazy holiday mornings spent with Mom. The week after Christmas before school reopened, Dad would head to the office each morning to catch up on paperwork while Mom tiptoed into Emily's room, their most recent read in hand.

Together they would lie nestled under the covers while Mom read out loud. The game was, Mom would read until one of their stomachs finally grumbled in protest. Whether she was in the middle of a sentence, at the crux of a cliffhanger, or only a few words into a new chapter, Mom would smile with a twinkle in her eye, tuck a bookmark between the pages and close the book before heading to the kitchen to prepare breakfast. The length of the morning shared enjoying both the classics as well as new releases remained dependent on the noisiness of one another's stomachs. Emily rolls onto her side remembering one evening when she ate an excessive amount of cheese and crackers before climbing into bed, just so her stomach would not be the first to grumble. They had been in the middle of one of the Harry Potter books and Emily was reluctant to stop the story until the last page had been read.

Within moments, the morning grogginess wears off and Emily is more awake than she would like to be. Her whirring brain and her grumbling stomach spur her into motion. Propelled from her mattress by her overzealous hunger and her need to outrun the vivid memory of Mom, she is on her way to the kitchen before the chilly floor can send her retreating to the warmth and seclusion of the covers.

With the water in the kettle set to boil, Emily whisks two eggs in a small glass bowl while the butter melts in a pan over the electric heat. Pondering her tasks for the day, Emily's eyes roam toward the calendar stuck to the refrigerator with a Patterson and Holt magnet. February features the image of a beautiful tree-lined park located somewhere in Seattle, reminding Emily of Veronica's invitation to visit Lake View Cemetery. The grassy and heavily treed historic cemetery sneaks into the periphery of her mind like a thief, ready to steal any potential for an otherwise good day.

The cemetery, established in 1872, was selected as the final resting place for Emily's parents by Colin and Veronica, the reasoning being her parent's deep connection to Seattle and its heritage. Given her inexperience with weighty decisions at the age of sixteen, she had little idea of what to expect on the day of the funeral. Shocked and a little more than unnerved, Emily was aghast at the sheer number of visitors strolling the grounds in the middle of winter, noisily interrupting what should have been moments of complete solitude as she buried her parents in the nearly frozen ground. Why hadn't the world stopped? Couldn't they see her life was in turmoil? All she wanted to do was push the pause button and step off the merry-go-round of life, if only for a few minutes of reprieve.

The experience at Lake View Cemetery was so unsettling that she has yet to return to pay her respects. A wave of guilt washes over Emily as she dips a tea bag into the hot water in her mug. Her eyes fixate on the transformation as swirling clear water spirals into deep brown tea.

Years later, Emily learned Lake View, nestled among cherry blossoms and panoramic views, is also the final resting place to some of Seattle's most prominent residents. Whether the disruptive visitors to the cemetery that paralyzing day were there to pay their respects to martial arts superhero Bruce Lee or some other historic Seattle native, Emily could care less. She has yet to forgive the visitors for the intrusion on what should have been a properly mournful experience.

The toast pops up in the toaster, startling Emily from her thoughts. She putters about her compact galley kitchen before scooping eggs onto freshly buttered slices of toast. Emily positions herself at the table with breakfast and reaches for the thick file containing the church's case brief.

Having read through the brief multiple times, Emily skims the text, flipping pages between bites. Forcefully pushing aside any thought of visiting the cemetery, Emily finds comfort in returning her attention to the needs and concerns of the church. The documents took up residence on the corner of the kitchen table the day they arrived in Emily's apartment, where they have been continually at the ready. The details of the legal case that has spanned not only years,t but decades helped her understand the need for her to quickly and diligently account for the church's records and archives. Archiving the extensive history is an immense task, but the brief serves as a motivator and a reminder of what is at stake. Reading the pages reaffirms Emily's belief in the congregation's right to do what they wish with their property, historic or not.

The case brief outlines the legal battle between The First United Methodist Church of Seattle and the City of Seattle Landmarks Preservation Board. The church leaders have spent many years in litigation with the city over a landmark status that the members of the church did not seek or want. The status was simply bestowed upon their property at 811 Fifth Avenue. As Seattle's downtown core changed, the church leaders found themselves in the center of a steadily growing business district, cut off from their congregation as Interstate 5 and office towers replaced residents' homes.

Founded in a log home with a handful of members in 1853, the First Methodist Episcopal Church was the first community church of Seattle. Over the years, the church expanded in response to its congregation's changing needs, building and moving three times. In 1910, supportive Seattleites gathered at the church's current home at Fifth and Marion to witness the building's dedication. The church fulfilled the needs of many citizens through the years, until the time came to find a new location. After several rounds of legal arguments, the church's case escalated to the Washington State Supreme Court, where it currently awaits a final decision.

Brushing crumbs from the table to her plate, Emily clears

her breakfast dishes to the kitchen. With reinforced confidence in the church leaders' legal right to sell the property and relocate to a community where they can better serve their congregation, she considers her plans for the day. Remembering the pile of thick beams and concrete blocks cluttering the concrete floor in the basement storage room, Emily contemplates the feasibility of building a makeshift shelving system. The shelves need to be sturdy enough for the interim but portable enough to relocate to a new church building.

Running a brush through her hair in front of the bathroom mirror, Emily pulls her hair into a tight ponytail before scrubbing the sleep away from her face with a washcloth. Though she's inclined to support the church leaders' position, others don't agree, as evidenced by her involvement with the archives. There had been grumblings within the community from those who wished to save the historic church building from the wrecking ball. Three weeks ago, those voices surfaced a little more loudly as an organized force. The news coverage on the Supreme Court case has done little for the church's side of the story. After years of costly legal pursuits, church board members and the congregation are tiring of antics that paint them as less than the loving, kind, and generous people they are.

Emily thinks back to the newspaper article quoting the group fighting to save the church and murmurs a sarcastic "thanks" to her reflection in the mirror. This escalation by the group known as the Friends of the First Church of Seattle prompted the church administrators to ensure all their historical records were in order. The effort to assure the community of the church's integrity regarding historical artifacts led to Emily's role in the case. She has been instructed to gather, sort, and organize the archives, in preparation for both a relocation and a favorable court ruling. A historical account of the church's history, spanning more than one hundred and fifty years, may help assuage the community's discontent in such a situation.

Swiping her lips with a sheer peach lip gloss, Emily takes another glance in the oval bathroom mirror. A barely there, neutral palette of freshly applied makeup warms her features. With a nod of approval, Emily retreats to her bedroom to dress for the day. She decides a pair of work gloves are in order if she is to build a shelving unit suitable to store the one hundred or more boxes she has yet to explore.

Dressed in jeans and a sweatshirt, she slides her arms into her camel-colored coat and loops a bright red scarf around her neck.

Emily sighs, the memory of her parents still tugging at her mind and heart. This archival project would be a lot easier if her parents had never set foot inside the church, much less chosen the building as the sacred space in which to begin their life together. With a final glance around the room, she shrugs off the tightness building in her chest, the kind that threatens to steal her forced composure. Emily pushes her keys and wallet into the oversized jacket pockets before heading out the apartment door. With her shoulders squared and her jaw clenched, she defies the emotions festering underneath her pale winter skin.

CHAPTER 7

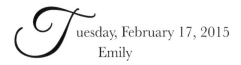uesday, February 17, 2015
Emily

The weather has improved over last night's rainstorm. Winters in Seattle often see snow, fog, sleet, torrential rain, and even spring-like days warm enough to encourage hearty flowers to pop through the hard ground. Though the clouds are heavy, layered and gray, a brightness to the day encourages Emily's purposeful steps toward the local department store. Pulling her phone from her bag's pocket, Emily calls Ryan as she navigates the rush-hour traffic along the wide sidewalks of downtown Seattle. When he doesn't answer, she leaves him a voicemail promising to talk to him later.

Ryan's confession of his desire for marriage tickles her memory, eliciting butterfly-like excitement in her tummy. She taps her toe as she waits impatiently for the traffic light to change. She and Ryan hadn't spoken of the future in such concrete terms before. With Ryan's confession, Emily delights at the tingle of hope for a happy future, one she wasn't sure she would ever have.

When the walk signal lights up, she steps off the curb and a crisp wind whips about her shoulders. Emily swivels her head to take in the view of Elliott Bay as she crosses the street. The chill is unsettling. Her mood shifts with the weather as the initial excitement of such happy musings of a future with Ryan mingle with fear, uncertainty, and guilt. The caveat is that he wants more from her. He wants her to share her feelings, bare her soul, and she isn't certain she can offer him that.

Her forehead crinkles, knitting her eyebrows against the chill and the problem before her. Why are the people most important to her so determined to see straight through her, to the past? She is determined to leave the past where it is. Her thoughts return to the cold, concrete-colored sky under which she laid her parents to rest only adding fuel to her already souring disposition. Who is she kidding? Happily-ever-after was never meant to belong to her.

Even from her favorite vantage point of the waterway that leads to the Pacific Ocean tucked between rows of towering buildings, Emily's shoulders sag. Since learning of her parents' connection to the church she now works within, she hasn't been able to settle this feeling. Stepping onto the opposite curb, Emily shakes her head with practiced stubborn determination. She tucks her emotions back into hiding while turning toward the water. Dodging morning commuters and the occasional brave tourist visiting the city in the middle of February, Emily walks toward the store. A big red circle with a dot in the middle is emblazoned on the side of the charcoal-colored building. Reassuring herself it is easier, better in fact, to let work consume her hours, Emily redirects her focus toward busywork instead of lingering memories.

The more physical the workload, the better for her emotional state, she reasons. Heading straight for the sparse gardening section, Emily spots a pair of sage-green gardening gloves among a few pots and a lonely bag of indoor potting soil. With her purchase in hand, she turns onto Union Street, making her way toward the church.

Grounded by her city and with the anticipation of the physical task ahead building within her, Emily raises her head, squares her shoulders, and musters on toward Fifth Avenue. Passing the library, Emily's steps slow long enough to raise her eyes upward. The glass building holds the promise of beauty and knowledge within its diamond-patterned exterior. *Dad would have loved this place.* Emily squeezes her eyes shut in a fierce blink, an effort to ward off the emotion building beneath her eyelids. Both her parents were avid readers, teaching her from an early age the importance of libraries. The love of spreading knowledge was at the core of such a building's creation. *Must they be everywhere?* she asks herself. Annoyance laced with growing weariness echoes in her sigh.

With another firm, scolding shake of her head, Emily sets her sights on the church building. Diving into the chaotic mess in the church's basement will be a far easier task than dissecting the disturbances currently running amok in her mind. Crossing over Marion Street, Emily takes another deep breath before whispering affirmations to herself. "All of it is easier than digging through my own past. I already know the past only leads to heartache."

Coming face to face with the ornate yet clean-lined beige building, Emily expands her posture with the manufactured confidence she has developed and improved over the years. The posture is intended to fool everyone, including Emily herself.

Climbing the church steps, Emily pauses briefly to

examine the front view of the Beaux-Arts styled building. Her heart stills and a question creeps into the corner of her mind, rubbing against her already frayed nerves. *What will the cityscape look like without this beautiful building here to anchor this corner?*

Brushing the question aside, Emily forces her attention toward more pleasant thoughts. Her favorite aspect of the building is hidden from the outside. The exteriors of the lovingly crafted stained-glass windows are muted with demure colors. But they shine brightly within the church's walls, casting fragments of light while adding a touch of magic to the space. *Windows to the soul of the building*, Emily ponders as she pulls on the large door and steps inside, onto the plush red carpet.

A hush falls over her as the outside world disappears. Like the air after a summer rainstorm, the silence of the massive entry hall exhales, adding a palpable tingle to the high ceilings and dark wood panels. Surveying the vast open area, Emily listens for the presence of Mrs. Peters, the stout church administrator who introduced her to the basement storage room yesterday. As Emily stands in the entryway, a wave of hesitancy swirls through her mind.

Pastor Michael suggested she get to know the church and visit the sanctuary, to gain a broader understanding of what she will find in the basement. A nervous bubble of emotion rises within her. The sanctuary lies a few short paces from where she stands. Her mind warns her not to, but the sanctuary's powerful pull nudges Emily to the right. She faces the narrow hall, where sunlight dances between the windows, casting shadow and light.

With a glance over her shoulder at the vacant narthex, Emily takes a deep breath, curiosity winning out over nervous anticipation. She takes a few strides into the scattered sunbeams decorating the plush red carpeting and pauses to examine the curved arches of the ceiling. Stepping into the sanctuary, another level of stillness descends over her and she catches her breath. The grandeur of the church's sanctuary stops her in her tracks. Like a whisper or a secret shared between friends, the sanctuary feels as though it has much to tell her.

Easing herself farther into the room, Emily's breath is tight within her chest. The hairs on the back of her neck bristle in subtle defiance of her forward motion, and yet she cannot stop herself from continuing into the heart of the room. She places a hand on the smooth rounded corner of a church pew, and images of her mother, dressed in white with a veil crowning her head like a halo, flit across her mind. Emily swivels to look behind her as the imaginary scene of her parents' wedding plays out in her head. The images are fueled by the framed photograph that lived on the fireplace mantel of her childhood home and by her recollection of stories shared by her parents throughout the years.

Turning her attention toward the altar, Emily takes another step forward before sliding into a cushioned pew. A rogue tear escapes her eye and slides down her cheek. The filtered light from the dome heightens the serene calm of the sanctuary, and Emily allows herself to be lulled further into a dreamlike state by the warmth and the quiet of the space. The pipe organ stands proud and tall on the upper balcony, like a soldier standing at attention, waiting patiently for someone to spur it to life. Through tear-blurred vision, Emily stifles a shuddering sigh as she imagines her dad standing at the front of the church. Beaming toward her mom, in his black tuxedo, his hair cropped short, and his posture exuding a mix of confidence and nerves.

Knowing that this church holds a piece of her parents'

past, Emily's heart lurches with longing for everything she has missed since their passing. Staring blankly at the dark paneled wood of the choir loft, she is unexpectantly struck with the realization that she could be about to lose another piece of them, another piece of their story. Fresh tears pool in her eyes at the thought of losing the building where her parents were wed. To have found this connection to them only to let it go is bittersweet. The realization is like a sword piercing her heart. A sword she was certain she had buried, along with two caskets laying side by side in the cold, dark ground.

Emily is not a religious individual per se. At least she hasn't been since her parents passed away. Her desire to commune with God, or with anyone else for that matter, all but vanished on that day. But somehow this space, this sanctuary, has cast a spell over her. Whether it is the knowledge of her parents' connection to the church or the church itself, she is drawn into a web of something unknown, something almost magical. Emily can't help but wonder if the sanctuary holds the memories, secrets, and stories of the past, as Pastor Michael suggested.

A shiver runs the length of Emily's spine, reminding her that she is at her current place of work. Here she sits, having an emotional meltdown at work—the last thing she wanted. Silently, she curses her overactive imagination. Unable to place her scattered thoughts into tidy columns, Emily wipes her face with the back of her hand. She stands and forgives herself for this one slip of emotional upheaval, while promising to think on these new conflicting points of view another time. She will ponder them once she has steadied herself again and is without a looming deadline and so much work waiting for her in the basement.

"Ms. Reed, there you are. I was wondering if you had arrived already." Mrs. Peters' singsong voice pierces the tranquility of the sanctuary as the swish of her skirt announces her small but rapid steps.

Emily struggles to find her words, startled by the presence of another person. "Mrs. Peters. Hello. I hope you don't mind. I wanted to take a peek at the heart of the building. I thought perhaps it would help me understand the history a little better as I delve into the archives."

"Not at all, dear. Not at all." Mrs. Peters pats Emily's arm. She tilts her head, an unasked question on her lips. "You are welcome here anytime you like."

Emily's cheeks pink with embarrassment as she dabs at what she imagines is a tear-mottled face. "Thank you. That is very kind of you," Emily stammers. She forces a smile and straightens her posture once more.

"You are settled, then. You have everything you need?"

"Yes, thank you." Emily walks up the aisle before pausing. "Oh, actually, I think I will need a ladder. I was hoping to use the old concrete blocks and beams to make a storage unit of sorts." Emily stuffs her hands into her jacket pockets and shrugs. "A little college student-inspired design, I know, but it should allow me to keep the sorted boxes separate from the ones still needing my attention."

Mrs. Peters taps a finger to her chin. "I suppose we can grab one from the janitor's closet. I am sure he won't mind." Mrs. Peters shuffles her feet before reaching out a hand to touch Emily's arm. "Just as long as you promise to be careful with it. I wouldn't want you to take a tumble, dear."

A friendly smile spreads across Emily's lips. Mrs. Peters, Emily has noticed, makes herself a surrogate grandmother to almost anyone she meets. Emily thinks back to their first meeting at the law firm offices and smiles at the memory of how Mrs. Peters doted on Emily's boss, Mr. Holt, just as she is doting on Emily now. "I promise to take the utmost care." She pulls a hand from her jacket pocket and places it gently on Mrs. Peters' shoulder.

As they walk side by side up the sanctuary aisle toward the hall entrance, Mrs. Peters prattles on about finding the key to the janitor's closet as Emily steals a last glance at the hallowed room. *Honoring my parents' memory is one thing but moving forward is productive. It has always been productive.* Emily reaffirms her commitment to tucking her emotions away once more. Emotions are messy and of little use. She shut them down quickly after losing her parents, and she has no intention of allowing herself to fall down that particular rabbit hole now, especially when the archives are waiting for her.

CHAPTER 8

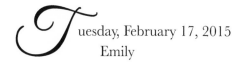uesday, February 17, 2015
Emily

The ladder scrapes along the concrete floor, emitting a squeal that is sure to echo all the way to the rafters. As she drags the metal A-frame ladder into place near the farthest wall of the overcrowded room, Emily imagines a flutter of pigeons taking flight from the church's domed roof in response to the ruckus. Leaving the ladder balanced against the wall, she reaches into the depths of her messenger bag, extracting a pad of sticky notes and a pen. Emily scribbles a quick note to the janitor about the whereabouts of his ladder and the extension cord she noticed hanging above the steel bucket and mop. She returns to the janitor's cupboard to leave the note and retrieve the extension cord.

Back in the storage room, Emily tugs free the tangled cord of a desk lamp. She plugs it into her newly acquired extension cord before beginning the hunt for a hidden power outlet. "Let there be light," she says out loud as she clicks the switch on the base of the lamp. The desk's surface is bathed in a soft yellow glow, eliciting a triumphant smile from Emily.

"And God said, 'Let there be light, and there was light.' " Pastor Michael's voice is soft but commanding as he pronounces the verse.

Emily turns toward him and smiles.

Spreading his arms wide, Pastor Michael continues. " 'God saw that the light was good, and he separated the light from the darkness. God called the light "day," and the darkness he called "night." And there was evening, and there was morning—the first day.' Genesis, chapter one."

"Good morning, Pastor Michael."

"It is indeed, Emily. It is indeed." Pastor Michael nods his head toward the lamp. "I see it is your resourcefulness that provided the much-needed light this morning."

"Well," Emily says with a childlike expression, "me, an extension cord, and Thomas Edison were all equally responsible."

Pastor Michael chuckles. "I see you are amenable to sharing credit where credit is due." His eyes twinkle with amusement.

Laughing in response, Emily is aware of the ease she feels in Pastor Michael's company. Perhaps the clergy collar makes her comfortable in his presence. Or maybe his likeness to Happy, one of Snow White's seven dwarfs, ushers in the softer side of her personality. "I visited the sanctuary, like you suggested." Emily winces at her somewhat juvenile but forthright announcement.

"Ah, I am happy to hear it." Pastor Michael tucks his arms, clasping his hands behind his back as his soft blue eyes rest on Emily's expression. "What did you discover in the sanctuary, Emily?"

"It is a beautiful space. Tranquil and——" Emily's eyes scan the boxes on the floor and then her own shoes as her mind rewinds the imaginary scene of her parents' wedding day. "It has stories to share, just like you said." Her voice is barely above a whisper. "I agree with you about the stories."

Pastor Michael nods in silent understanding. The air in the room seems to shift, and Emily wraps her arms around her shoulders to ward off the sudden chill. "I'd better get started, then." Emily forces a wide smile, hiding her slip of vulnerability while pulling the gardening gloves from her bag.

"Take care with those beams, Emily. They are much heavier than they first appear." With a nod, Pastor Michael disappears through the door.

More than an hour later, as Emily is shoving boxes away from the wall where she intends to place the shelving unit, a thought crosses her mind. *How did Pastor Michael know I was planning to use the beams?* She clears a fresh path from the pile of beams in the corner of the room to the space in front of the concrete wall. Dragging the last box out of the way before wiping sweat from her forehead, Emily decides Pastor Michael must have spoken to Mrs. Peters before he ventured down to the basement to see her this morning.

Thinking of Pastor Michael, Emily's mind takes a detour, returning to the imagined scene of her parents' wedding day. A world of love shone from their eyes, bringing tears to her own. Just as she remembers their wedding photo doing, the pretended unfolding she fabricated in the sanctuary is infused with a deep sense of hope. A trickle of sweat runs down her temple, sending a shiver through her body. "Get your head in the game, Em." She scolds herself for the interruption and turns her attention toward the yet-to-be-built shelving unit.

Gritting her teeth, Emily places her gloved hands on either side of a gray concrete block, half carrying, half dragging it into place against the wall before retrieving two more. With three blocks spaced evenly against the wall, Emily pauses for a drink of water before assessing the feasibility of dragging a beam to the same location.

"This would certainly be easier if I had help." With her hands resting on her hips, Emily contemplates the insanity of believing she could build the shelf alone. "Life would have been easier . . ." She stops herself from saying out loud, *if they had lived*. The fastest way to a defeated state, she learned ages ago, is to put voice to the things you cannot change. She isn't willing to give those thoughts power, especially in this church, where their past is far too entwined with her present.

Never one to back down from a task, Emily tightens her ponytail and heaves one end of a beam into her arms. She shuffles to face forward, dragging the beam down her narrow path. At the wall, she places the end of the beam on top of a concrete block before scooting to the opposite side of the beam. Kneeling, Emily gives the beam a hefty shove with both hands and slides the full length of the beam into position on top of all three concrete blocks. She steps back to admire her handiwork, sweat streaming down her face.

With weeks of organization ahead of her, Emily can already imagine the space beginning to appear bigger as she makes progress sorting, filing, and storing. Reorganizing has always made Emily feel satisfied, and her task at the church should be no different. Both the physical release of the work and the sense of a job well done appeal to her pragmatic, type A personality. *If only my mind could be reorganized with such ease.* She reaches for a misshapen box near the desk, pushing aside for what feels like the hundredth time today thoughts of what her life could have been like if her parents had lived.

With the box's lid removed, Emily gently scoops up a thin stack of yellowing newspaper articles, setting them on the desk with care. A larger item wedged into the confines of the box draws her attention. Pushing the side of the box against her hip while pressing on its opposite side with one hand, Emily creates enough space to insert her free hand between the cardboard and the object. With a twist and a pull, the solid object comes free, leaving the cardboard box empty and far from square.

Dropping the empty box to the floor with a thud, Emily places the square brown case on the desk. Turning the case around, she fiddles with the brass clips. After releasing the clips, she easily lifts the lid off the case and finds a vintage record player, complete with a crank handle. Within the case, two locking fasteners secure a large needle arm in its molded storage compartment.

Placing the player's lid upside down on the desk, Emily spots a black grooved record cloaked in brittle and somewhat tattered paper, secured with two elastic straps against the case's lid. Extracting the record from its enclosure, Emily places it atop the player. She inserts the crank's arm and winds it before steadily lowering the needle onto the first groove of the record.

Crackles and pops fill the room before the orchestra breaks through with the snappy tune of "Sweet Georgia Brown." Emily beams and her toe taps as the song plays in the manner it was originally intended to be heard. The added fullness of the music is rich with the history of the 1920s. Charmed by her musical find, Emily hums along as she flips through newspaper clippings. Emily startles in response to the sound of a voice as the song ends.

"What a marvelous start you have made on the room, Emily."

69

Emily turns toward the door. "Pastor Michael, you startled me." The cool air in the dingy basement chills the perspiration clinging to her skin.

"I apologize. It was not my intention." With his hands tucked behind his back, he nods toward the initial layer of the newly erected shelf. "You are a resourceful one, aren't you? Well done, Emily."

She reaches a hand toward the back of her neck at his compliment, feeling a flush of heat rise to her cheeks. The way he praises her with sincerity makes her feel as though she has been invited into a fold of familial compassion, one she hasn't felt since her parents' deaths. "I think it will work." Emily stands a little straighter while giving the shelf a once-over.

"It most certainly will, my dear." Pastor Michael moves a few steps nearer to the desk, peering past the old record player, which is stuck thrumming against the innermost, music-free grooves of the dull black record. Craning his neck slightly to the right, he narrows his eyes toward the newspaper clipping in Emily's hands. "What have you found there?"

"I'm not entirely sure just yet." Newspaper clippings lay scattered on top of the desk. Plucking another from the pile and unfolding it gently, Emily reads the first line in bold black letters. "They look like newspaper articles from the 1920s. Says here that Mother Reynolds was thanking the prominent citizens of Seattle for the newly constructed home for children."

"Ah, Alberta Reynolds." Pastor Michael's smile broadens. "Now there was a woman with tenacity."

Emily swivels the wooden chair around, drops her bag to the ground, and sits. She leans forward in anticipation.

"Some say that Mother Reynolds, or Alby, as the community called her, created the first unofficial orphanage of

70

Seattle." Pastor Michael grins. "Now, *unofficial* describes exactly how she operated. She kept no records of comings and goings, much to the chagrin of city officials from whom she frequently requested funding and donations. She quite literally opened her doors to whomever was in need. In addition to children, she took in unwanted individuals society had shunned. Husbandless women who found themselves inconveniently with child. Aging women without the financial resources to feed and clothe themselves. Female prisoners and prostitutes. All were welcome in Mother Reynolds' cramped but kindly quarters."

Pastor Michael gives a single nod before continuing. "She offered both long- and short-term shelter. Some came for a night, a hearty meal, and a warm bath. Others lived among the brood and squalor until they were old enough to make their own way in life. According to some estimates, Mother Reynolds housed and cared for thousands of children during her years in Seattle. She did so with community support. Many community members willingly gifted whatever they could afford, while others were more or less coerced into loosening their purse strings."

"That is a fascinating story." A laugh escapes Emily's lips and she reaches for the newspaper article once more, squinting at the small black-and-white photograph of a stern-looking woman. "Not an overly flattering image, but she does appear to be as tenacious as you say. I'd certainly give her whatever she was asking for."

Pastor Michael's smile is kind and thoughtful. "I believe you would, Emily." He turns on his heel with a swift and silent motion and wanders toward the shadowy doorway. Before she can utter even a thank you, Pastor Michael has left Emily alone with her thoughts and the article in her hands.

. . .

TANYA E WILLIAMS

Mother Reynolds Finds a Home to Call Her Own
April 17, 1920

Best known to most Seattleites as Mother Reynolds, Alberta H. Reynolds and her self-made orphanage have finally found a home. The new location will offer support for children without family, soon-to-be mothers without husbands, and elderly persons in need of assistance.

Mrs. Reynolds arrived in Seattle in 1881. Grief-stricken over the death of one of her own children, Mother Reynolds set out to help the children of a neighbor who passed away. Mother Reynolds adopted the four neighbor children, and soon her goodwill led to the addition of twenty-five more children to her home. She filled every nook and cranny of her house with children in need of care, becoming Seattle's first unofficial orphanage.

With little resources to her name, Mother Reynolds sought community support in the form of food, clothing, and financial donations. Though Mother Reynolds has on more than one occasion butted heads with Seattle's higher-ups over her lack of record keeping, she continues her work, spurred on by the need that exists within the city.

One of this reporter's favorite tales involves Mother Reynolds discovering that many of her children required new shoes. She marched those children down to the local shoe mercantile and initiated a sit-down strike, refusing to leave until the proprietor surrendered and gave each child a fresh pair of durable shoes. On her way out, Mother Reynolds thanked the businessman and told him he could consider the shoes his donation to Reynolds' House for the upcoming year.

After reading the newspaper articles, Emily records each clipping in her binder. Her brow furrows in concentration as she writes a brief note for each article, including the publication name, the date, and a description. A squeal through the pipes makes her jump almost entirely out of her chair. After clutching at her heart, Emily reminds herself it is just the heating system Mrs. Peters warned her about.

Scanning the poorly lit and desolate-feeling space, Emily shivers. Her eyes search between the boxes and piles of miscellaneous items for a grate or radiator, something to provide a little warmth to the dungeon. *With all that racket, you would think there would at least be some heat in here.* Shrugging on her coat, Emily thinks back to the day Mrs. Peters introduced her to a list of quirks specific to the basement room she was soon to be working in. As they sat in the offices of Patterson and Holt, a pot of tea between them, the kind church administrator peppered her with details woven among apologies for a room Emily was not yet familiar with.

"The building is heated with hot water that runs through pipes," Mrs. Peters said. "The system emits excess steam into the street above, but I am sorry to say, the basement seems to be the most ill-equipped to receive much warmth from the ancient design."

Emily hadn't given it much thought at the time other than to appreciate the allure and charm of oddities such as the heating system that exists within the unique building. But with personal experience now on her side, the luster of charm has diminished significantly in the cold basement.

It is well past five o'clock by the time Emily has finished recording the newspaper clippings. She places them in a protective plastic sheet before returning them and the old record player back into their original misshapen box. She labels the exterior of the box in a tidy, practiced hand with a thick black marker. Emily's stomach grumbles, letting her know she has worked through lunch again. Skipping lunch becomes a habit for first-year lawyers, who are used to battling the clock to log case hours. When Emily took on the archiving project, she decided to stick to her usual office hours. Fearing she might lose her edge, she was determined to remain conditioned for her eventual reentry into the law office's busy environment.

Emily slides the box under the beam, pleased that her homemade shelf is the perfect height for bank boxes, of which she has hundreds to process. She grabs another box from the floor with both hands and heaves it onto the desk. The scent of aged books wafts up to greet her as she lifts the lid. Childlike delight spreads across her face as Emily, an avid reader from a young age, takes in the gold mine she has uncovered. She first notices Agatha Christie's *The Mysterious Affair at Styles. Ulysses* by James Joyce, *The Great Gatsby* by F. Scott Fitzgerald, *The Sun Also Rises* by Ernest Hemingway, and *Mrs Dalloway* by Virginia Woolf.

Emily fingers the Christie spine as a memory and tears race to escape from their sequestered state. Agatha Christie is a Reed family favorite. Some of Emily's earliest memories are of her dad reading the Detective Hercule Poirot novels out loud. "Oh, Dad." A strangled laugh escapes from deep within Emily's throat. "This must be where my overactive need to solve mysteries came from." Her voice cracks with emotion. "Not now," she mutters under her breath, deflated by the memories that have been assaulting her, holding her hostage with only foolhardy emotion as company in this desolate church basement. She pinches the bridge of her nose in an effort to banish any moisture.

Her eyes fall upon the box of books. Avoiding the Christie novel, Emily scans the other titles and finds her eyes drawn to *Mrs Dalloway*. She picks up the book, turning it over in her hands as she examines the cover. Emily's attention is drawn farther into the box when she notices a second layer of smaller, squatter books lining the bottom. Placing *Mrs Dalloway* on the desk, Emily gently removes the entire collection of classics, placing them on the desk before reaching toward the previously hidden row.

Pulling one book after another from the box, Emily realizes they are not books at all, but a collection of diaries. A few leather-bound editions feature the word *journal* or *diary* in fine gold embossing. Flipping through the pages, Emily notes dates in 1912 and 1918. "What on earth are someone's diaries doing in the church's archives?" A shiver runs the length of Emily's spine and the hairs on the back of her neck rise to attention. Her curiosity wins out, and Emily flips to the first page of each journal, searching for a name. Learning to whom the diaries belonged may help her understand how they fit into the history of the church.

Emily's phone moans like a foghorn from her jacket pocket, pulling her attention from the journals. The alarm is for the weekly reminder she programmed into her phone's calendar months ago, after a somewhat heated discussion with Ryan about her overtime hours. Together they decided Tuesday night would be their nonnegotiable date night. The screen lights up with the message she wrote for herself: *Ryan 6:30 Theatre One.* During a brief phone conversation last week, they decided to see an action movie and Seattle's Theatre One is Ryan's favored location to grab dinner and a movie.

Checking the time, Emily calculates how long it will take to walk home and change. She'll need another thirty minutes to walk to the theater. She is tired and more than ready to call it a day. Emily layers the novels at the base of the box before tending to the smaller diaries. The diaries intrigue her, and she places them within easy reach inside the box. Emily contemplates whether she has time to flip through a journal or two. She'd like to solve the mystery of the diaries' owner. A slight frown forms across her lips as she decides better of it. After all, choosing Ryan over work was the point of date night. She slides her arms into her jacket sleeves and grabs her bag. Flipping off the light, Emily walks out the door.

CHAPTER 9

*W*ednesday, March 4, 2015
Emily

A few weeks later, Emily steps into the basement room, having refilled her water bottle at the cooler located on the upper floors of the church building. Last night's date with Ryan ran late into the evening, both of them unwilling to leave the comfort of one another's snuggles. They sat tucked into her sofa while an old movie played on the television. The hours passed in their quiet but comfortable companionship. Emily stifles a yawn mixed with a smile as she thinks of Ryan and their relationship being back on solid footing. Both of them forgave and moved on from any earlier tension.

After the late evening and this morning's task of wrangling another beam onto the second level of concrete blocks, she is ready for a break. Pulling her thermos from her bag, Emily unscrews the lid, letting the steam escape before pouring the tomato soup into the lid, which doubles as a cup.

The box of diaries is on the floor to left of the desk. Emily picks up the edition she began reading yesterday. The muted wine-colored spine yawns slightly as she opens the page to her makeshift bookmark, a yellow sticky note. Emily flipped through several journals before discovering they belonged to a woman named Elizabet Thomas. Though she has not yet determined why they are here within the church's archives, she has been captivated all the same.

March 26, 1917

Dear Diary,

What a night! To be honest, I was less than pleased when Rupert presented the tickets to me several evenings ago. His face, though, was reminiscent of a boy who had just been given a lollipop, and I knew that I could not refuse him this outing. I am so pleased I decided to refrain from offering my opinion as we would have missed the game that I am sure will land the Seattle Metropolitans in hockey history.

The Seattle arena was filled to the brim as the Montreal Canadiens took to the ice, the fans all a twitter over the Flying Frenchman and his teammates. I wouldn't be surprised if many Seattleites wagered against their hometown team, given the reputation of the famed hockey phenom. But in the end our Metropolitans became Stanley Cup champions, with a final score of nine to one. What a night indeed!

Emily picks up her phone, intending to search the internet for confirmation of a Seattle hockey team. As a Seattle native, she has never heard of such a team's existence, and the Stanley

Cup win sounds more like fiction than reality. A frown creases her forehead as her phone is unable to connect to the world beyond the basement.

Slurping the remnants of soup, Emily wipes the lid with a paper napkin before placing the sealed thermos in her bag. She stands and stretches the kinks out of her back and then returns the diary to the box beside her desk.

Hours later, as the afternoon draws to a close, Emily is hunched over the desk, sorting documents into stacks by year. Her mind revisits the idea of a Seattle hockey team.

"Ah Emily. Hard at work, I see." Pastor Michael wanders into the room, quiet as a church mouse.

With the question still burning in her mind, she greets him with a brief smile before launching in. Their daily conversations have created a comfortable and easy familiarity between them. "Did you ever hear about a Seattle hockey team that won the Stanley Cup in 1917?"

"Why yes. It was quite the brouhaha, or so I have heard." Pastor Michael paces slowly back and forth, just inside of the basement room's door. "I remember my father speaking fondly of the championship as a child. Why do you ask?"

"Something I read in a document had me wondering. I questioned the story, since I have never heard mention of professional hockey existing in Seattle."

Emily's mind wanders to her dad and his love of the game. "My dad was an avid hockey fan and I just thought—" Emily's voice cracks slightly under the weight of sharing information about her parents. "I guess, I figured he would have known about the history of the Metropolitans, and that he would have shared the story with me. I was curious is all."

"Sounds as if you were close with your father." Pastor Michael meets Emily eyes.

"I was." Emily's smile is sad, her eyes showing her worry

over the thoughts running through her mind. "Not with regard to hockey, but yes, we were close."

A light laugh leaves her lips. "When he discovered I was not cut out to spend hours balancing on thin blades on top of a frozen bit of lake, he wasn't hurt or disappointed. He simply switched gears, and by spring I had a brand new baseball glove."

"Ah, so you found a sport you enjoyed." Pastor Michael beams, his friendly face an invitation for her to continue.

"Lemonade and glove oil." Emily's expression softens at the memory. As the weeks she has spent in the church continually press her memories forward, Emily is becoming aware of and a little more used to the nostalgia.

"What is that, Emily?" Pastor Michael nudges her to continue.

"Friday afternoons from May to September," Emily offers in a quiet voice, "I could count on finding Dad sitting on the back steps, waiting for me with a glass of lemonade in one hand and a bottle of glove oil in the other. We would sit for hours talking stats and favorite players. He used to coach me on the subtleties of the game."

Pastor Michael leans in, listening intently, his interest conveyed by his posture.

"I played shortstop on the neighborhood team," Emily announces with a steady voice before the words trail off, a memory captured. "I always knew my glove was the softest on the team. He never missed a game."

Swiveling her chair to face Pastor Michael once more, a sheepish expression rises on her cheeks as she collects herself. "Anyway." She clears her throat and sits a little taller in the hardbacked chair. "I wouldn't think a sports achievement such as winning the Stanley Cup would be overlooked by Seattle sports fans of any era."

"Perhaps it was overshadowed by other events. We were in the thick of World War I, and then there was the Spanish flu after that." Pastor Michael lowers his chin, his eyes finding interest with the concrete floor as he ponders Emily's observation. "I suppose folks had other things on their mind, and a sporting event was a short-lived boost in morale."

"You are probably right." Emily rocks slightly in the chair as her head bobs in agreement. "I don't imagine it was the easiest of times."

"I do remember my father telling me the oddest thing." Pastor Michael's eyes twinkle with mischief. "There was a tradition in the chase for the cup. Since the two teams in the final games were usually from different leagues, with different rules of play, they would alternate rules. In 1917, games two and four were played under six-man rules. Each team had six players on the ice, and forward passing was not allowed. However, games one and three were played under seven-man rules, with seven players on the ice and allowable use of the forward pass."

"Really?"

Pastor Michael chuckles lightly. "I still can't imagine how the players managed to keep those rules straight night after night."

Emily joins him in a laugh, shaking her head in disbelief. "Not to mention how confusing it must have been for the fans." Regaining her composure, Emily adds, "I have to say I am learning about things I never expected to find here in the church. There really are a multitude of stories hidden within all this disorganization."

"Precisely why your job here is so important, Emily." Pastor Michael turns toward the door. "Stories are only valuable if someone is willing and able to share the knowledge. And if someone else is interested in hearing them." He steps over the threshold. "To be of any value at all, a story requires two participants."

Emily swivels her chair to face the desk. The stories she holds onto about the life she shared with her parents may lose their value if she continues to keep them to herself. The awareness of such a possibility agitates her.

She wants to ask him if he truly believes this to be the case with all stories. She turns her head to raise the question, since she hasn't heard him set foot upon the stair's squeaky tread, when the squeal from the hot water pipes startles her. The sound interrupts her thoughts and any desire to remain in the dark basement room. She straightens the papers before her and decides they can wait another day. Gathering her coat and belongings, Emily takes a last glance at the work in progress before switching the light off and closing the door.

CHAPTER 10

hursday, March 19, 2015
Elizabet

I've become accustomed to having her around over the past several weeks, but seriously, how could I not watch the girl? She was reading my diaries again. My private thoughts and contemplations. My hopes and dreams, along with my grief and troubles, right there in my own hand. It's certainly an intrusion into the confines of my mind, and yet it's a gift of sorts, I suppose, if I am honest with myself.

The first day she reached for the box, a keen interest etched in her expression, I had been watching her from the corner of the room. I was curious as to why she was still here. Having cleared the area around the old desk, she continued to riffle through boxes, one after the other. Observing her was interesting enough in the beginning, hearing remembrances of friends' achievements and celebrating all over again, as if they were happening before my eyes.

As Pastor Michael told the glorious tale of the opening of The Fresh Air Cottage, I remembered the event with fondness. We devoted many months of work to raising the funds necessary to build the children's orthopedic hospital. I organized a knitting bee, and many of the women of Seattle knitted socks, hats, mittens, and the like to sell at the church holiday bazaar the winter before The Cottage was to be built. We were a proud lot, seeing what we had achieved with a bit of yarn and determination. We helped make our city the best it could be.

Years later, after dear Rupert had passed, our home became *the* place for socials, oftentimes functioning as a headquarters for fundraising events as we ladies endeavored to help those less fortunate than ourselves. For me, the polished silver and punch bowls became a distraction. I immersed myself in the events to forget my grief. We once hosted a gala evening with the theme *literary delights*, since us women had originally come together through our joint interest in literature.

I remember our first literary meeting well. Rupert and I had only recently begun courting, and though my interest in education was already well established, he ardently encouraged my learning. He even offered his home's library for our first literary meeting, where we discussed Arthur Conan Doyle's latest Sherlock Holmes title.

Those were the days. A smile tugs my cheeks upward, even after so much time has passed. I was immediately smitten by Rupert, and the love that never died, even when life itself no longer remained. Despite our age difference, his willingness to accept both my intelligence and my hand in marriage was one of the greatest pleasures of my life. Never had I felt so at home. Twelve years of marriage was far from enough. I hung on afterwards, as a shadow of the woman I was before, I am sad to say.

I slide closer to Emily, peering over her shoulder at the diary in her hands. She shivers slightly beneath the coat that lies across her shoulders. After I passed, Rupert wasn't where I expected him to be, in this church. Thus, I suppose I am trapped in a world between the last one and the one that, according to Dorothea, still lies ahead of me. Perhaps Emily has the information I require. Perhaps she is here to show me the way to my beloved Rupert. I lean a little closer, reading the open page that has captured her attention.

August 26, 1920

Dear Diary,

Today is a glorious day for our state and our country. A day that has been hard-won. A day that shows this grand nation of ours what it means to have equality among men and women. Women have secured the national right to vote, and I am eager to exercise that right, with all women across our nation. For us Washington women, this has been a journey long in the making.

When I was a small child, my mother used to regale to me with a story of when Washington was a mere territory in 1883. Apparently, women were granted the right to vote, and in Seattle that meant the creation of the Apple Orchard Convention. The party won every seat in Seattle government the next voting year, save for the position of city mayor. However, the party's monopoly over Seattle politics and our right to vote were short-lived. Thus, it has been a lengthy thirty-two years since

Washington women have been provided a voice in any governmental election.

I feel as though I should pinch myself to believe the news. The Nineteenth Amendment is finally a reality. We will march to the polls at the first opportunity, with our heads held high, and will cast our votes as we see fit. A glorious day indeed. May our great nation come together as one and do right by each and every American among us.

My eyes fall back to the diary's page. I remember the day clearly. Pure, ecstatic delight vibrated within me as I heard the news on the talking box. Rupert and I crammed ourselves together onto a single chair so we could share the headphones. Later that same year, on November second, we listened together again as KDKA provided the results of the first presidential election to be broadcast over the airwaves, eventually announcing Warren G. Harding as the next president of the United States.

Emily pauses before turning the page, and I wonder where her thoughts are taking her. Little does she know how instrumental and resourceful we women have been throughout the years. We arranged dinner parties to include those who were to be influenced along with those capable of doing the influencing. A lengthy seven-course meal provided ample opportunity for coercive conversation, and we dictated where the guests were to sit.

We threw galas in the name of charity, while letting the prohibition reserve pour freely, loosening up the tongues and wallets of those in attendance. Whether at a simple dinner party or a well-orchestrated gala event, the women working behind the scenes were a penetrating and mighty force of stained lips and sheer determination.

Flipping through the pages, Emily stops abruptly, and I lean in for a better view.

September 18, 1920

Dear Diary,

The news is dreadful. What should seem like a million miles away feels far too near and unnerving. Less than two years free of the Great War, and already a catastrophe on American soil. The papers announced the tragedy this morning, the details sparse but the terror overwhelming.

Two days ago, under the clear skies of an almost perfect late summer afternoon, there was an explosion at J. P. Morgan bank located on Wall Street in New York City. The blast rattled every building in sight, killing thirty individuals immediately. Several with life-threatening injuries were taken to a nearby hospital. A bomb is believed to have detonated during the lunch hour. Sadly, this was the busiest timeframe for the area, as employees from surrounding businesses ventured out of doors in search of their lunchtime meal. Many employees, with only a short thirty-minute window for lunch, walked hurriedly by, paying little attention to the horse and cart parked in front of the dome-roofed building.

My heart is sick with the news and has forced me to bed in the middle of the afternoon with a cup of tea and an unhappy disposition. Rupert is scheduled to visit New York City, departing a mere three days from now via train, first to Chicago and onward from there. Business calls him to the opposite side of the country, and this I find distaste with.

In an attempt to calm my nerves, Rupert ordered a gin and tonic be sent to my room, though the gin these days is lacking in quality and the tonic does little to ease the pain in my head. I have tried to distract myself with a needlepoint project, but unless Rupert is able to confirm his travel plans have been altered, I fear I am in no state to venture outside of this room.

A dreadful day it was. That was one of the few arguments Rupert and I participated in during our twelve years of marriage. I was filled with fear for his safety, as his heart had already begun to give him cause for concern. I had his best interests in mind, but a stubborn man will do what a stubborn man will do. And Rupert was indeed a stubborn and strong-willed man. It was what made him so exceptional at running his many companies. Seldom did he view a challenge as anything but an opportunity, positively convinced any obstacle could be surmounted.

Rupert did indeed venture to New York City that fall, though he delayed his travel one month in an attempt to appease my nerves. Rupert's health was my primary concern during his last few years on earth. The Spanish flu hit Seattle with a vengeance in September 1918, and Rupert fell ill with the disease within the first two weeks of its arrival in our beautiful city. The disease spread like wildfire, closing down public spaces, meetings, and schools. Rupert was one of the fortunate few who recovered from the epidemic, none of us knowing how or why some were spared while others were not so fortunate.

I tended to him night and day, dismissing most of the household staff, both for their personal safety and to allow them to care for their own family members. It was a wretched time. I watched death play with lives like a cat plays with a field mouse, batting it to and fro with little regard to the pain and damage it inflicts.

As quickly as it swept in, the flu vacated our city and much of our state. By the time spring arrived, over fourteen hundred

Seattleites had perished, leaving businesses and loved ones behind. For Rupert, the flu left a weakened heart. Times were indeed difficult, but we managed through it all. Through the war. Through the flu. Through the terror come to our nation's soil.

At the time, I considered myself a woman of strength, of resilience. I had experienced more hardships than any one life should hold. But I also considered myself a woman of great fortune. I had found the love of my life, and he took care of me just as I took care of him. We had few wants, as Rupert was a sturdy provider, even building me a dream home upon the hill. Even as his health burdened him, I felt fortunate and blessed.

Two years later he was gone. In 1922, at the age of forty-seven, I found myself anything but strong and far less resilient than I had thought myself to be. I was no longer myself. Though I moved through grief, pasting a socially suitable smile upon my face when necessary, my life and my heart never recovered from losing Rupert.

A faint scent of flowery perfume permeates the room, pulling me from my reverie and from Emily's side. I whirl to find Dorothea lingering about the wall closest to the door, wavering against the shadowy light. Hardly a tentative woman by nature, she hesitates. I assume she senses my grief, and despite the loud and righteous opinions others may have of her, Dorothea is a woman of great compassion. She is my silver lining in this beloved building, this place in between worlds.

"I thought I might find you here." Dorothea edges closer, her double-wrapped strand of pearls rattling as she moves. Once Dorothea discovered the styles of the 1920s flattered both her flamboyant tastes and her less than narrow waistline, she never ventured far from the 20s fashions, even after the decade had passed her by. "You wouldn't happen to be avoiding me, would you?"

I roll my eyes in her direction. "Why would you think I was avoiding you?" I incline my head toward Emily and the diary before her. "I've been busy is all."

"Elizabet dear, you cannot outrun the gravity of the situation any longer." Dorothea's blue eyes settle on me like a mother with an argument to win, determined to gain my undivided attention.

"I am not running." I cast her a cheeky glance. "Does it look as though I am running?"

"Come now. I know you are feeling unsettled. The news is long in coming." Dorothea's eyes soften. "But ignoring the very likely possibility that this church will soon be gone is no longer an option."

"The news, as you put it, has been long in coming for close to twenty-five years. What makes you think it will end this time?" I am aware that my logic is unfounded, but my distaste at discussing such thoughts has left me irrational.

Dorothea, undeterred, presses on. "Elizabet, The Supreme Court is the final step. There is nothing beyond its decision. I think it is time to discuss what will happen when the sanctuary ceases to exist."

"I don't understand why we cannot simply wait for news." My voice wavers, and fear wraps around each word like a ribbon weaves through a strand of hair.

"You must understand, dear. Time is running out." Dorothea's voice is both soft and firm. With her peace said, she moves to leave. "We are not finished discussing the topic, Elizabet."

I straighten my spine, infusing a strength I do not currently possess into my message. "Until we know for certain, I will remain precisely where I am." In a much quieter voice, my true feelings on the topic slip past my lips. "Rupert may still show himself, you know."

Dorothea sighs, retracing her path toward the door. "I believe you will wait for him for eternity, my friend. It is why I worry for you so."

CHAPTER 11

*M*onday, March 23, 2015
Emily

As Emily opens the door to the archives room with a tentative nudge of her shoulder, cool air whooshes toward her. The chill has been locked away all Sunday long while the church was full of congregation members and sermons. Emily imagines that, on this Monday morning, the chill is eager to play after its confinement.

When Emily flips the light switch, the light trembles before coming to life, bathing the basement room in a wash of muted yellow. Emily moves toward the desk, which she repositioned again last week, with a great deal of muttering and a substantial amount of sweat. She guided the solid wood beast toward the most well-lit location. As she strides into the room, she is pleased to find that the pile of rubbish has finally been removed from the area beside the door. Over the past month, the pile of old and broken furniture—along with items she

categorized as less than useful, with no historic designation—
made their way to the ever-expanding pile.

Plunking her bag onto the yellowed wooden office chair,
Emily empties its contents onto the desk before glancing
around at the space the removal of the junk pile has created.
Her homemade shelving unit has progressed to four levels,
which she has filled with archived bank boxes, each labeled
with black ink.

A pattern has emerged for Emily over the past several
weeks. Six mornings a week, she arrives on the corner of Fifth
and Marion just before the clock strikes eight. With a thermos
of tea in one hand and her messenger bag slung over her
shoulder, Emily lifts her eyes to the sanctuary's domed roof. As
the weeks in the basement pass, she begins to contemplate
how the skyline will appear without the church present. For a
second or two each morning, the thought of such a future
steals her breath.

The morning passes with speed as Emily hauls another
three boxes into place on the fifth storage shelf. She realizes
she cannot stack the boxes any higher, not to mention the
beams and concrete blocks. She would need the help of
another person or, at the very least, a much sturdier ladder.
Emily pulls her phone from the back pocket of her jeans and
checks the time.

She is accustomed to the long workdays, but the physical
intensity of the task at hand and the mental puzzling of dates,
names, and records has drained her. Each day, she sits and
recharges with lunch and a cup of tea, either packed from
home or enjoyed at Murph's, to maintain her productivity.
Drawn time and time again to the box of diaries, Emily soon
discovered that reading the almost fictional account of
Elizabet Thomas' life helps her maintain her mental fortitude.

With half a ham sandwich in her left hand, Emily uses her

right to lay flat the diary page. At first, the slanted penmanship of an era long since passed proved challenging to decipher. But the process has become easier after a month of practice reading historic documents. With the assistance of her trusty desk lamp, Emily hunches over the journal and continues where she left off last Saturday.

March 29, 1922

Dear Diary,

My heart is heavy. Sobs come in uncertain waves like an ocean washing over me, pulling me under, leaving me scrambling for air. Today, I buried my love, my best friend, my Rupert. His heart, weakened by the strain of a deadly flu and the passing of years, was unable to beat any longer.

I am filled with gratitude for the years we had together, though I know happiness will never again be wholly mine. They were beautiful years, filled with love and laughter and hope. I suspect it is the hope I will miss the most. When one has something to hope for, one has life. Without it, what is left?

Emily's head lifts from the diary page. The scent of sweet vintage perfume fills the air, drawing her head toward the archive room door, where she expects to see Mrs. Peters or another lady of the church. Seeing no one, Emily returns her attention to the pages, eager yet also tentative to read of Elizabet's loss.

A trickle of guilt snakes through Emily's mind as her eyes return to the spot her finger has marked, aware she is intruding on someone's privacy by reading the diary entries. Elizabet's words are honest and beautifully written. They tug at Emily, burrowing themselves deeper within her heart. The connection Emily feels to this woman, this stranger, is both foreign and familiar. The familiarity of Elizabet's circumstance wiggles beneath Emily's skin like a tick, threatening to poison its new host stealthily and without warning. Though Emily does not understand why she feels compelled to read Elizabet's journals, she dips her head and begins again.

When one has something to hope for, one has life. Without it, what is left?

But it was all worth it. I wouldn't change a thing. The grief that wraps around me like a straitjacket today can never outweigh the love and joy. I won't let it Rupert. I promise you that.

There is never enough time. That I am certain of. If my beloved Rupert and I had spent every waking moment of every day together, we would not have had hours enough to fill me up for the rest of my days. The trick now is to be grateful for the ones we did share.

Rereading the passage twice more, Emily's eyes brim with tears. Her chest constricts with emotion as she feels the straitjacket Elizabet wrote about tightening its bind. "It is always there." The sandwich falls to its wrapper on the desk, spreading lettuce and mustard beyond the crust's edges as Emily's tears turn into sobs. "No matter how much I push away the grief, it's always there. The knowledge that life will never be the same again."

Emily's heart pounds in her chest as her thoughts turn to the reality she has tried desperately to ignore. *I will never hug my mom again. My dad's laugh will forever be missing from any home I live in. How can I have a future when theirs was cut so short? This isn't fair. They should have been here to see me graduate from law school. They should be here now so I can tell them about my work in the beautiful building where they said "I do." They should be here so I can explain to them how I am falling in love with the church, just as I imagine they did.*

A convulsive sigh erupts from Emily's chest, causing her entire body to shiver. Hastily flipping the diary over, Emily reaches for her thermos and gulps hot tea in an effort to shoo away both the wrought emotions and the cold. Swiping in frustration at the tears on her cheeks, Emily is startled by Pastor Michael's voice. Biting the inside of her cheek to stop herself from cursing in his presence, Emily wonders how in the world Pastor Michael continues to sneak up on her without warning.

"Ah, Emily." Pastor Michael's concern is etched into his deep blue eyes. "Is everything all right?"

Emily smiles sheepishly, finding comfort by focusing on the gray concrete floor. "Yes. Yes, of course. I was caught up in some reading and it—" Emily's pause, she realizes too late, acts more like an invitation than a request for privacy.

"Made you sad." Pastor Michael finishes her sentence for her.

Shrugging her shoulders, Emily blinks several times, the tears still eager to return. "It's—it's just that . . . Well, I don't know." Emily squares her shoulders and forces a smile. "I'll be fine. Nothing to worry about."

Pastor Michael returns her smile. "What you read made you think of your parents?"

Emily's eyes grow wide in disbelief. "How did you know? Who told you?" Stammering her way through incomplete sentences, Emily leans on the edge of the desk for support. "I don't mean to be rude, Pastor Michael, but I don't want to talk about it." Emily nods with certainty in a desperate attempt to close the conversation.

Pastor Michael's eyes twinkle with a hint of dwarf-like mischief. "This isn't my first rodeo, you know," he says with a wink. "Not wanting to talk about something and not being able to are very different things, Emily." Pastor Michael clasps his hands behind his back, in what Emily has come to think of as his thoughtful stance. "So, what was it you were reading?"

Relieved to move the conversation away from herself, Emily flips the diary over. "I came across a box of diaries a few weeks ago. Elizabet Thomas' diaries. To be honest, I am not really sure why they are here in the archives. I've been reading diary entries here and there. I've found entries from as far back as 1915, but I haven't yet been able to sort out a starting point."

Nodding his head, Pastor Michael seems to weigh his words before speaking. "Elizabet Thomas and her husband, Rupert, were members of our congregation for many years. They were married here in the sanctuary. In fact, they were the first to wed in this building, if memory serves me correctly." After searching the ceiling for his recollection of events, Pastor Michael turns to Emily with renewed enthusiasm. "Well, where did you leave off? Let's hear a little of what Mrs. Thomas has to say for herself, shall we?"

Not wishing to begin anywhere near the emotional entry, Emily thumbs several pages ahead in the diary, attempting to put distance between herself and any mention of Elizabet's grief or Rupert's passing. She finds an entry that, from the first few words, promises to be uplifting. Emily glances at Pastor Michael and begins to read out loud.

July 19, 1922

. . .

Dear Diary,

I had the most unexpected meeting today when I went to the church to visit Rupert. So often, I find myself alone in the sanctuary during my weekly Wednesday morning visits. To be honest, I was startled at first by the presence of another individual in my sacred space. A plume-hatted head was bowed low in prayer several pews in front of my usual place.

Once I regained my composure, I steadied my posture and found a spot among the many empty rows. I lowered my own head, closed my eyes, and waited for Rupert's presence to wash over me. Instead of being engrossed in the memory of my beloved, I found myself distracted by the sweet, flowery scent of a woman's perfume.

I was at first annoyed by the intrusion into my weekly ritual. But then I found myself captivated by the scent, and the memory of a garden party years before appeared in my mind's eye. I remember the party well, as it was where Rupert and I first met. He was talking with the gentlemen as I mingled among the ladies, but wherever I ventured around the grounds, his eyes seemed to find mine. After several hours, filled with mini sandwiches and potato salad, Rupert approached me and introduced himself in a polite and assured manner.

The afternoon bled into evening, and by the time I was wrapping a shawl around my shoulders, Rupert had invited me to dine with him the following week. I was unaccustomed to male attention, to say the least, given my preference for higher education over marriage. His rapt intensity, waiting to hear what I had to say, was more than enough to intrigue me. However, it was his wink, directed solely at me as I bade farewell, that won me over in the end. There before me was a man who valued all of me, intelligence, opinion, and female form.

The woman finished her prayer and was about to exit the sanctuary. The swish of her fashionable skirt and a stronger whiff of her perfume drew me back to the present. I opened my eyes and met her startling blue ones. She gave a polite but curt nod in my direction, and as I stood, hustling my stride to reach her before she left, I realized with slight embarrassment who the woman was. The awkward state in which I found myself flushed heat onto the back of my neck as I stood before a woman who I certainly knew by reputation but had never before engaged in conversation with.

"Ms. Graham," I stuttered. "If you have a moment?"

"Mrs. Thomas," she said, with a put-upon smile and false friendliness. "What can I do for you?"

"Oh, Ms. Graham. I am sorry to interrupt you. I was just wondering if you could tell me the name of your perfume? You see, it reminded me of a happier time, and I thought— Well, I thought perhaps it would be useful to have some in my collection, so as to brighten a day here or there." My cheeks blushed asking this of Ms. Graham, madame of Seattle's most well-established brothel.

"Mrs. Thomas," she said, "I was very sorry to hear of your loss. My condolences to you."

I must have been out of my mind with grief to ask such a question of her, but I asked anyway. "Did you know my husband, Ms. Graham?"

Her blue eyes lit up with a smile. "Not in the way you are asking, Mrs. Thomas. Your husband was a principled man who cared deeply for the people of Seattle. That is all we knew of one another, rest assured."

She reached out and patted my arm, and I have to admit that a bubble of relief welled up inside of me. One thinks they know their husband, but the lack of his daily presence and too much grief-stricken time can let the mind run amok. One cannot help but wonder who he might have been prior to marriage, and thoughts never allowed entrance sneak in and begin rearranging the house.

"I will send a note with the name of the perfume, Mrs. Thomas." With that, Ms. Graham and her flowery perfume wafted out of the sanctuary.

In hindsight, I must giggle at myself. What an unlikely encounter for

99

two women to have. Church might have been the last place I ever expected to see the likes of Ms. Graham.

A boisterous laugh escapes Emily's lips. "I am really growing fond of our Elizabet."

Pastor Michael stifles a chuckle of his own. "Please, do continue, Emily. This most certainly is amusing."

July 25, 1922

Dear Diary,

A package arrived today by way of a long black Studebaker. It was from Ms. Graham. A bottle of her flowery perfume was wrapped in tissue with a note.

Dear Mrs. Thomas,
 I hope this small token will aid in easing the pain of your heart.
 My thoughts and prayers are with you during this difficult time.
 Yours sincerely,
 Dorothea

I knew in that moment I had stepped beyond societal bounds and made a friend. I hope I can somehow be of service to her in the coming years.

. . .

A smile slides onto Emily's lips. Sniffing the air discreetly, Emily is certain she can smell the sweet scent of perfume as she shifts in the chair. Her toes tingle in her shoes and Emily stands to rejuvenate her blood flow. "Do you know if the two women became friends or whether the social structure of the day kept them apart?"

"Oh, they became friends indeed. Lifelong friends." Though his words answer Emily's question, she suspects there is more that Pastor Michael isn't saying.

"Was Dorothea really the town's madame?" Emily can't help but ask.

"Oh yes. The town folk called her Madame Lou. She ran the biggest brothel in Seattle for many years. Though I cannot condone her chosen profession, she was most certainly a clever businesswoman in her own right." Pastor Michael places a hand over his heart. "She also had one of the city's biggest hearts. Quiet about it always, but deeply generous to the town and its community members." Pastor Michael lets out a guffaw. "It's been said that, in those days, more business was done at Madame Lou's than ever was at city hall."

Emily shakes her head in disbelief. "They talk about Madame Lou on the tour beneath the city. It's been ages since I visited, but I remember a photograph in the gift shop of her with some of her girls."

"This building has stories to share, Emily." Pastor Michael's voice is serious once more. "Yes indeed. Weary hearts to console and stories to share. I hope you will read on." Pastor Michael inclines his head toward the box of diaries at the foot of Emily's desk chair. "There is much to learn from the past. I'm not sure this building has told all of its stories just yet. It would be a shame to lose the stories along with the building, don't you think?"

Emily's stomach lurches at the mention of losing the

church. Emily feels her connection to the church and its history weaving its way into the fabric of her being. Her analytical mind reminds her the legal situation is well out of her control. The church's future lies with the courts now, and it is far too late to think that an alternate solution might exist. She could spend time hoping, but she isn't convinced that any measure of hope would do her or the church any good.

Strolling toward the door, Pastor Michael turns back to her and lays a finger to the side of his nose, much like Emily imagines a real-life Santa Claus might do. "Weary hearts yet to console, Emily."

Emily offers a brief wave as Pastor Michael sweeps out of the room. She listens with an ear cocked toward the door, but the squeaky staircase beyond offers no sound, no mention of someone upon its treads.

CHAPTER 12

 ednesday, April 1, 2015
Emily

A text from Ryan earlier this morning said he would be at the church by noon. Excited about the midweek lunch date and about Ryan visiting the archives she has worked tirelessly to organize for the past month and a half, Emily climbs the stairs to the narthex a few minutes before twelve.

She pushes on the heavy wooden door, cracking it open to breathe in the day's chill, and examines the sky. There is still no rain in sight and not a single dark-rimmed cloud hovering above. The dull color of the sky indicates no coming precipitation, but the temperature suggests winter has yet to vacate the city.

Taking in the view from the top of the church steps, she notes the tall buildings that shroud the church from every angle. Tossing around in her head the argument that has plagued her for the past week, Emily finds it easy to empathize with the congregation and administrative staff. The church no longer seems to belong here, at least not when viewed from this vantage point. No wonder they feel the need to relocate.

Emily shakes her head as her brain swirls with competing thoughts. Without question, she began work on the archives with her feet planted behind the church leaders' legal right to sell the property. She believed in their right to move on, for the betterment of their congregation and their pocketbook. At first, she didn't give the controversy much thought. Her job as a lawyer is to support her clients, regardless of her personal beliefs. But somewhere along the way, or somewhere within the dimly lit and far from hospitable basement storage room, she was pulled in another direction. Wrapping her arms around her body for warmth, Emily admits to herself that she no longer wants to see the church destroyed. She no longer wishes to see the memories, both those in boxes and those within the walls, crumbled by a wrecking ball.

Having mulled the situation over in her head with nauseating repetition, Emily is teetering on the edge of wishing the Supreme Court would rule in favor of the city instead of the church. Her secret wish is cloaked by fear that she might inadvertently speak the words out loud. The niggling contemplations have cost her several nights of sleep. They run through her dreams, leaving her with bloodshot eyes and the belief that giving this opinion a voice might also give it strength. Emily knows that this revelation does not need to gather strength beyond the safety of her own carefully fenced-in mind.

As a lawyer, Emily is trained to work toward the goals and resolutions of her clients. But as a researcher who rubs elbows with the past, she cannot help but root for history and memories to win. Rational thinking aside, Emily has fallen in love with the church and, more specifically, with the sanctuary.

With her heart tugged toward the magic of the space, Emily is in awe of the sanctuary. Despite the surrounding noise, traffic, and human motivations, the sanctuary remains a place of reprieve. A place to sit in contemplation, be inspired, and become whole again.

Each morning, Emily enters the sanctuary, a hush washing over her as she sits in a pew and casts her eyes about the immense space. A few moments is enough to invigorate her spirit, drawing her closer to something she can't quite put her finger on. Emily has yet to determine whether it is magic, foolery, or divine grace. Though her pragmatic mind is usually in constant motion, Emily shushes her brain into submission in the sanctuary, experiencing the place through the beating of her own heart.

"Hey." Ryan climbs the stairs two at a time, his long legs striding with ease. His messenger bag is slung over his broad shoulder, the epitome of a young professional on the verge of conquering the world.

Emily smiles at him, an automatic response to his beaming face. "Hey." She opens the door wider to allow him to squeeze past her, into the warm air of the church's front hall.

Removing his hands from his tailored dress jacket, Ryan rubs them together before wrapping Emily in an embrace. "Cold out there today."

With his chilled cheek against her head, a fresh shiver sneaks along Emily's spine. She inhales, catching whiffs of his cologne, a familiar and comforting scent. "I just need to grab my jacket, but come, I'll give you the twenty-five-cent tour." Unwrapping her arms from around his waist, Emily purposefully steers him away from the sanctuary doors, not trusting herself to allow Ryan direct access to her recently unearthed vulnerable side.

Tugging his arm in the direction of the basement staircase, Emily motions toward the low ceiling. "Watch your head."

"Did you talk to Colin and Veronica about the weekend?" Ryan ducks his head while placing a steadying hand on the outcropping of the ceiling's drop.

"I did." Emily smiles over her shoulder at him. "They understand we won't be with them for Easter dinner. Besides, who wouldn't think an Easter getaway to Whistler is a wonderful idea?"

Descending the last step, Ryan pulls her into a tight embrace before kissing her nose lightly. "I know I am looking forward to getting away with you. Three entire days." Ryan pulls back and gives her a quizzical look. "I don't think we've ever spent three full days together. Whatever will we do?"

Emily snuggles in a little closer, inhaling his cologne while allowing his afternoon stubble to rub against the top of her head. "I'm sure we can think of something," she murmurs into his chest.

"Look." Emily pivots, still wrapped in Ryan's arms. "I am no longer working in a dungeon. This is now officially the archives room." She points to the small dark blue sign, engraved with clear white letters.

"Moving up in the world. Look at you," Ryan teases as Emily reaches for the doorknob, pushing the door wide in one motion.

Emily steps over the threshold and moves to the side of the entrance so Ryan can take in the entire room with a single glance.

"Wow." Ryan moves into the vast room, beaming with pride. "This is amazing, Em. Given the photographs you showed me after your first day, I am impressed. You did all this yourself?"

She nods, pride bubbling up within her. "Well, most of it. I had some help with a ladder or two."

Ryan turns and places a gentle hand on Emily's upper arm, squeezing her bicep in playful mockery. "If the next project offers the same workout routine, you can cancel your gym membership." His eyes wash over the room once more. "It really is something, Em."

"Thanks."

"May I?" Ryan motions to the wall lined with the rudimentary but sturdy shelving unit.

"Of course." Emily follows behind him as he scans the rows of neatly labeled boxes.

"And all of this is documented as well? It goes back as far as 1900." Ryan's surprise at the dates penned on the first row of boxes is palpable.

"Yep, since the beginning of the church, actually, in 1853. Though items from that time period and the early 1900s are sparse. The records are mostly marriages, births, deaths, baptisms. Maintaining a wider variety of documents and artifacts seemed to become more important after this building opened in 1910." Emily rests her hip on top of the corner of her desk. "I wonder if it became more feasible to store items since they had more space once the church was built."

Pointing toward a box labeled *Christmas 1912*, Emily continues. "They kept everything, from important church records to more personal mementos. I even found several handmade angel costumes, complete with halos, from the 1912 children's reenactment of Jesus' birth. Somebody from the church will go through some of the boxes to decide what to keep and what to toss, but I couldn't bring myself to put a single angel costume in a garbage bag." Emily shrugs as a tinge of embarrassment creeps onto her neck and cheeks. Those words she let slip reveal a sentimental side of herself that she rarely shares with anyone.

"It's incredible, Em. Truly incredible. I can see how it has captivated you so intensely." Ryan moves from one wall to the next before edging to the center of the room where the desk sits. "Interesting spot for a desk." His eyebrows reach toward his hairline. "Do you want help moving it? It looks heavy."

A laugh bursts from deep within Emily's throat. "I'll have you know I did move it." She pats the desk's worn surface with a gentle hand. "It is heavy. Extremely heavy actually, and perhaps a bit stubborn too." Emily slides her hip off the edge and backs up a few steps to examine the beast of a desk. "I explained to Pastor Michael when he teased me about the very same thing. After days in this shadowy light, attempting to read hundred-year-old documents written with vintage handwriting, I tested the room's light by moving about with a document in hand." Emily spreads her arms wide, palms up to encompass the whole of the desk's positioning. "This was the most well-lit spot in the room, and thus this was where the desk needed to be."

"You are tenacious, Em. I'll give you that." Ryan's grin teases her. "*Stubborn* might be another word for it. I would have brought in a lamp myself."

Emily playfully swats him with a diary she picked up from the desk. Feigning indignation, she says, "I did that too. I'm not a complete idiot, you know."

"I said nothing of the sort. You know I think you are brilliant." He leans over and kisses her again. "So, what is that? A new discovery?" Ryan points to the book in Emily's hand.

"This is just another rabbit hole I've scampered down." Emily holds the book out for him to examine. "It is a diary. So far, I've found three boxes of them. All written by one woman, an Elizabet Thomas."

"Why would someone's diaries be in the church's

archives?" Ryan turns the book over in his hands. "How old is it?"

"I haven't looked through them all, but from what I can tell, they began the year she was married, 1910. That's the same year the church was officially opened to the congregation. It looks like the diaries continue until her death in 1935." Emily moves closer to Ryan as he skims the pages. "I'm told the diaries made their way here after Elizabet's passing. She had no family to speak of, and she left all of her worldly possessions to charities. These diaries were the only thing of a truly personal nature found in her mansion. Her friends couldn't bear to dispose of them, and so they agreed that the church would store them until they could find a more permanent and suitable home for them."

"But Em, that was eighty years ago." Ryan's face contorts with a lack of comprehension. The neat freak in him clearly cannot understand why anyone would hold on to anything for that length of time.

"I guess they haven't found a permanent home yet." Emily's shoulders creep toward her ears. "To be honest, I'm glad they didn't. If they hadn't been here, I wouldn't have had the opportunity to read them, to get to know her." Emily's words hang in the air between them as she admits to another way in which the archives have captured her attention and her heart. The hot water pipes squeal to life.

Ryan looks over his shoulder toward the sound.

"It's the heating system," Emily explains, moving the conversation away from her attachment to Elizabet's diaries. "Not that you would think one exists when you are tucked away down here."

Ryan is still flipping through the diary. "So, how many of these have you read?"

"A few." Emily's finger traces the grooves in the desk's top as she considers whether to tell Ryan of her conundrum over the fate of the church.

The silence between them feels heavier to Emily than it did only moments ago. The room grows stuffy. Though she is certain it is a figment of her imagination, Emily feels as though the air itself is being sucked from the space.

Ryan is engrossed in reading something within the diary's pages as Emily argues with herself. She thinks back to the many times Ryan has asked for more from her. More sharing. More honesty. *Tell me how you feel, Em.*

She steals a glance at his expression, and before she can talk herself out of it, she squeezes her eyes shut and confesses. "I think they should save the church. I—I mean, I don't want to see it destroyed."

Ryan looks up from the journal. "No offense, Em, but I don't think you have much to do with deciding the outcome of this building."

"I know. I mean, I get that it is in the court's hands now." Emily examines her fingernails, picking at her thumb. "But what if I could save the church? What if I could convince the church administrators and Mr. Holt to look for alternatives?"

"Come on, Em, you can't be serious. You'd be committing career suicide. And for what? Because you read an old lady's diary and now you think you should try to save everything? You'd ruin your own life at the same time." Ryan closes the diary and drops it onto the desk.

"No. I mean, yes." Emily's chin falls to her chest. "I don't know. I just think the church is worth saving. I think it is worth fighting for." A lengthy sigh leaves her lips. "I've spent a lot of time here these past few months and I've come to see things differently. I'm not so sure this church is done giving yet. It isn't just for me, you know." Emily's eyes flicker sheepishly upward, barely meeting Ryan's gaze. "This building holds a piece of my parents too."

Ryan sighs as his hands move to rest on top of the desk, his head lowering in what Emily interprets as contemplation. "I am sorry, Em, I just don't agree. Saving the church won't bring back your parents. It won't even bring back their memory." Ryan turns to face her, reaching a hand out to lift her chin. "The memories you have are the only ones you are going to get. I don't see how putting your career on the line by not abiding by your legal oath will make life any easier."

Emily pulls back her shoulders, her face transforming into an expression worthy of stone. "You wanted to know how I feel about things. You've been begging me for months to confess all my emotions. 'Tell me what you're thinking, Em. I won't marry you unless you open up to me Em.'" Emily's hands go to her hips. Her raised voice echoes around the room as her bruised heart and righteous spirit spew words laced with indignation. "Sound familiar? Don't be such a hypocrite, Ryan. You wanted more from me, and now that you have it, you don't like what you've got. Convenient. Very convenient." Emily crosses her arms across her chest and grits her teeth in frustration. "I shouldn't have trusted you. I was better off keeping my feelings to myself." Her jaw aches as she unleashes another whip of words. "I should have known better."

"Emily, that isn't fair." Ryan's face reddens a shade as his fists open and close repeatedly at his sides. "Do you even hear yourself? Emily, your job isn't to save this place. Your job is archiving the contents so they can be saved." Taking a deep breath, Ryan steps toward her. "You are doing something good here, but you aren't responsible for saving it all. Just because I don't agree with what you said about the church doesn't mean I don't want to hear what you have to say."

The first tear escapes, navigating a slow and steady path down her cheek, gaining momentum until it becomes lost in the stream of tears spilling from both eyes.

Ryan's face softens. He takes another step toward her, his arms outstretched, inviting her into his embrace. "Let's think about this rationally. You are upset. I get it. But Em, you said it yourself. This church has been through countless years of legal battles. Do you really think it is wise to step in the way of this particular moving train?" Ryan's voice carries a plea. "Why don't we go to lunch?"

Emily shakes her head firmly and takes a step backward, away from Ryan. "You can go now."

"Em, this is crazy. We can talk this through."

"I'm not crazy," Emily fires back at him before turning her back.

"I didn't say you were. I said . . ." Ryan runs his fingers through his hair.

Whipping around once more, Emily points toward the door. "I said you can go now." The words come out loud and full of anger. "I will be sure to give Colin and Veronica your regrets over Easter dinner. Have a pleasant trip to Whistler."

Ryan's head drops to his chest. "Fine. I'll go. But I want you to know I am proud of you for all the work you've put in here. Maybe once we've cooled off, we can talk more." Ryan reaches the door, the hall light filtering around him. "Just so you know, I am well aware this isn't about the church. I hope you can see that in time." Placing his foot on the first step, Ryan turns and meets her eyes with his own moist ones. "I love you, Em. I hope you know that too."

She waits until Ryan has had enough time to vacate the building before grabbing her things and heading to Murph's in search of a glass of wine and a deep plush booth to sulk in.

CHAPTER 13

ednesday, April 1, 2015
Elizabet

Emily left in a rush today, after her argument with the boy. I worry about her, as much as I can worry about a girl I barely know. There is something fragile, something childlike, behind the stone exterior she so often shows the rest of the world. Losing decorum is not usually one of Emily's habits. If there is anything about her that I've admired these past several weeks, it is the way she conducts herself in a polite, put-together manner. Though some might say Emily too thoroughly controls her existence, she appears to be a young woman of great propriety, which is most certainly something I can relate to.

I am certain there is more to her story than meets the eye. I've given it some thought—so much so, in fact, that I've noticed she seems to be able to tuck away rogue emotions on demand and become a slave to whatever task is at hand. I have only recently begun to witness teary eyes turn into waterfalls, and today is the first time I have watched her frustration morph into a release of real anger. Even the almost immovable desk and wooden beams far too heavy for one person to lift didn't bring about the frustration she unleashed on the poor boy this afternoon.

This isn't the first time I've wondered about her, sometimes hours after her departure. Perhaps my own daughter would have been like her. The daughter I never had. I chase my thoughts away from what was not. I must stop this maudlin. It does me no good to pine for a life that, for whatever reason, wasn't meant to be mine.

"Well, isn't this interesting? Emily has a beau and a very handsome one at that. Odd that we haven't met him before, don't you think? Given all the hours the girl spends here." Dorothea interrupts my thoughts, speaking plainly though a mischievous smile plays about her dark stained lips.

"You are the eternal matchmaker, aren't you, Dorothea?" I roll my eyes at my friend.

"I can't help it. Matchmaking is what I was born to do." She curtsies mockingly. "You don't think it strange, given the days and nights she has spent holed up in here, that this is the first indication of someone important in her life?" Dorothea glides toward the box of diaries, peering at the neatly piled books with a hint of longing.

"I don't think it is any of our business what Emily does or does not do. But yes, I suppose you are correct. She is a bit of a closed-off sort of bird, if I do say so myself."

"You are one to talk. Is that the kind of thing only one closed-off sort of bird can say about another?" Dorothea nods her plumed hat in my direction, as if she is a teacher pointing out the correct answer to one of her students.

I ignore her wry comment and twirl once more around the room, grateful for a floor free of clutter and perfect for dancing. "She started talking to me today, Emily that is." I drift about the room, slowly gauging Dorothea's response from every angle. "Pastor Michael encouraged her to read my diaries. Did you know?"

"*Ptsh*, Pastor Michael. What is that old fuddy-duddy up to now?" Dorothea waves her hand in the air, the scent of her perfume washing over me as I glide by. "Of course I didn't know." Her voice sounds sure enough, but her inability to keep her hands from fidgeting shows she is evading the whole truth.

"At first I was taken aback. Eight minutes and eighty years feel all too similar to me now. My past life feels so real, so close, but it is all muddled up into one big recollection." I hold my arms out as if I am accepting a dance partner, tilt my head, and begin anew with a fresh round of music playing inside my head. "My words, the ones she reads from the pages of my diaries, seem to resonate with her. She talks out loud. Did I tell you that?" I laugh as I twirl. "Her one-sided conversations amused me in the beginning." I drop my arms and shrug. "But then again, who am I to judge. I talk to ghosts, after all." I tease Dorothea with a wink.

"Nobody is forcing you to talk to ghosts, you know. And I've told you before, Elizabet, I am a spirit. You are the ghost. Besides, you are quite welcome to find your own little corner to sulk in. Might I suggest somewhere near the pipe organ? This building is quite large enough to accommodate the two of us in separate quarters." With her back turned to me, Dorothea puts on airs that she is offended by my words.

"Now, now, dear friend, you know I would be lost without you here with me." I soften my tone as if talking to a small child whose feelings have been bruised. "How fortunate we are to have bonded over the love we share for this building. Well, that and your perfume, of course." Dorothea turns to face me, cheeks full and round, and erupts into a raucous laugh. Her laughter, bold enough to belong to any jubilant male, brings to mind an image of her surrounded by men in her large, stately home. Her home doubled as the town brothel, and men would hang on her every word as she made crass jokes, purely for their entertainment.

Dorothea's earsplitting laughter makes me giggle, but within moments she shifts her attention back to Emily's visitor. Old habits die hard. "Do you suppose they've been courting long? I didn't see a ring, so I don't suppose marriage is on the table as of yet. But he did seem quite smitten with our girl, despite her outrageous outburst."

My mind is racing as fast as my feet are gliding across the concrete floor. "Dorothea, seriously. Did you not see what I saw?" I stop mid-twirl as an idea begins to take shape. "She was furious with him. You can't tell me you didn't notice their argument." I move in Dorothea's direction, puzzle pieces clicking into place as I consider Emily's words.

"What?" Dorothea is upon me, tapping the toe of her high-heeled shoe impatiently. "What are you mumbling about over here?"

"Emily. Why do you think she is here? I mean really here?" The buzz about my head is growing louder. "Do you think she is in this church for something more than cleaning up the storage room?" My eagerness at the possibility of a project ignites something deep within me. Having been trapped in this world in between for more years than I am comfortable counting, I feel excitement simmering inside me. I feel something I haven't felt in far too long. Something resembling a purpose.

I continue without waiting for Dorothea's reply. "Pastor Michael has been awfully suspicious of late, don't you think? The way he has been coaxing the girl. Suggesting she look in this box or that. He almost pushed her into the box of my diaries, now that I think of it. Perhaps Emily has been brought to us on purpose. Perhaps she is the one who will save the sanctuary."

The awareness of my discovery is tantalizing, and I am giddy at the notion. Though how or why the girl might do this is beyond my scope of understanding, I am intrigued. "She said it herself, Dorothea. She thinks the church should be saved. Don't you see? The girl is on our side after all." I step away from Dorothea once more and begin to pace around the room. "But how? We need to find a way to encourage her forward."

"Encourage her forward in life or solely in an effort to save your current residence?" Dorothea raises an eyebrow at me as she runs her fingers through the length of pearls wrapped around her neck.

The sarcasm is not lost on me, and I shoot Dorothea a look of disdain. Her comment, though intended to prove a point, only adds fuel to the fire burning within my mind. "We can do both." The dark navy folds of my ankle-length skirt sway as I move excitedly toward Dorothea. "Have you noticed the sense of melancholy Emily seems to carry?"

"I can't say I have, but then again, I haven't spent nearly as much time in the girl's company as you have, Elizabet."

I ignore the slight and try again. "Perhaps we can find a manner in which to assist Emily while encouraging her to rally in support of saving the sanctuary."

"Ooooh. Perhaps we can have our hand at matchmaking, then. Surely, she could use a little encouragement in that department." Dorothea's motives are written all over her eager expression.

"If that is what Emily needs." I pause, considering our options while searching for appropriate words to quell Dorothea's excitement over Emily's love life. "It may be prudent to focus on the girl and the sanctuary first."

"What shall we do, then?" Dorothea's eagerness at the task is comforting. Knowing I will not be alone in this endeavor bolsters my enthusiasm and calms my nerves.

"We need to gain her attention." My mind is whirring with ideas. The quandary spurs my problem-solving brain into action.

"But how?" Dorothea asks with seriousness. "If you haven't noticed, we can't exactly invite her to tea."

"No, we can't. But . . ." A small smile curves my lips as an idea takes hold.

"But what? Please, Elizabet, do not start holding out on me now."

"Have you noticed how Emily sniffs the air and looks toward the door when you draw near to her?"

"Can't say that I have. I expect I am much more interested in reading your diary entries if she has them open. My favorite is the description of the day we first met. You remember the one?"

"Yes, yes, of course." I offer a quick smile to appease Dorothea's feelings. I am often surprised by how easily she is put off by sentiments, both said and unsaid. "It was a day that was meant to be, now wasn't it?"

"It was indeed." Dorothea spins around, the gathered skirt of her shimmering dress swishing to and fro. "Friends for life, you and me."

"Friends for life." I repeat her words with a confident nod. "Yes, indeed." I pause a moment, ensuring the sentiment has registered before proceeding. "I suspect Emily is able to smell your perfume."

"No! That isn't possible." Dorothea shakes her head adamantly.

"I think it is true." My eyes soften as Dorothea considers the idea.

"But how? All these years, no living person has been even slightly aware that I am nearby, unless of course I intend for them to know." Dorothea winks, wearing a mischievous smirk. "But then again, I haven't paid that much attention to be honest." Shrugging at her own lack of interest in the living, she continues. "Anyway, Elizabet, given my state of dress"— her fingers flow through the silky shimmer of her 1920s-style attire—"a modern-day interaction with the girl would be difficult, now wouldn't it?"

"Yes, I suppose it would." I temper my words so as not to offend. "I believe an opportunity still remains, Dorothea dear. Do you remember how I used to tease you about the strength of your perfume? The way I suggested that perhaps you shouldn't bathe in it, but be content with a spritz or two?"

"You weren't actually serious?" A quiet moment lingers between us. "Were you?" Clearly appalled at my mention of the unflattering moment, Dorothea is well on her way toward a sour mood. "I mean, certainly Elizabet. You were the only one to say such a thing to me. Ever!"

"Please don't take offense, Dorothea. You must remember, I was your only true friend. My intention was never to hurt your feelings, only to alert you to the possibility that more is not necessarily better. Sometimes more is just, well—more." I sigh, gathering up a compliment, albeit a slight one. "Your perfume, in whatever quantity, is going to come in handy now. The solution is what we should be focusing on. Don't you think?"

"I suppose so." Dorothea's eyes bat slightly, a sign that she has granted forgiveness. "If you think I can truly be of assistance with Emily, then I suppose I can forgive your words."

"I do. I do indeed. Now, let's put our heads together and make a plan."

CHAPTER 14

hursday, April 23, 2015
Emily

Settling into the red vinyl booth of the diner, Ryan sits across from Emily, instantly engrossed in the menu before him. She watches his eyes as they scan burgers and sandwiches. A rush of adoration for him mixes with a healthy dose of stubborn pride. The argument they had over three weeks ago pushes to the forefront of her mind. Emily contemplates the potential outcomes of the conversation before deciding whether to share how much she has missed him.

"What is going on in that head of yours?" Ryan's eyes flicker up and seek hers. "Anything you want to talk about, Em?" Setting the menu aside, Ryan folds his hands on top of the table and gives Emily his full attention.

Aware of where the conversation could go, Emily switches gears. "I am glad you got to see the church." Emily reaches for his hands. "It means a lot to me that you are interested in seeing what I have been doing all this time."

"I've always been interested, Em. I am interested in anything that has to do with you. I thought you knew that about me." Ryan's smile fades, and his face takes on a shadow of what Emily interprets as sadness.

Reading the signs, Emily jumps in with what she deems is an appropriate answer. "Yes. Of course I know. I do know. *Really.*" Her eyes seek his in an attempt to convince him.

"But that doesn't change the rest of it, does it, Em?" Ryan's question signals a sharp left turn, and Emily finds herself heading the wrong way on a one-way street as the conversation veers toward the last time they saw each other.

A waitress in a pale pink, 1950s-style uniform interrupts, and Emily breathes a sigh of relief. "What can I get you?" Her pencil hovers over a notepad. Her pink glossy lips match the bubblegum she is chewing between words.

"I'll have the bacon cheeseburger with fries and a strawberry shake." Ryan licks his lips and Emily smiles at his childlike appetite, while coveting his hollow-leg metabolism.

"For you?" The waitress turns toward Emily, her lack of inspiration for her job manifesting in subtle impatience.

"The half sandwich and daily soup special please. Just water to drink."

"All righty then." She gathers the menus and taps them on top of the table. "It'll be out shortly."

Waiting a beat for the waitress to move on from their table, Emily leans in toward Ryan. "I don't want to argue with you. Like I said on the phone, I am sorry. I overreacted." She pauses in order to construct her next sentence. "I overreacted because, well, quite frankly Ryan, it took a lot of courage for me to share my thoughts about saving the church with you. I know you think me wanting to rescue an old building is crazy, but—"

Ryan cuts Emily off mid-sentence. "But you don't really care what I think, do you?" He sighs, running his fingers through his hair. "You are as stubborn as an ox, and you have a habit of digging your heels in and doing whatever you need to do in order to feel whole." Ryan shakes his head in disbelief. "What amazes me, Em, is how you don't see what is happening to you. I'm not sure you are aware of how shaky the ground is beneath your feet. I can see how precarious your emotions are. I know you better than you think. It's been like this ever since we met."

Ryan's eyes dash around the diner as he contemplates his next words. "You have a tendency to keep your pain just beneath the surface. Hidden away from the rest of the world, covered by a polite smile and a strong work ethic. The thing is, even though most people are fooled by your upbeat demeanor, the pain is always there. It follows you like a shadow. Lingering close enough to affect your mood and the way you view the world. Heck, even how you feel about that church. I just don't think your current method of dealing with life's challenges is sustainable. I'm worried about you. I am worried about us."

Ryan lets the air whoosh past his lips in a slow exhale. "You are hiding behind this archiving project. Saving the church is just a substitution. I think this is how you avoid being alone with yourself, with your emotions. This is you trying desperately to find a foothold in your life."

Emily's eyes drop to examine the green swirls within the laminate tabletop. She is not proud of how she responds to these conversations, always finding herself ill-equipped to deal with Ryan's concerns. "I am not trying to push you away, Ryan." Emily tempers the cadence of her words in an effort to control her emotions, an ability that has been less reliable recently. "I care for you. I want you to know how much I care for you. I—I'm just not sure I can give you what it is you need."

The waitress appears again, halting the conversation. She leaves Emily's ice water and Ryan's milkshake topped with whipped cream and a maraschino cherry.

Ryan steadies his attention on the straw as he unwraps it from its paper binding. "Emily, the point is that you are missing the point. Entirely. All together. Completely. Yes, it is true that I don't understand why you would risk your career, your financial stability, and your reputation by breaking the legal oath you swore to uphold, especially for an old building probably already slated for demolition." Ryan plunks the straw into his thick shake and takes a sip. "The bigger issue is you, and everything that you are avoiding."

Ryan's words sting as they land squarely on Emily's shoulders. She shakes visibly in response, his words penetrating the walls she has so diligently laid in place for protection.

"And just for the record, this has absolutely nothing to do with what I need from you." Resentment fills Ryan's words, and the couple seated in the booth next to theirs glance over as his voice rises in frustration.

Emily lowers her eyes as embarrassment creeps in. The tears she's been holding back prickle at the corners of her eyes.

Lowering his voice, Ryan continues. "I've never met anyone like you, Em. You are incredible. You are fun to be with, and you are ambitious. But you seem to be under the impression that you can outrun your pain. You are a master at hiding from anything and everything that might hurt you. You can outmaneuver, sidestep, and outwit like no one I've ever seen." Ryan shakes his head as his voice wavers. "You do everything in your power to hide the pain and the memories away as if they never existed, as if they never happened. But they did exist, and they did happen. The closet you are hiding them in can only get so full before there isn't any more room for the difficult stuff, and eventually it will all spill out. To be honest, I am more than a little terrified of what will happen to you when all the grief and disappointment spills out of that closet. What happens then?"

Emily's chin quivers, and her attention turns toward keeping her emotions in check. *I will not cause a scene. I will keep it together, no matter what.*

Ryan reaches for her hand. "I have no idea what it must be like to lose your family so young. I don't know how it feels to be you. You are so incredibly successful at everything you put your mind toward, but knowing they will never see it . . . I can't imagine what that kind of knowing does to you. They will never see you succeed, Em, and I know that has to hurt." Ryan's chin drops to his chest. "I want to be with you, by your side, to witness every success, every milestone. I know I can't replace your parents, but together, I think we can create a new kind of family. I want us to be happy together, Em, but . . ." Ryan pauses, his words ripe with the emotion of his own unshed tears. "But I think you have to grieve. I think Veronica is right. You need to seek counseling. And I hate to say it, but I think you need to *want* help before we can have even the slightest chance of being happy. To be honest, I'm not quite sure how to navigate that with you. I'm not sure you even want me to."

Sitting in silence, staring at the table, Emily is certain that any normal girl would look at this amazing guy sitting across from her, full of love and compassion, and immediately do somersaults to keep him with her. A man who clearly sees her flaws and still wants to walk through life by her side. *Why can't*

I give in and concede he may be right? It isn't as if he is wrong exactly. Why can't I just say yes to everything Ryan is offering me? A partnership, a future, a family, someone who is there solely for me.

The cost is too high. In the quiet of her mind, Emily's knee-jerk response argues back with lightning speed. She wants nothing more than to give herself and all of her pain to him so they can walk forward together. But doing so is precisely the thing she is certain will destroy her.

It is true, she has felt herself leaning into her past a little more as she works among the archives. Pastor Michael's stories and Elizabet's journal entries have given her much to think about, but she knows enough to keep these thoughts and memories to herself. Ryan is desperate for her to unearth her emotions, and it feels as if he is asking her to step off the edge of a cliff without a parachute. Despite knowing wholeheartedly that she wants Ryan in her life every day going forward, this is something she is not prepared to do.

Emily squares her shoulders. She has let herself slip into unfamiliar territory by allowing the memories of her parents to tug her this way and that. In the comfort of the church, her reminiscences felt magical, almost meant to be. But now, in front of Ryan, she knows her experience within the church was an illusion. And illusions are dangerous things.

"All I know is how to be strong." She cringes slightly with immediate regret as the whispered words tumble out. Strong is the last thing she feels right now, and yet she cannot offer Ryan any other explanation.

The waitress approaches the table with two plates in hand. Her eyes slide from Ryan to Emily as she places his burger and Emily's soup and sandwich before them. "Can I get you anything else?" Her voice trills as if she is trying to release the tension in the air.

Emily pastes a smile on her lips. "This looks great. Thank you."

Ryan shakes his head and, without another word, begins devouring his burger. They eat in silence, each focused only on their plate. Halfway through her sandwich, Emily wonders if Ryan's burger is lacking in taste as much as her food is. She stops herself from commenting on the cardboard-like nature of the meal and presses on, occupying her hands and her mouth with eating.

With little conversation between them, lunch is finished, and dishes cleared with record speed. Ryan pays the bill, waving her off when Emily offers to cover her half. He holds open the door for her and they exit the restaurant, standing to the side of the entrance in the warm spring air.

Emily feels the need to fill the silence, but aware that her words won't be close to enough, she says nothing at all.

Ryan leans in and kisses her cheek. Catching a whiff of his cologne, Emily's body gravitates toward the warmth of his embrace. He steps back before she can connect with him and finds herself jolted into the reality of his disappointment with her.

"I'm sorry." Emily's voice is quiet. "I'm sorry I disappoint you. I—I understand it may not seem like it, but I am doing the best I can at the moment."

"I'm not disappointed in you." Ryan runs a hand through his hair. "I'm worried, Em. There *is* a difference." Ryan pauses to glance at his watch. "Look, I have to go. I have a meeting with the head architect."

"Of course. Sorry to have kept you." Emily's words sound less friendly than she intends. Her guard is up again, protecting her from further hurt.

A heavy sigh passes between Ryan's lips. "Maybe I am not the one who can help you, Em. I'd like to be, but I don't know." Ryan reaches for her hand and squeezes it tightly. "Why don't we give ourselves some time and see where we are then?"

Emily nods in agreement, but her heart is pounding with fear. He has never wanted time away from her before. These past three weeks alone have been agony. Emily is desperate to say something, to fix this mess. But she finds herself at a loss for words, and all she can do is watch him walk away. A single tear runs down Emily's cheek and she wonders if all the habits that used to keep her safe have now turned against her. What if she is the cause of her own pain?

CHAPTER 15

hursday, April 23, 2015
Emily

Emily's walk back to the church is slow. She shuffles her feet in
a dawdling and forlorn manner as her mind whirs around in
an overactive frenzy. She is in no hurry to reach any
destination. Her instinct to curl up in a ball and close out the
world is immense and stifling. She unzips her light spring
jacket, hoping to usher in fresh air and relief. If she had the
keys to her apartment and her bag, she would hail a cab and
head straight for home, to a warm bath, a comforting dish of
mac and cheese casserole, and a good book. Comfort seems to
be the sole solution to what plagues and overwhelms her
senses.

The keys and the bag, though, remain in the safety of the
church archives room. Emily releases another heavy sigh and
begins the arduous task of navigating back to the cavernous
basement room of the church, her legs heavy with self-

loathing. These last few weeks, the basement invigorated her, as it was filled to the brim with the evidence of her focused and diligent work. Emily's blood, sweat, and tears turning the chaotic mess into an organized and catalogued historical account of the church's history.

Her mind reels with Ryan's words. *He is probably right about the sanctuary. The building is quite likely a lost cause, but he is wrong about me. He thinks he wants the puddle-of-emotions Emily, oozing my sadness like a fountain spurts water. I am well aware, however, that nobody wants to be around a grief-stricken version of anybody, no matter how much they think they do. I saw it firsthand in the weeks following the funeral. People become tired of and even uncomfortable with someone else's grief. The sane thing to do is tuck that grief away, out of sight. It's for everyone's best interest.*

Maybe that is where I went wrong in thinking that I could save the church. Perhaps I was looking for something to save, the same way Ryan is looking to save me. "Useless goals, both of them," Emily mutters under her breath. Another sigh escapes her lips, and distraught thoughts spiral her demeanor downward, into a foul mood. Her dad used to say she was too stubborn for her own good, though his words always ended with a lighthearted chuckle.

Less than an hour ago, Emily was proud of her work with the archives and uplifted by the progress she made in only a few months. Now, her heart is full of worry over what will come of her relationship with Ryan and returning to the archives room feels arduous at best.

Climbing the steps to the church's front door, Emily's exhaustion is fully realized. Her athletic legs give way, morphing into heavy tree trunks. Tugging on the oversized door, she steps inside. The familiar scent of candle wax—the flame snuffed out days before—greets her with a wave of intimacy.

The hush and solitude of the aging building hangs in the air, gently but firmly pulling Emily toward the sanctuary. Stepping into the inner sanctum, she exhales. The sanctuary is vacant, yet Emily feels anything but alone. Meandering down the center aisle, she runs a hand along the smooth, rounded corners of each wooden pew. The feel of the polished wood grounds her in the quiet of the chapel.

In the center of the room, Emily slides onto one of the narrow benches. Her eyes are locked on the altar. The tall golden candleholders anchor the space, surrounded by white cloth, white banners, and white candles. The landscape of white relaxes Emily's eyes, encouraging her vision to blur and swim in the grace of the simplicity surrounding her. Sitting in complete silence without thought, Emily sinks into the luxuriousness of this state between chaotic daily life and a deep-rooted sleep. It is almost as if she is dreaming, fallen asleep but still aware.

Images filter through her memory like sunlight through a patch of evergreen trees, seeking out spaces between the branches. Emily's attempt to guard herself from such memories seems futile as her energy is already depleted and she has little fight left.

In the memory, she is a child. The sun is shining, warming her face as her head tips upward. Iridescent bubbles float against the blue backdrop of the clear, cloudless sky. Laughter fills the air as more bubbles cascade around her. Emily feels her cheeks tighten as her smile grows wide upon her young face.

She holds her arms straight out at her sides like an airplane about to take off, and her body spins, slowly at first before picking up speed and blurring her vision. As she twirls, her eyes glimpse familiar wide-striped, peach and white fabric. A laugh escapes her lips and Emily tips her head back farther, enjoying the thrill of the spinning sensation.

As the next revolution draws nearer, the fabric comes into better view. She recognizes Mom's favorite shirt. Arms reach out for Emily, and she feels the strength and security of her mom's embrace as she scoops Emily up and spins them both around together, locked in a whirling hug. Laughter fills the surrounding space. The memory of Mom's laughter transports Emily back to a time when all she knew was love and pure, innocent joy. A time when the only running she did was in a game of tag. A time when Emily knew for certain where she fit in the world, and herself was all she had to be. Back to a time when Emily felt safe and assured and happy.

"When in doubt, start at the beginning, my dear."

The voice wrenches Emily from her remembrance. Pastor Michael's words echo in her mind. Emily's eyes fly open and scour the sanctuary, looking for the kindly man dressed in his dark clergy attire, whose words linger in her consciousness long after he's finished speaking. His words have more than one meaning, Emily suspects. She's endured sleepless nights as dreams echo Pastor Michael's phrases. Despite not always understanding Pastor Michael's intended meaning, Emily feels in her gut that his hidden message is yet to be revealed. He seems to hold a secret, a key, but she knows neither the secret nor what the key unlocks. The intrigue of it all keeps her guessing.

Gaining her bearings, Emily touches her face and discovers it is wet with tears. She swipes away the tears with the back of her hand and takes a deep breath. After not shedding a single emotional tear in years, she's had several outbursts in a few short months. Shaking her head in disapproval at the state she finds herself in yet again, her eyes glance up toward the pipe organ. The sheer size of the instrument anchors the room in a steadfast manner, like a father at the head of a family's dinner table or a judge on the bench in a courtroom, the galley filled with spectators watching in awe. If the organ could speak, it would whisper words of comfort to anyone in need.

Letting her eyes roam about the sanctuary, Emily thinks about the many prayers spoken and the countless tears shed. She wonders how many times forgiveness has been granted within these walls. The archives hold an immense volume of historical accounts, but as she gazes about the sanctuary, she is struck by the awareness of how much this sacred space has witnessed.

Perhaps this is the source of the comfort, the hush, the solace. This knowing, loving space consoles those in need, shares the delight of those joining in marriage, and mirrors and celebrates the love of a congregation in worship. Perhaps this is the reason Emily finds herself unable to do anything but let her guard down in the sanctuary.

She waits in silence for several minutes, scanning the room. The comfort of the peaceful environment washes over her and calms her overwrought senses, allowing her to think clearly once more. She understands now what she must do. She is determined to push away any self-pitying despair. Her job is in the archives. There is no need for her life, present or past, to get tangled up with a job that will be complete in a matter of months. With assuredness restored within her, Emily stands, forcing a smile and squaring her shoulders before turning to exit the row.

As she strides back down the center aisle toward the sanctuary door, ready to retrieve her belongings from the basement and head home, a pew creaks beside her, splitting the silence of the air into tiny fragments. The groan of the aged wooden bench sounds as though someone has stood up from the seat. Emily halts, one foot lifted in mid-stride as a fresh shiver runs through her body. She squints her eyes, scrutinizing every inch of the vacant row. Her researcher brain is curious and intrigued, but the unnerved little girl within her wins out. Emily moves past the pew, determined to cross the threshold as quickly as possible.

As she walks a few paces beyond the pew, Emily notices the sweet scent of vintage perfume in the air. Resisting the urge to turn around and examine the sanctuary once more, Emily inhales and tucks the memory of the perfume into the back corner of her mind. She continues toward the exit, doing her best to pretend as if she has noticed nothing out of the ordinary. The ability to push past that which is uncomfortable has served her well enough all these years, and Emily is certain it will help her vacate this building, leaving her curiosities behind. Emily pulls her shoulders into a straight-backed posture and asserts her strength. She decides with assuredness that there is no point in sharing her inclination to save this building with anyone from the church or the law firm.

Her mind is filled to the brim with competing thoughts as she walks with purpose down the hall and toward the archives room. After the argument with Ryan, the stroll through her childhood memory, and the quiet moments within the sanctuary, Emily is more than ready to call it a day. Already anticipating a late afternoon nap in the comfort of her apartment, Emily's mind is elsewhere as she descends the stairs toward the basement.

There is music coming from the archives room. Emily lingers near the second-to-last step, wavering in her decision to descend farther. The creaking pew in the sanctuary has unnerved her more than she would like to admit. She contemplates running in the opposite direction in search of Mrs. Peters and the comfort another person might bring her.

Holding her breath, Emily listens intently. No voices. No movement. Only music. A waltz perhaps, but if so, it is one she is unfamiliar with. With a rising unease and uncertainty of what to do next, Emily listens with rapt attention to the music, searching for a clue to who or what is behind the closed door.

Pastor Michael once told her, when speaking about the many great and resilient women of Seattle, that one only had to be brave for a short moment at a time. His statement answered Emily's question of how Seattleites, female ones in particular, managed to do such incredible things in an era lacking today's technology and ease of lifestyle. Over the past two months, those words have run through her mind more times than she would care to admit, as she has desperately tried to puzzle out their true meaning. She has questioned her own courage and her own reactions to life situations real and imagined. But before now, she hasn't attempted in real life that which Pastor Michael's words suggested. Now faced with this situation, Emily grasps tightly to those words of wisdom. Her role at present is to be brave for a short moment. Emily takes a deep breath and steps quietly down the two remaining steps before pushing open the door to the archives room.

CHAPTER 16

 hursday, April 23, 2015
Elizabet

Dorothea rushes in to find me in the basement storage room. Her plume-hatted head bobs as she hurries toward me.

"Emily is on her way." Dorothea fans the air before her, dousing the room with the floral scent she adores bathing in. "I didn't think I would arrive in time to tell you."

"Time to tell me what, dear friend?" I incline my head and wait patiently for Dorothea to calm herself.

"She is in a state, Elizabet." Dorothea spins around as the door opens with a burst of force. "She is in a state for certain." She whispers the last words as her blue eyes narrow toward the girl.

I almost burst out laughing as Emily races into the room. The poor girl looks something between terror stricken and bashful. Guilty as a cat caught with a field mouse between its teeth. Dorothea and I watch from the corner of the room as the door flies open, catching all of us by surprise.

"Oh, Ms. Reed. You startled me some." Mrs. Peters' head snaps up, and she clutches her heart with both hands.

"Mrs. Peters," Emily stammers. "My apologies. I hadn't meant to startle you. It's just that I heard the music." Emily's cheeks turn pink as her eyes drop in what I assume is embarrassment. "I suppose my imagination got the better of me. I thought— Well, never mind what I thought." Glancing about the desk, Emily's eyes fall on the record player. "I didn't realize you needed the record player? I could have brought it up to you."

"Oh, no dear. Not to worry. I found this old album misplaced in one of my ancient filing cabinets this morning, and I thought you could store it. I remembered you mentioning we had an old player down here somewhere and when I did a quick scan of the boxes, it was right there, neatly labeled in your handwriting." Mrs. Peters' smiling face exudes appreciation for Emily's months of dedicated work. "I must say, dear, the room is coming along nicely." Mrs. Peters nods toward the shelving unit filled with boxes. "Everything upon that wall is complete, then?"

"Yes." Emily's face is flushed, and mottled blotches across her cheeks are evidence of recent tears. "I have recorded the contents of each box in a master list. One copy will remain with the church administrators, and another will be stored in a fire safe at the law firm. Just as a precaution," Emily adds with a reassuring smile.

"Wonderful. Just wonderful, dear," Mrs. Peters says in a delighted tone of voice.

Dorothea and I exchange looks from the corner of the room. Dorothea's knowing nod says, *I told you so*, with regard to Emily's current state of mind.

Dorothea waited impatiently in the sanctuary for Emily to return from her outing, a task she first balked at. She was certain Emily would return directly to the basement. But having witnessed the girl settling into the sanctuary in recent weeks, I suspected she would venture there first. Her mood had been shifting toward melancholy since her argument with the boy. The sanctuary has always been a place of great solace for me, and I suspect it has become one for Emily as well.

Emily takes a few steps toward the desk and Mrs. Peters. Emily has visibly relaxed, having recovered herself. "What have you got there? You found it in your filing cabinet, did you say?"

"Yes, odd spot I know. One never knows where these things will pop up." Mrs. Peters' lightheartedness at having found an old record tucked within the church files comes across as absentminded. But her tone sets my teeth on edge, and I wonder if I am reading more into the church lady's motives than is necessary. "I used to adore such music. Once I found the player, I was easily cajoled by long ago memories to play the record." Mrs. Peters traces the edge of the record's protective cover.

"It is like stepping back in time, isn't it?" Emily smiles as she reaches for the record player's handle and places the needle atop the record. The music booms, vibrating out from the little box, and Dorothea and I watch intently as both Mrs. Peters and Emily close their eyes and let the music carry them away.

Emily sways with the song, her lightweight jacket swishing softly in rhythm with the waltz. I am eager to join in and want nothing more than to twirl myself about the room. Dorothea's eyes plead with me, telling me to restrain myself. We wouldn't want to startle the poor girl any further. She has already had quite the shock today, and we need to be patient. Watch and wait. Dorothea's hands motion for me to settle myself.

My concern for Emily has grown immensely in the past months. Watching her was at first a form of entertainment but has now become much more pressing. My connection to the girl is beyond anything I can make sense of, but it exists, nonetheless. Given my natural inclination to be a productive woman, I am at the ready to do what is needed to help save this girl.

The song ends, and Mrs. Peters' face is alight with pure bliss. "It is a lovely song, Mrs. Peters." Emily pats the woman's arm in a friendly gesture.

"It is indeed, Ms. Reed." Lifting the record from the player, Mrs. Peters slides the black disc back into the protective sleeve before securing the player's lid.

"Do you happen to know if the record belongs somewhere specific?" Emily's eyes roam about the room's perimeter. "I am not familiar with the musicians or the record itself. Perhaps you know the era? I can sort through the boxes of the most fitting decade and see if I can find it a good home."

"No. I am sorry to say I have no idea where the record belongs. Perhaps there are more records you have yet to locate." Mrs. Peters casts her eyes toward the pile of boxes Emily still has to navigate. "Did you know the church hosted a yearly ball?" Mrs. Peters waves her hand in the air. "Nothing too fancy, of course. Not like the grand events thrown in the mansions up on the hill, but we served tea and cake. The couples of the church would come together for an evening of music and dancing." Mrs. Peters' eyes glaze over with remembrance mixed with a touch of emotion. "I met Mr. Peters at one of those balls, I did. He was so handsome in his suit." Mrs. Peters lays a hand on Emily's arm and gives it a squeeze. "He was new to town. A mutual friend brought him along to the church ball and introduced us." Mrs. Peters shrugs, a smile painted across her peach glossed lips. "I guess you could say the rest is history."

"That is so sweet." Emily smiles.

Lifting the record player from the desk, Mrs. Peters begins to return it to the misshapen box. Emily offers and takes the player in her hands as Mrs. Peters holds the sides of the box. Together, they return the player to the shelf.

Mrs. Peters slides the rogue record to the opposite corner of the large desk. "I'll leave it here for now. When you come across the other albums, you can add it in with them."

Emily nods her head. "I'll be sure to keep the player handy, and I'll let you know when I find the rest. Perhaps we can enjoy a little music over a cup of tea in the coming weeks."

Mrs. Peters points to the diary left open on top of the desk. "I noticed you were reading one of the diaries. How far have you gotten with them?"

"Oh, yes." Emily blushes, I assume embarrassed to have been found out. "I've kind of fallen down a rabbit hole of sorts. I've been reading a few entries here and there, when I stop for lunch. I find them . . ." Emily pauses as she fingers my open diary. "Well, they certainly add some color and context to the other archives."

"I thought you might say that." Mrs. Peters bends and plucks a diary from one of the boxes. "I think you might find it helpful to start from the beginning." She hands the diary to Emily. "The Thomas diaries begin right around the same time this church was opened. Experience the history of this great building from all of its angles. There are so many stories within these walls, dear. It would be a shame if someone who had the opportunity to learn of those stories didn't take the time to do so."

Emily nods, and I imagine I hear her mind whirring behind her eyes. "Mrs. Peters, I must say, it seems this building is quite well loved. So why the persistence to relocate? Why has the church administration fought so diligently against the landmark title?"

"To put it plainly, we simply can't afford the upkeep." Mrs. Peters' shoulders rise and fall. "After the earthquake highlighted all the ways in which our 1910 building is not up to the current building codes, the push was on for us to locate a solution that our now much smaller congregation could afford. Our plan is to build a new church of a more appropriate size, in a location that is easier for our congregation to access. The interstate and the growth of downtown Seattle has fenced us in, making our location and thus our services less than appealing to both current and potential members."

Emily nods again as Mrs. Peters makes her way toward the door. "Well, I'd better be off. The filing cabinet is organized now, but the rest of my office is in such a state that I'd be embarrassed to have God himself pop by for a visit." Mrs. Peters turns at the threshold. "Don't hesitate to call for me if you need anything at all, dear. And Ms. Reed, try not to worry. You never know, there is always room for a miracle."

Emily smiles politely. "I suppose one never knows." Though her words are cordial, I can't help but sense a lack of belief at the mention of miracles, and I wonder briefly whether the girl holds a belief in anything at all.

As she closes the archives room door, Mrs. Peters looks pointedly toward the corner of the room where Dorothea and I are hovering. She grins, nodding her head in Dorothea's direction. Mrs. Peters issues a wink of her eye, which elicits an almost imperceptible nod from Dorothea. My mouth falls open, aghast at what I am confused to learn is some sort of communication between the bumbling little church lady and my dear friend. I am eager to understand what I have missed. How is it possible that the living and the dearly departed are not only communicating but are somehow in cahoots, while I am on the outside of it all?

Emily moves closer to the boxes, pulling my attention from Dorothea and her secretive venture. I vow to needle my friend as soon as Emily departs for the evening. Until then, I watch the girl kneel on the concrete slab and remove diaries from a box. "When in doubt, start at the beginning," Emily says out loud, and Dorothea and I share a nod.

Emily is engrossed in the task of sorting my diaries. She begins by removing all of the diaries from one box and piling them on top of the desk. She systematically examines each book, noting the month and year, before placing them into piles. She first sorts them according to year and then into months, until she has arranged them chronologically.

Upon completion of her sorting process, Emily has three empty boxes. Several stacks of well-worn, personal accounts of my days line the wall nearest to the desk. After extracting the first diary from the long row, Emily settles herself into the desk chair. I smile when I realize she is indeed taking Pastor Michael's advice and starting at the beginning.

CHAPTER 17

hursday, April 23, 2015
Emily

Desperate to escape the conversation with Ryan that's playing on repeat through her mind, Emily directs her attention toward the boxes of diaries and approaches the research as she would any other such task, in a systematic and recordable way. An hour and a half later, having sorted the diaries into chronological order, Emily is confident that all the diaries are accounted for in the row of books, stacked with their spines up. Mrs. Elizabet Thomas seems to have seldom missed a day of recording her experiences. Emily plucks the first diary from the row and settles herself at the desk. Leaning over the journal with elbows bent and hands cupping her face, she takes a deep breath and reads.

April 17, 1910

. . .

Today was too momentous of a day to not record its splendor. I am committed to this new habit of writing, given the delightful turn of events in my life. I wish to create a record of my experiences within these pages, through the writing of daily journal entries from this day forward. So, without further delay, I begin my daily practice of journal writing.

Dear Diary,

It may sound a little childish, but to whom else would I address my private thoughts and experiences?

Today, our beloved church at Fifth and Marion was officially dedicated. The festivities were full and filled with joy. Though I had hoped the building would be ready by Easter, the dedication was splendid, nonetheless.

Many Seattleites gathered this morning to join in the celebration of our beautiful new church. It was such a pleasure to give them a tour of the building. They oohed and aahed when they entered the stunning new sanctuary. Everything the eye could touch shone brightly, and it felt as if God himself was beaming down on us.

The sermon was a fitting one. Rupert and I sat proudly among our families, friends, and congregation. It was difficult to suppress a wide smile when the announcement of our upcoming wedding, which will be in a short two weeks' time, was proclaimed to all within the sanctuary's round walls. Rupert's smile matched my own, and I was reminded of how loved he has made me feel. I am eager to become Mrs. Rupert Thomas.

. . .

Emily smiles as Elizabet's joy spills from the page, seeming to fill the basement. Pulling a pad of yellow sticky notes from her bag, Emily writes down a reminder to visit the Seattle Room in the downtown library. Emily's interest in Elizabet is deepening, and she is keen to see a photograph of the woman. Having spent many days and evenings within the library's glass walls, Emily knows that, if anyone in the city has photographic evidence of Elizabet Thomas, it will be the well-established library. The library houses both the heart and the fringes of Seattle's heritage. Sticking the note onto the outside of her reference binder, Emily turns the page in the diary.

April 20, 1910

Dear Diary,

The final fitting for my wedding dress was today. I am a vessel of excitement, as Mother mentioned with slight irritation this afternoon as I fidgeted with pins and ribbons.

When the veil was placed upon my head and I caught my reflection in the mirror, I almost had to pinch myself. I am truly a bride to be. Never in all my life have I dreamed my own wedding day would come. I have never held the belief that one should tiptoe around others' feelings, simply because the facts of life might not be that which they wish to hear. I have been well-aware from a young age that I was not one to be thought of as the marrying type.

Instead, I filled my days with books and learning, and I sought to live a full life of knowledge in place of one filled with marriage and children. It is not lost on me that my love of knowledge is precisely what drew Rupert to me. He told me once that he fell in love with my smile at first glance but was so deeply smitten by my brain that he had no option but to pursue me with the utmost vigor.

God most certainly does work in mysterious ways, and I am ever so grateful that He does.

Emily's thoughts turn to Ryan and his recent mention of marriage, and then to the weeks of tension that lie between them now. A frown creases her forehead and her mouth. She flips past a few pages of diary entries, glancing briefly at the words. At twenty-six years old, most women would be thrilled to have a man like Ryan in their corner, rooting for them, loving them, offering a lifetime of togetherness. Even though Elizabet appears heartfelt and honest in her writings, the guarded and wounded realist within Emily can't help but wonder if Elizabet was simply caught up in the excitement of a wedding. Perhaps marriage was another thing altogether.

The hurt she feels over Ryan, in truth, she hadn't seen coming. She's balanced her life these past two years with him in her world. Well, at least she has appeared to have her life balanced. The fresh sting from the current level of distance between Ryan and herself causes Emily to stand abruptly, sending the chair careening backwards, all four wheels trying desperately to keep up with the unexpected motion.

Trying to clear the fog from her thoughts, Emily paces around the room. Even in times of heartache, she has difficulty settling and listening to the wisdom of her own heart. She clings to rules set in place by emotional trauma so deep that she would do anything to avoid experiencing it again. Her stone wall of protection rises up within her, commandeering her thoughts, fueling her internal discord with half-truths. "But Ryan hurt me too!" Emily calls out to the empty room. "He hurt me first." She slams her hand flat on the desk.

Emily casts the throbbing in her hand aside, the same way she shoves her own guilt over the situation away from her awareness. *Relationships always end badly.* She consoles herself with thoughts of the few breakups she's experienced during her dating life, purposefully ignoring the fact that she never came remotely close to feeling for another what she feels toward Ryan. *I'm sure there isn't any other way for things to end.* Emily's head aches at the pressure building at the back of her skull. Rubbing the tension from her neck, she wonders if Elizabet was truly happy in her life. The later diary entries seem filled with such grief, such heartache. Having felt something similar after the death of her parents, Emily reminds herself that no amount of happiness is worth that kind of pain.

"Emily, is everything all right?" Pastor Michael's voice spins her around, toward the open door, her face flushed with embarrassment and emotion. "I thought I heard you yelling. Did you say you are hurt?"

Busying herself by guiding the desk chair back to its usual place, Emily shakes her head somberly. "No, I'm fine. Just talking to myself." A shrug she hopes will halt any further inquiry is followed by a weak smile.

A tilt of his head indicates Pastor Michael's disbelief in her words. "Come, child." He taps the white collar tucked into his dark blue dress shirt. "This makes me a skilled listener, you know."

Emily can't help but offer a weak smile at the kind gesture. Sitting with a thud onto the hard wooden chair, Emily sighs. "I think I've just broken up with my boyfriend."

"Ahhhh. I see." Pastor Michael clasps his hands behind his back and meanders back and forth across the room. "Affairs of the heart are often the most challenging." He inclines his head to meet Emily's eyes. "But they are also the most rewarding."

Emily shrugs, her disagreement with his comment evident.

"Can I tell you a story?" Pastor Michael's blue eyes twinkle when caught in the beam of muted light. "It's a story about a young couple about to be wed."

"Sure." Emily swivels the chair to face him and reclines, crossing her arms lightly across her chest.

A smile lights up Pastor Michael's face. "I once knew a happy young couple. I always delighted in seeing them, as they seemed to make each other blossom into the best versions of themselves. I was confident in their love for one another and for the path they were choosing to take. It was two weeks before the day of their wedding when the soon-to-be bride came to me in tears."

Emily's elbows move to her knees as she leans forward in the chair, Pastor Michael's storytelling voice drawing her into the tale.

"She was devastated. Distraught and barely making any sense at all when she rushed into my office, announcing the wedding was to be canceled." Pastor Michael casts his gaze to the ceiling. "Oh, how my heart went out to her. The burden of her anguish was clearly heavier than anything she had ever experienced."

"What did you do? What did you tell her?" Emily's eyes follow Pastor Michael as he resumes pacing.

"I asked her several questions. Did she still love the man? She did. Was the argument about something so unforgivable that she would not be able to look him in the eye without resentment? It was not. Had fear or anger driven her to call off the wedding? 'Anger,' she replied. The man had disappointed her greatly, and that made her angry." Pastor

Michael steals a glance, ensuring Emily is listening. "'So, you are afraid?' I asked the young woman." Pastor Michael's mischievous smile is barely masked. "'No,' she replied. 'I just told you, I am angry.' I said, 'Yes, but my dear, anger is merely the cloak of fear.'"

Emily sits upright, sliding her body back in the chair as she braces against the hard wooden back, her face a shade paler than it was a moment before. In a whisper, she repeats to herself, "Anger is the cloak of fear."

Pastor Michael smiles as understanding dawns and settles on Emily's face. Clearing his throat, he continues. "So, we talked some more and determined that the young man, also under the pressure that wedding plans and new beginnings often bring, was still human. She agreed it was reasonable to assume he did not set out to hurt or worry her. She spoke to me in great detail of her own fears and realized with clarity that their fears mirrored each other.

"This, my dear Emily, is the double-edged sword of a relationship built upon a solid foundation. When two people are intertwined with truth, love, and respect, in times of uncertainty or stress, their burdens become each other's. Separating the two is often a challenging endeavor. My best advice is this. When a relationship offers two people everything they desire, God will make sure they experience everything they need. This does not guarantee smooth sailing, nor is it an excuse to treat one another poorly in any situation, difficult or not." Pastor Michael's eyebrows raise in an authoritative and knowing manner. "Instead, it is a promise that you will be provided with both that which you want and that which you need." Pastor Michael's face softens as he winks at Emily. "Keeping in mind that what you need isn't always what you think it is."

"What did she say? Did she think it was all worth it in the

end?" Emily's voice is as quiet as a child's, cracking with emotion as the question leaves her lips. "Even though she knew there were sure to be challenges big enough to break her in two?"

Pastor Michael nods. "Even though it may cause you discomfort, wounded pride, or even pain, if you truly love someone, you owe to it yourself and to him to love each other all the way through it."

Emily is lost in thought as Pastor Michael turns to leave. As he nears the threshold, she asks, "What happened to them?"

Pastor Michael swivels away from the door and meets her gaze. "They married two weeks later. That was back in the 1980s."

A soft smile forms on Emily's lips as her head dips up and down, still deep in thought but pleased by the happy ending. Pastor Michael is through the door when Emily remembers. "My parents were married here. In this church. In 1983." Though she says the words out loud, Pastor Michael has already left the room.

CHAPTER 18

hursday, April 23, 2015
Elizabet

Emily's outburst is as startling as Pastor Michael's story is endearing, leaving Dorothea and me to linger in the shadows in silence as the afternoon's events unfold. Whatever he intended, Pastor Michael's words seemed to have calmed the girl. Within moments of his departure, Dorothea and I are once again gathering closer, reading my diary over Emily's shoulder.

June 23, 1910

Dear Diary,

. . .

Summer is well upon us in Seattle as the sun shines its glorious rays onto my flower garden. Rupert's allowing me to carve out a space all my own is another example of how well this man knows how to love me. The roses will be in full bloom in no time, and I am eager to see their bold colors through the sitting-room window.

Though his home is more than amply sized for the two of us, Rupert has delighted me by acquiring a large piece of property on the outskirts of the city. The sloping land on the hill offers a distinct vantage point of our beautiful city and boasts a clear view of the water's edge.

We've begun to discuss plans and timelines, though Rupert has suggested we wait to finalize details. At least until we've had the opportunity to travel together, seeking out the world's best design ideas as we go. The one room we've agreed upon is a nursery. Though we hope to be blessed with news of a baby soon, we continue to enjoy one another's company in the meantime.

Our travel plans have been set for August. We will journey to Europe and visit several castles in Ireland and Scotland before setting sail to Asia. A trip of a lifetime I am certain this will be, and I am delighted to have Rupert's knowledge of worldly places as well as his companionship as we journey together.

As Emily continues to peruse my diary entries, I think back to our trip of a lifetime and remember with fondness the days and nights we spent abroad. Oh, how Rupert doted on me, spoiling me daily with exquisite foreign teas for breakfast and the most beautiful hats a lady could desire. The hats were such glorious creations. I can hardly imagine the cost to ship the various styles and sizes of hats back to Seattle. But ship them he did, packing each one carefully into a hatbox and crating the whole lot back home to wait for our arrival.

Dorothea is eyeing me from Emily's other side, subtle signs of concern etched into the corners of her downturned mouth.

I move closer to Emily as she flips another page. I am eager to relive those glorious early days of my life with Rupert. I would give anything to be with Rupert now. Despite what Dorothea may think, I've tried to push the longing away, occupying myself instead with memories of the past. Try as I might, I want nothing more than to be with him in eternity. Alas, I remain here, stuck somewhere in between worlds, with only memories to occupy my overabundance of time.

Dorothea is a good friend. But I have suspected for some time now that she has knowledge of the way beyond this world in between. I've almost uttered the question of how I might leave. But I falter each time, not certain I can muster the courage needed to leave this place with no guarantee that Rupert is waiting for me on the other side. I believe Dorothea would have told me if she knew for certain that he would be there. Perhaps she remains with me, faithful and humorous all these years, because she is not certain.

I glide over to Dorothea as Emily reads from the notebook filled with records of purchases acquired during our travels abroad. She flips through pages and pages of items, along with notes of where and from whom they were purchased. As I became more thoughtful regarding our future home, I added another column indicating my desired placement of each treasured item within the mansion that would one day be ours.

Dorothea raises her eyebrow. "I thought I was a shopper, but you, my dear Elizabet, put me to shame. An entire book? Really, my dear?"

A sheepish smile creeps across my lips. "It was a bit extravagant, wasn't it?" I crinkle my nose in mock embarrassment, but I know in my heart that I would not have changed a thing. The experiences, more than the purchases, made the time so memorable. "In our defense, we did make good use of each and every piece of furniture, and not a single painting was stuck hiding in a back closet, gathering dust. All of them were proudly hung in our home, on display for all of our friends to see. Sadly, Rupert did not live long enough to see our home complete and decorated as we imagined during those days spent traveling together."

"Humph. Not all of your friends." Dorothea crosses her arms across her ample bosom, and I suspect she is changing the subject in an attempt to draw me from a potentially melancholy mood. "Don't forget, Elizabet, I was never one of those friends. Never one to attend your fancy balls or fundraisers."

"Come now, Dorothea. You spent plenty of afternoons in my company at the house. And you know you were always welcome." I tuck my chin and meet her disgruntled expression. "As I recall, you were also invited to more than one of those 'fancy balls and fundraisers.' Perhaps it was you who chose not to attend."

"Wasn't the sort of thing a lady of my standing in the community could very well attend, now was it?"

"I hate to be a naysayer, Dorothea, but that too was your choice." I raise my eyebrows at her self-pitying banter. Her chosen profession as the owner of the city's finest brothel was entirely her own doing. "I've never snubbed my nose your way, dear friend, but certainly one should own the choices one makes in life."

"You don't say?" Dorothea pivots in place, a wide smile replacing her previously sour expression. "Would you agree, then, that one should also own the choices one makes in death?"

My eyes have been following Emily's movements as she tries to gain a comfortable position in the desk chair, but Dorothea's comment commands my attention. "I suppose so, though I am not entirely certain of how one would have any choices in death."

"Ah, so your being held hostage here in this church has nothing to do with choice?" Dorothea's voice is smug at best, challenging at worst, and an unsettling feeling comes over me as I contemplate her meaning.

"I've no idea what you are talking about." My voice is sharper than I plan for it to be. "I am here because of Rupert. He should be here. I know he should. I just—" My voice quivers with uncertainty. "I just don't know what could be keeping him is all."

Dorothea glides closer toward me, a sympathetic expression on her rounded face. "Come now, Elizabet. Certainly, you must realize, dear."

"Realize what? Speak plainly. Please." Frustration laces through my words as I plead with Dorothea. "What are you not telling me, Dorothea?"

"You are the only one holding yourself back from moving on in death. All of this is in your hands now." Dorothea places a hand atop my own gloved hand. "Your future, Elizabet, has always been in your hands."

My heart aches as if a dagger is being plunged directly through its center. My eyes are wide, my mouth agape. I am losing all decorum, whether due to Dorothea's knowing gaze or the fear of eviction from my home of eighty years. I do that which is all I know to do. I turn abruptly and flee from the archives room.

The church building usually feels plentiful with space. Never have I felt penned in by its large stone structure. Until now, that is. I meander the halls, the clergy's office, and the kitchen until I find myself hovering about the entrance to the sanctuary.

I pause before entering. This is my sacred space, the only

place of true comfort and solace since Rupert passed. How could Dorothea say such a thing? How could she think that I would ever abandon this hallowed ground for a place of uncertainty? Perhaps she is simply spouting off, trying to cause mischief.

Lost in my thoughts, I move toward the third pew from the front, the one Rupert and I used to share with our friends each Sunday morning. I am deep in thought, trying to locate a kinder meaning in Dorothea's words, when Pastor Michael's familiar voice startles me. Taken aback by the presence of another, I turn left and instead position myself into a shadowy corner of the rounded sanctuary walls.

"Though in order to understand where we have come to be, we must begin with the beginning. Asking ourselves, how did we arrive here? What choices did we make along the way? Examining one's choices, though, is merely the first step in a long journey. If it is salvation we truly seek, we must proceed along the path laid out before us. We must find the strength to not only move forward, but also to allow our hearts to experience every pain, every heartbreak, every speck of grief along the way. For it is through the pain that we shall find salvation."

Pastor Michael's firm but soft voice preaches to the empty sanctuary. For a man of somewhat shorter stature, he appears larger than life behind the pulpit. For the first time in all these years, I am struck by the immense calm of his presence as I tuck myself into the quiet corner to watch and listen. Pastor Michael is dressed in his dark blue suit, and his white clergy collar is a stark and noticeable contrast to the dimming afternoon light of the sanctuary.

His voice booms out as he reaches the core of his message. "Strength and resilience are two attributes of a life well lived. A life well learned." His voice softens as a low chuckle escapes his lips. "However, the irony of becoming an individual who embodies strength and resilience is that you first must find yourself in a position of weakness. One of vulnerability. Oftentimes, this includes an experience filled with grief. Whether you grieve the loss of a lifestyle or the loss of a loved one." Pastor Michael's eyes seem to locate mine in the shadows.

"Whether you grieve over the loss of oneself or something outside of yourself, you must give yourself two things. Two very contradictory things. You must first give yourself time. Time truly does soften the edges of all things, my friends. But time alone will not result in strength or resilience." Pastor Michael's eyes seek out every corner of the sanctuary. He is a master at delivering his message to everyone in attendance. Sadly, there is no one present to hear his words today.

"You must also be prepared to give yourself grace." Pastor Michael steps away from the pulpit, his shaking finger pointed toward the empty rows. "*Grace*, you think. *Well, certainly grace must be as easy as time.* Ah, but not so fast, my friends. Grace is a tricky one, you see. Yes, grace asks us to be kind to ourselves, gentle and forgiving. But what you may not realize is that grace also asks us to move past our pain. Through our pain. Ah, not so easy anymore, is it?"

Pastor Michael returns to stand behind the pulpit. "Time gives us grace, and grace pushes us through time. If we persevere and walk the path before us, eventually we find ourselves on the other side, with our new companions, strength and resilience, walking right along beside us." Pastor Michael beams at his imaginary audience as my mind races with his message, wondering if his words could have been intended solely for me.

His final words break through my searching thoughts. "The journey is yours to take. Free will isn't always easy, but it is always available to you." With a nod, Pastor Michael's eyes wash over the room once more, landing at last in the shadows of the corner I am sequestered in. "You always have a choice. Choose wisely, friends."

With his sermon delivered, Pastor Michael vacates the sanctuary, leaving me alone in the corner to consider his words. I contemplate my past choices, searching for moments when I felt strength and resilience by my side. The oddity is that I have never felt like a weak individual. I was quite accomplished as a woman, as a wife, as a Seattleite. When things became difficult, I simply pulled up my sleeves and got to work. Never did I shy away from a bit of hard work to see a situation righted or another person assisted. But somewhere in the depths of my awareness, I sense that Pastor Michael's words are more applicable to me than I care to acknowledge. I fear I am missing some key piece of information, which I would need to make a choice I have no desire to make.

CHAPTER 19

 riday, May 1, 2015
Emily

Glancing about the room, Emily estimates she is about halfway through the archiving process. All five levels of her frugally designed shelf are fully loaded, and a slew of larger boxes and oddly shaped artifacts have taken up residence in a dark corner of the room.

Having leafed through more than a dozen of Elizabet's diaries, Emily has come to learn the woman was diligent about recording her thoughts, life events, and even her worries. Not for the first time, Emily wonders if the church leaders recognize the gold mine it has in Elizabet's historical account of Seattle. Making a mental note, Emily decides to mention the collection more pointedly to Mrs. Peters the next time she sees her.

Standing to stretch her legs, Emily places the journals she has already perused into a box, laying them end to end in preparation for storage. She places the stack of diaries she plans to read next onto the desk's surface. When she flips open the first cover, she comes face to face with dates matching the years of the Great War.

Of course, Elizabet wouldn't have called it such when the war began in 1914. Back then, before America entered the war, they referred to it as the European War. Emily remembers from high school history class that the war had three names: the European war, the Great War, and World War I. Sadly, no change in label could alter the reality of what occurred between 1914 and 1918.

September 30, 1918

Dear Diary,

The war rages on. So many families have lost their sons, husbands, and fathers in this dreadful and gruesome war. In town two weeks ago, I counted the mourners dressed in black. I was overcome with sadness as the number grew in my head.

Even though war is more than enough, it seems war is not all we will have to contend with. Rupert is unwell. Very unwell. And to be honest, I am unsure of what more I can do for him. The doctor was called for, but due to the illness hitting Seattle with a vengeance over a week ago, it might be days before he is able to check on Rupert.

I was instructed to send all unnecessary staff home. The flu is spreading and leaving only a fortunate few untouched. I have not left Rupert's side for two days, save for fetching him cool cloths, chicken broth, and more blankets than I imagined any one person could ever need.

Tonight has been the worst of it so far. I fear what state this dreadful disease will leave him in, should it decide to vacate his body and our home. Lord, I pray it decides to leave.

I have set up a temporary bed next to his, and I wake each time the fever and restlessness are more than my strong, loving husband can handle. I have tied a kerchief over my nose and mouth in hopes of denying the flu a home within my own body. I must be quite the sight, with my frizzy hair about my face and my clothes damp with sweat and water from the basin I dip the cloth into.

I am desperate for Rupert to come through this, and tonight I will spend every spare moment in prayer for his survival.

Emily instantly notices the gap in diary entries. She reasons that Elizabet likely had her hands full dealing with Rupert's recovery from the Spanish flu. Emily flips the pages back and forth, searching for even the slightest insight into what transpired during those weeks, wishing for the time to appear on the pages before her. Disheartened by the lack of entries, Emily catches her unfavorable mood and scolds herself for feeling disappointed. This is not fiction, but actual lives with genuine fears and suffering.

She turns the page and begins again.

November 11, 1918

Dear Diary,

Peace! Peace at last. The Great War is over. This morning's newspaper told us Germany has surrendered and our boys are coming home. Relief is the most prominent sensation coursing through my exhausted body, as there is now one less battle to worry myself with.

Rupert is recovering well, though at a slow pace. His heart has been weakened, and stairs and too long walks out of doors still challenge his enthusiasm daily. He is a sturdy man, and though his physical strength is coming along slower than he would like, his sense of humor is well intact. He amuses himself quite well for a man recovering from such a devastating ordeal.

Today, we have returned to taking our meals in the dining room. Having taken them in his bedroom since late September, it will be a pleasant change of view, with ambiance reinstated to our mealtime conversations. I may even polish up the silver and break out the tall candlestick holders for the occasion. I have missed the dining room, though it seems a silly notion. I must admit, a change of perspective can perk an individual up a bit. Both Rupert and I could use some perking up, and so we will once again dine like civilized human beings.

A laugh sneaks past Emily's lips as she turns the pages past several more accounts of life returning to normal at the Thomas house. "The simple things in life. It is always the simple things in life that make us feel human again," Emily muses out loud as she scans the pages for points of interest, having realized several hours ago that it will not be physically possible to read each diary entry. She adjusted her goals a few diaries ago and is spending more time skimming and searching for key insights. Given that the official church records don't require an entire account of the diaries' contents, Emily is now reading for her own entertainment or, perhaps, for her own escape.

Emily pulls her phone from her jacket pocket to check the time. She discovered months ago that the archives room is not unlike the internet. Both of them are time warps that can suck a person in for hours. Glancing at the screen, Emily contemplates her next move. It's six fifteen on a Friday night, and her stomach has been shouting at her, telling her to find some food. She grabs her jacket and plucks two diaries from the pile. *I'll multitask*, Emily thinks to herself as she heads for the door in search of a warm meal and a more comfortable chair to read in.

By default, Emily's feet carry her in the direction of Murph's. She glances around the dimly lit environment, before heading straight to the back, toward her reserved semicircular booth. Sinking into the soft velvety green cushions, Emily slides herself into the farthest corner.

Allison appears from behind the tall-backed booth seats. "Emily, I thought I saw you come in. How are you today? You seemed a little . . ." Allison pauses, flattening the empty tray against her hip. "Sad. You've seemed a little sad the last few times you have been in."

Swallowing the lump in her throat, Emily forces a smile. "It's been a tough couple of months." Emily's eyes fall to the dark wood of the table as she contemplates how much to share with this girl she hardly knows, though Allison's company is oddly comforting. Clearing her throat, Emily decides to start at the beginning. "My parents died several years ago, when I was sixteen. Just before I began work at the church, I learned that they were married there. I guess things have kind of gone off course since then, memories and such." She shrugs in an attempt to lighten the words, and she peeks at Allison's expression. "I didn't expect it all to hit me so hard. It just kind of caught me by surprise."

"Oh, Emily. I didn't know." Allison's free hand is on Emily's shoulder in an instant, giving it a squeeze of support. "I am sorry for your loss. No matter how long ago, loss is loss." Allison's smile fades. "I lost my older brother when I was a kid. Nobody really gets it, you know?"

Emily's eyes snap up to meet Allison's. "No, they don't." Emily blusters forward. "Even my boyfriend, Ryan—well, I think he might be my ex-boyfriend now—doesn't understand. He keeps waiting for me to . . . I don't know, come apart at the seams, implode." Emily nods as Allison's support bolsters her beliefs. "You are right, people don't get it." Emily straightens her posture with self-infused determination. "I find it easier to move forward with my life. Stay busy and do everything I can to keep from dwelling on the past." Emily stammers out her last words, unexpected shame poking her in the ribs as she realizes her ardent approach has waffled over the past several months, while she has been working in the archives. "I am sorry for your loss also," Emily offers in a quiet voice, trying to distract from her out-of-control admission.

Allison nods, but something behind her eyes tells Emily she doesn't agree. "I'd like to tell you it gets easier. Living without them, that is. But it doesn't, not really. Life moves on and the pain's sharp edges dull, but things never go back to the way they were before. The single most difficult thing about losing someone you love is that life is never the same again. The thing is, Emily, grieving is an important part of the process. Don't discount it entirely." Allison touches Emily's arm in a gesture of understanding. "You can't move forward in life if you haven't grieved what you've lost, where you've been. It takes time for sure, but you have to allow yourself to really feel the grief. All of it. You know what I mean?"

Emily nods, but Allison's words feel as if they have landed near her instead of within her. *Perhaps I am warding them off, instead of letting Allison's advice settle.* The two women stare at one other, no further words needed. Complete understanding somehow exists between them now. Emily considers that she may have underestimated the benefit of having someone to talk to about her parents' deaths. Someone who grew up with loss, whose world was shaped from a young age by the lack of something important in their life. Someone who knows there are no words comforting enough, no hugs strong enough, no time long enough to replace what was lost.

Emily drops her eyes and examines her hands, hoping to elbow away the unease that has settled beside her in the booth. She prefers to maintain the path forward, never looking back. She cringes a little knowing her secret is out in the world, even if only with one person. She has worked so tirelessly to hide the scars, to ensure nobody looks at her with pity. Emily steels her resolve, blinks hard, and meets Allison's eyes again.

"So, wine?" Allison's lips curve upward in a cheeky smile. "I've found it best to celebrate the days I do have." She tilts her head to one side, eyeing the books on the table. "What have you got there? A tad bit smaller than what you usually lug in here."

Emily looks over at Elizabet's diaries. "Yes. To both wine and my smaller haul today." Emily touches the cover of the top diary. "I am off the clock tonight, but I've been reading these for the past few months, and I can't seem to stop. They are the diaries of a woman who lived in the early 1900s."

"That is amazing. And you're reading them all? How many are there?" Allison leans over the table to get a better look at the cover.

"Three boxes full, but I won't get through them all. There are too many for the time I have." Emily pauses, and her stomach grumbles its displeasure. "What is the soup today?"

"Broccoli cheddar, and it is so yummy. I had some on my break earlier and would definitely recommend it." Allison flips the tray in her hand. "I'm sure they loaded it with cream, but maybe the tiny bits of broccoli outweigh the calories."

Emily laughs at Allison's humor, knowing full well not to ask about the soup's calories if she wants any hope of savoring a bowl. "I'll have the soup and half a roast beef sandwich, please. Oh, and wine. I will definitely have the wine today."

"You got it." Allison flips her tray again and heads toward the computer to enter the order.

Emily is lost in thought, her head in her hands as conflicting topics race in circles within her mind. Pastor Michael's story about the young couple and the value of seeing love through, sweet as it was, has grated on Emily like a scouring pad set to skin. Too scared or perhaps too proud to reach out to Ryan, the strain over the unresolved situation has grown with each passing day.

Allison places the glass of wine on the table. "You aren't going to rush out of here again, are you?" Her forehead creases as she waits for a reaction.

"No." A nervous laugh leaves Emily's lips. "I am sorry about leaving in such a hurry that time. It was a full day. They all seem like full days now." Emily's voice falters, eliciting a concerned look from Allison.

"You have a lot on your plate. How are things going at the church? I haven't read anything new in the paper lately." Allison's intuition to change the subject is correct, but not without consequences.

Emily's deep sigh creates a deeper line of concern across Allison's forehead, so she attempts to lighten the kind waitress' concern by focusing on the positives. "The archives are coming along nicely."

"But?" Allison's chin drops with the question. "I can hear it in your voice. Something is troubling you."

Another exasperated sigh whooshes past Emily's lips. "I

don't know really. I guess I am on the fence about what should become of the building. There is so much history there. And stories. Oh my, it would take weeks to tell you all the incredible stories I've discovered there. But at the end of the day, the decision isn't up to me."

Emily waits, breath held in anticipation, watching Allison's reaction. Allison's smile is wide and full of understanding. "I can see why you are so glum. Lots of unfinished business running about in your life." Allison looks over her shoulder before leaning closer. "My dad likes to say that everything works out the way it is supposed to. So there's no need to get caught up in presuming to know what is supposed to happen."

Emily can't stop herself from smiling. "My dad used to say something just like that." A laugh bubbles up inside of her, and without force or coercion, her mood lightens. "It is good advice, and to be honest, there is little I can do about any of it until the Supreme Court hands down its ruling. I will just keep doing what I am doing and see what happens."

"That's the spirit. No point worrying about the things we can't control." Allison nods at the glass. "How is the wine?"

Taking a sip, Emily stifles a giggle. "I promise I'll stay and finish both my meal and my wine this time." She raises the glass in a mock salute before opening the diary to where she left off.

CHAPTER 20

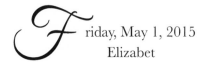riday, May 1, 2015
Elizabet

"You always have a choice." Pastor Michael's words from last week seem intent to remain with me. I exit the sanctuary just as Emily is walking out the door, two of my diaries tucked under her arm. She didn't seem agitated, which I interpret as a sign that she will return once again, likely with my diaries intact. I must admit, though, I am not fond of the idea of having my personal journals removed from the safe and private sanctity of the church's basement room.

I linger about the hallway, not wanting to return to the sanctuary but unwilling to return to the basement storage room, where I anticipate Dorothea will be waiting for me. She seems to have taken a greater interest in my whereabouts since our argument over the choices she presumes are not in my best interest. I pace back and forth, my feet hovering just above the thick red carpet, the shimmering beams of light creating shadows on the walls and floor.

Dorothea is quite committed to the idea that I am somehow capable of altering my situation here. I tuck myself above a window ledge and gaze longingly at the darkened Seattle sky. Oh, how I miss strolling the streets of my city. Rupert and I used to bundle ourselves up and walk arm in arm, my hands tucked into a warm muff and his tightly gloved in brown leather. We strolled the parks and the waterfront even on the coldest nights.

Conversation was plentiful, but even in silence, there was a comfort between us. *What God has joined together, let no man put asunder.* I hoped the words from our wedding ceremony would last both our lifetimes. I suppose I was naïve to think we would have that long together. I blissfully ignored the realities of our age difference as we courted and married, choosing instead to live in the fairytale that was our daily life, never thinking ahead to a day when we would no longer be together in this world.

There is that word again. Choice. When it comes to the choices I have made in life, I've nothing to be ashamed of. I made decisions with the right mix of intelligent thought, heartfelt contemplation, and time spent in prayer.

I sit up straight, an idea percolating at the edges of my mind. Choices, Emily, my diaries. Emily is most certainly in need of our assistance. She needs to make a new choice to snap her out of the melancholy she has been carting around for the past month. She needs a new direction, to find the happiness and usefulness she is currently missing. Poor girl, she is sadder than ever, it seems. I may not be able to mend her broken heart, but I can most certainly help her find purpose. If saving the sanctuary makes her feel useful, I can help the girl and my beloved sanctuary at the same time. My diaries may indeed be the best way of showing her what is truly important.

Fueled by the revelation, I descend the stairs at once to find Dorothea. Rushing down the stairs, I am brought up short by the sign. The janitor posted the rectangular placard a few weeks after Emily began dragging things about the room. Nothing like the word *archives* to make you feel older than your memory thinks you are. I rush into the room, calling out to her. "Dorothea. Dorothea dear, please forgive my sour mood. I am sorry to have been so difficult this past week."

I smell her perfume well before I see her form. "Well. It is about time you returned. All done with your huffy attitude now?"

I glide toward her, ignoring the huff in her own voice. "I think I finally understand how we can help both the sanctuary and Emily."

"Well, get on with it then. What is your brilliant idea?" Dorothea's impatience, and quite possibly her worry over our exchange of words regarding my supposed choices, causes her to fidget with her hands.

"I believe Emily is heartbroken. Not just about the boy. Something else troubles her." My revelation doesn't light up Dorothea's face as I expect. I pause, waiting for Dorothea to say something. "What? Am I wrong?"

"No, you are not wrong." Dorothea steps toward me, speaking in a hushed tone, though no one could hear us. "Emily lost her parents. Many years ago, in fact. An automobile accident, I believe it was."

"Oh my, the poor girl. Those wretched motorized beasts. I never trusted those tin cans on wheels, Dorothea, not for a moment." My heart feels heavy at the news, and I have the sudden urge to feel a seat beneath me. "How do you know about this, and for heaven's sake, why have you not told me before now?"

"I heard Mrs. Peters talking with one of those men. You know, the ones who come often with papers and rolled-up architectural drawings." Dorothea, pleased with her knowledge, sways back and forth like a cat who has successfully caught the canary.

"The lawyers. Do you mean the men in charge of Emily's work?" I am still recovering from the news, and my mind spins to make sense of Dorothea's information.

"The same ones. A few days before Emily showed up, they came and chatted with Mrs. Peters about Emily's anticipated arrival. Mrs. Peters recognized her last name, I suppose. She asked a bunch of questions and shook her head with a sad expression painted on her face. Apparently, Emily is the daughter of two beloved Seattle lawyers who were killed several years ago. I heard something about how Emily's parents helped Mrs. Peters' brother and his wife find their way back to a happy life together when they came to their law office seeking a divorce." Dorothea tilts her head toward me, eyebrows raised. "They were family lawyers, it seems, heavy on the *family*."

"I see. Well, now I do understand why Emily needs our assistance and a new project. She is truly lost, Dorothea dear, and we must help her find her way again. It is our duty to do so. We owe it to the poor girl to guide her through."

"And how exactly are we going to do that, Elizabet? You said it yourself, the girl is one closed-off sort of bird."

A wide smile emerges on my face. "The diaries. We will reach Emily through the words that are already written. She is already immersed in them. She can hardly put them down. I am certain I must have written something wise and worthy that will guide the girl toward happiness. And along the way,"

I say, pausing for effect, "she might just save the sanctuary as well."

Dorothea eyes me warily.

"Did you see her leave with two of my diaries tucked under her arm?" I shake my head with concern, thinking of my diaries leaving the safety of the church's basement. "We must become the source of grace that will help push her forward in life. She needs a project. The girl is a doer, after all. She seems to gain the most value in life by taking action, so let's nudge her into action."

"Push her we will." Dorothea's face is alight with a playful smile. "Directly into Mr. Right's handsome embrace."

"Oh, come now, Dorothea. Emily's reason for being here is not merely about us sorting out her love life. This is truly important. For all of us."

"Fine. I will help you." Dorothea rolls her eyes with exasperation. "But I want to be clear, Elizabet. I am helping for the girl's sake and the sanctuary's sake, not for your sake. I am not agreeing to the line of thinking that you should remain any longer in this church should the building survive in the end. Are we clear?"

I feel slapped by Dorothea's words. I back away from her, finding myself in need of a little breathing room. "Nobody asked you to stay." The words spew from my lips in an unkind tone. As they land, I realize too late that they are quite likely to sting her as much as her words have stung me. They are true but unkind all the same, and I regret them even before they roll off my tongue. "I'm sorry. That is not what I meant to say. Forgive me?"

"Forgiven. But on one condition." Dorothea watches my expression as she continues. "Once we have Emily sorted out, you and I will begin our own transition."

"Transition? Transition to where?" I hold my face as expressionless as possible.

"Oh Elizabet, there is so much more waiting for us. We need only be brave for one small moment."

A burst of laughter pushes past, and I cover my mouth in embarrassment at my outburst. "You've been listening to Pastor Michael again, haven't you?"

"He does say some rather inspiring quips from time to time, you know. Besides, I am sure you can agree he is spot on regarding the women of Seattle and all they have accomplished. Seattle women have always been and always will be trailblazers in their own right. We, my dear Elizabet, are no different." Dorothea tucks her chin and winks at me. "We can and we will be brave. Even if it is merely for one moment at a time. Do you agree to my conditions?"

"Yes. I suppose I can muster up a little extra bravery for whatever you have set your sights on." My words come out stronger than I believe them to be, but I console myself with knowledge I learned long ago. Just because you are brave doesn't mean you aren't also frightened. The two often go hand in hand. Being brave, I've heard said, is more about acknowledging you are frightened and choosing to move forward regardless of your fear. *Choosing to move forward.* That phrase might just be the death of me if I were still alive.

"I am so pleased to hear it." Dorothea beams at me with childlike enthusiasm. "I may not agree with your motives, Elizabet, but at least we are both rowing in the same direction now."

"Getting down to business." I glance at the long row of diaries lined neatly against the wall. "How are we going to accomplish all of this?"

Dorothea places one hand on the brim of her hat, while

the other hand runs through the plume situated there. "I have my ways, Elizabet dear. I have my ways."

"Yes, but what are they?" I lean in, anticipation mingling with the worry building in my chest.

"Elizabet, are you sure you want to ask questions you don't want the answers to?"

My mind reels with possibilities, the recent encounter between Mrs. Peters and Dorothea at the forefront. "No, I suppose not." Shyness over my uncertainty of Dorothea's capabilities causes me to refrain from asking anything further. "But I am curious."

"Curiosity killed the cat, or so I've heard." Dorothea bats her eyelashes at me.

"Well then, I suppose curiosity cannot cause me any harm." Together we laugh, friends again and frustrations between us forgiven.

CHAPTER 21

 riday, May 1, 2015
Emily

The soup and sandwich arrive, accompanied by a second glass
of wine. Emily's entire body relaxes as the first few slurps of
warm soup provide nourishment and comfort. She glances
about the restaurant between bites, taking in the scene.
Couples share intimate conversations at candlelit tables. With
date night in full swing around her, Emily's thoughts return to
Ryan. She checks her phone, desperate for a message to
appear.

Nothing. Not even a text. The last communication
between them was a voicemail. Ryan left the message midday
on Monday, informing her that he was being sent out of town
for a conference. He was filling in last minute for a colleague
who had found himself in the emergency room the night
before with his appendix about ready to burst. All week,
Emily's disquieted imagination has been whispering that he

probably left the message when he was certain she would be in the archives room, out of cell service—a convenient tactic to avoid her.

The saner part of her brain notes the last-minute nature of the situation, holding fast to the knowledge that Ryan's motives should not be in question. Emily's emotions are running amok, like a train with no more track in front of it. She considers what life might be like without Ryan in her corner.

I haven't taken him for granted, she argues with herself as she chews thoughtfully on her sandwich. *I am a lot of fun to be around. We enjoy the outdoors and the same kind of movies. We seldom argue about where to eat, and at the core of things, I believe we hold the same high standards about how to treat people and what we want in our lives.* Emily bolsters herself with memories of happier times spent together. Kayaking on the lake. Hiking the many trails in and around Washington State. Sunday morning brunches complete with mimosas and waffles, followed by snuggles on the sofa while old movies played on Emily's television.

Taking another bite of roast beef, Emily reminds herself that Ryan is indeed a stand-up guy. He is thoughtful and kind and generous. She once watched him help an elderly lady across the street when it became apparent the woman would not beat the walk sign. Emily smiles at the memory of his tall frame crouched over, holding the elderly lady's elbow as he waved off the horns from disgruntled rush-hour motorists. She had known it then, watching Ryan step up to help someone in need. Without a doubt, Mom would have adored him. With her puppy-rescuing, hug-giving, exuberant personality, Mom would have fallen head over heels for Ryan. Even though this thought is tinged with sadness, Emily tucks the sentiment into the back corner of her mind. *Maybe it isn't too late for us after all.* Emily thinks over the possibility as she wipes mustard from the corner of her mouth.

The wine eases the roadblocks she has set up, and Emily finds herself being unabashedly honest with herself. She admits that Ryan reminds her of her dad. The awareness of this knowledge has poked at her from time to time over the past two years, but she has deftly swept aside the connection, preferring to see Ryan for himself. At least that is what she told herself. With her thoughts tuned in on memories of her parents, Emily wonders what they would think about her current predicament. It was their church, though she hadn't known that when they were alive. Perhaps they would feel as passionate about saving it. Being attorneys, though, they might side with the law and accept the church's fate, despite their personal feelings.

Emily's thoughts are running away from her, out of control, in the precise manner she usually commands them not to. One solitary question whirls through her brain. Why has she never thought to ask what her parents would do? Those answers could have guided her life, her choices, perhaps even her reactions. If she had thought to ask sooner, would she even be a lawyer? She certainly doesn't feel like a model lawyer at the moment, questioning whether she is for or against the case of her clients. Maybe she wouldn't have even pursued law school. Just because it was their path doesn't mean it was the only path for her.

Emily cringes as she swirls the remaining wine around her glass. Her gut tells her that if she had asked what her parents would do, she likely would not be in her current dilemma, with regard to both her career and her relationship. Emotion fills Emily's eyes. *If my dad were here, I certainly wouldn't sweep him aside. I would cherish every moment. Every smile, laugh, and embrace.* Taking another sip of wine, Emily pushes the plate and bowl to the opposite side of the table, attempting to jolt herself from a pointless and potentially embarrassing line of thinking about things she cannot change. Eager for a distraction from her own thoughts, Emily opens the red leather diary to a random page and delves back into the life of Elizabet Thomas.

December 24, 1922

Dear Diary,

I can hardly believe nine months have passed without my Rupert by my side. The new house is lonely, despite the staff I keep on to guarantee another person is in the house with me at all hours of the day and night. Not that I seek them out much. I tend to spend my days in my bedroom, comforted by a roaring fire. The flickering flames make shadows across the intricately painted tile facing surrounding the grate.

Not a single design element was left unthought of. That was Rupert for you. Every detail was completed to his exact instructions. The wood paneling of the smoking room, the dish warmer in the kitchen. Even the nursery was outfitted with the latest designs. Bay windows were set in place to provide ample natural sunlight for the child we desperately wished to have. I am surrounded by his thoughtful details, and yet I am alone. The nursery is now forever empty, the smoking room unused by the man of the house. My coveted dish warmer will never see the elaborate parties that we intended to host together.

I moved into the home a month after Rupert passed. What should have been a celebrated day felt like a second funeral. Once the furnishings were in place and the artwork hung, I retreated to my room. With a view of the lake and another of the carriage house and grounds, there is plenty within eyesight to entertain a heartbroken old biddy such as myself.

The pastor says I will move on in time. The grief will subside. I was too ashamed to admit to him that I have no desire to move on. If Rupert exists only in my memories, then that is the only place I plan to be from now on. We can be together forever in a memory.

Emily looks up from Elizabet's words, trying to puzzle out Elizabet's grief-stricken state. The difference between Elizabet's and Emily's situations is glaringly obvious, though Emily wonders if one approach is healthier or perhaps even gentler than the other. Elizabet preferred to live in her grief, almost marinating in it, as a way of remaining close to Rupert. Emily, on the other hand, has done everything in her power to avoid feeling any grief at all. To control the trajectory of her life, Emily chose to get as far away from the pain as possible. She's been stuffing it down for so long now that she's uncomfortably uncertain of what might spew forth should she uncover it.

Taking another sip of wine, Emily is overcome with a desire to know if Elizabet found peace by immersing herself in her grief. She quickly flips pages, seeking a date far enough from the previous entry to help her understand. Nearing the last pages of the red diary, Emily realizes the last entries are too close together for her to gain a true understanding of Elizabet's mindset going forward. She reaches for the green diary, opening to a page a quarter of the way into the book.

July 27, 1923

. . .

Dear Diary,

The summer sun shines down on the garden this morning. The roses in full bloom made me smile as I rounded the corner and witnessed their vibrant colors. Rupert planted them for me, before the house had even been completed. I am so grateful he saw fit to think ahead, as I find the garden a delightful place to spend time out of doors. Rupert's memory is always right there beside me.

Tonight, there is to be a fundraising ball, so I wandered out to the garden early to cut roses for the occasion. There is simply nothing like vases filled with lightly scented blooms to offer an exuberant welcome to our guests. The ladies from the Sunshine Club of Seattle are organizing the gala. Seeing that we have such a large ballroom, our home is a frequent host for many of the organizations I've volunteered with over the years. The thought has crossed my mind that some events may be less than necessary. I wonder if my friends are simply attempting to draw me back into society. I appreciate the sentiment and am becoming more aware of what is expected of me when I am in company outside of this bedroom.

Last night, though, I must admit with a slight blush to my cheeks, I was found out by the in-house maid. I knew I would be missing Rupert dearly at this evening's event, with the music and dancing and wine. So when the maid ventured out for an evening with her beau, I donned my most exquisite shimmering blue gown from 1915 and descended the stairs to the ballroom on the ground floor. The dress was one of Rupert's favorites, with its gold-trimmed lace and trailing train. The plunging neckline was perfect for displaying the shimmering blue sapphire and diamond necklace Rupert had given me the Christmas before. All I was seeking was a small piece of solace as I called up Rupert's company, preparing for the onslaught of guests the next evening.

The waltz was playing, booming out from the gramophone loudly enough that I didn't hear them return from their outing. I was surprised and a little embarrassed to find them standing in the doorway, watching me glide around the parquet dance floor, my arms held high as if I held Rupert within them. I gathered myself up hastily and dashed from the room, leaving them to turn off the player and the lights.

I can only imagine what they must have thought of me. A sad old woman, dancing alone in her mansion. What a sight I've become. Despite the obvious, embarrassing situation, the dances enjoyed, imagining Rupert in my arms, were worth a moment or two of discomfort.

Emily looks up from the diary once more and reaches for her nearly empty glass of wine as Allison approaches the table. Allison smiles at her as she stacks the soup bowl onto the empty plate before taking them into her free hand.

"Soup is good, right?" She beams at Emily with a knowing smile.

"So good." Emily marks her place in the diary with one hand as she holds the glass with the other. "Thank you for suggesting it. I would definitely order it again."

"Another glass of wine for you?" Allison nods toward the glass, its contents dwindling.

"No, thanks. I had better stop at two." Emily laughs as she becomes aware of the warm sensation flowing through her.

"On the tab, then?" Allison asks as she turns to walk away.

"Yes, thanks. I'll just finish this up and be on my way." Tipping the glass back and emptying its contents, Emily reaches for a clean cocktail napkin. She folds it in half before placing it within the book's pages to mark her spot.

Scooting out of the booth and sliding her arms into the sleeves of her jacket, Emily shivers as the inner lining chills her skin, reminding her of the cool night air beyond Murph's comfortable interior. She decides to take the long way back to her apartment. Despite the chill, a walk along the water's edge might do her good. It may even clear some cobwebs from her

181

head. Needing time to think, time to consider Elizabet's words, Emily hopes the thoughts that have dogged her for months will be gone by the time she arrives at her apartment. Though she is not quite ready to embrace the idea completely, the similarities between Elizabet's struggles and her own are difficult for even Emily to ignore.

Though decades separate them, it is like Allison said. *Loss is loss after all.* Emily tucks the diaries under her arm and heads toward the door, offering Allison a final wave as she leaves.

CHAPTER 22

*W*ednesday, May 6, 2015
Elizabet

I've never considered my existence in this world in between to be boring. Full of heartache and longing, yes, but not particularly boring. I suppose I've always had my memories to keep me company. Thoughts of Rupert and our days together are as fresh in my mind today as they were more than eighty years ago. But this week seems to be dragging on for an eternity, and I know all too well how long an eternity is. I pace about the archives room, finding myself bored and anxious. I am bored because little can be done until Emily arrives in the archives room and anxious to start setting right the girl's life. I'm ready to put in motion our plan to save the sanctuary.

I have grown fond of the girl. She is a complex one, and if there is anyone living today I desperately wish to speak to, it is her. She clearly needs a mothering hand in her life. I would be delighted to take on that role for her, if she would have me, of course.

I admired what I originally thought was her strength while watching her during the first month she spent in this room. Now, I realize it was all a ruse. Not an unkind one, like when someone tries to pull the wool over another's eyes, but the most damaging and detrimental kind of ruse. The kind that allows a person to lie to themselves.

Emily is certainly most achieved in the lying-to-oneself department. Given what I know now about her loss and struggles, I can see through her paper-thin exterior and into the heart of where she holds her insecurities, her unshed tears. I don't blame her, and I would never scold her for such behavior. Instead, my concern for her propels me forward. I want to help her rise above what life has handed her. She will be successful in whatever she decides to pursue, I've no doubt. But her being happy is not a forgone conclusion, unless of course we can help her see the error of her ways. I've considered my role in her life, and I have determined that I am to assist her in seeing all of her options so she is in the position to make wise choices on her own.

The strength she portrays is merely a facade of strength. A good facade—I will give her credit where credit is due—but a facade, nonetheless. Her ability to close off her emotions and put difficult things aside, regardless of their importance in her life, is of epic proportions. This is what must change. This is the biggest lie Emily has been telling herself all these years.

She is a strong young woman. She has muscled her way through the physical mess of the storage room and will come out on the other side accomplished and with her goal achieved. Along the way, though, I've begun to see her steel exterior crack. Whether the fissures are due to Pastor Michael's constant delivery of thoughtful tidbits or the hours she has spent in quiet contemplation in the sanctuary, I am not certain. But the crack will benefit both Emily and my plan to help her. A crack is where the light gets in, after all, and this poor, defeated, heartbroken child is in desperate need of some light. I have no doubt that our plan to help her embrace the idea of saving the sanctuary will be the first step in saving herself as well.

The door to the archives room opens and Emily flicks on the light before stepping toward the oversized desk. She drops her bag in its usual place and scans the room, her eyes roaming over the neat boxes and the unorganized pile yet to be sorted. Sliding her jacket from her shoulders, Emily pushes up the sleeves of her sweatshirt and moves to stand before the row of diaries. With her back to me, her expression and her state of mind are a mystery.

I glance nervously at Dorothea. Our plan to coax the girl is set to begin. Our intention was to watch her this morning, patiently gauging her mood until the time came for her to eat her lunch and read from a diary. I move closer to Emily's side, trying to read the expression on her face.

Dorothea sweeps closer, and the scent of her perfume wafts through the air. Emily steals a glance to her right before crouching low to examine the row of my diaries with more intent. Her fingers caress the upright spines, and I motion for Dorothea to come closer. It seems that we won't have to wait until lunch after all.

A moment passes and then another. If I were alive, I would be holding my breath, I muse. And then it happens. Emily looks up and sniffs the air, and a soft smile spreads across her lips. It is difficult to tell whether she is aware of our presence or merely the whiff of Dorothea's signature scent, but I am confident in the moment before us. We have the confirmation we were seeking. We have found a way to communicate with the girl.

I nod toward Dorothea, and she moves into action, positioning herself near the stack of diaries that have the words I wish to impart to Emily. I motion for Dorothea to move about and draw Emily's attention. I step back to provide Emily the room she needs to move down the row of diaries.

In true Dorothea style, she shuffles the shimmering layer of her skirt, runs her fingers through the plume of her hat, and begins to dance, moving her high-heeled toes back and forth near the preselected row of diaries. I stifle a giggle and watch as Emily stands and takes a few steps along the row, toward Dorothea and the waiting diaries.

I have set my sights on the 1925 collection. Emily squats in front of the books once more. Dorothea's face is aglow with a look of success. I nod my appreciation toward my friend and attempt to coax Emily with my thoughts, nudging her to peruse the editions located farther to the right, where I am certain I have written in great detail about my love of and appreciation for the sanctuary.

Several minutes pass as Emily's fingers dance above the spines, lingering over them as if waiting for the diaries to speak directly to her. Her back to me, she shifts, blocking my view of her face once again. My eyebrows knit together in concentration and concern as I hold myself back from moving closer to gain a better vantage point. Before I can even conjure my next thought, Emily extends her arm and plucks a diary from the row. Dorothea's smile drops to a frown, and I feel the opportunity slipping through our fingers like sand. Emily is bracing one hand on the concrete floor and gathering herself to stand when I catch Dorothea's movement out of the corner of my eye.

With a nudge from the toe of Dorothea's rounded high-heeled shoe, the diary we had set our sights on shifts and draws Emily's attention as it falls. My wide eyes scuttle back and forth between the diary laying askew and Dorothea's pleased expression.

"What?" Dorothea says with an impish grin tickling the edges of her lips.

"You can move things?" My shock is palpable and only delights Dorothea further.

We watch as Emily scoops the fallen diary into her arms before standing and returning to the desk. "I am not like you, Elizabet." Dorothea eyes me sideways, gauging my reaction as she speaks. "I've told you before. I am a spirit. You are a ghost."

I shake my head, indicating my lack of understanding. "I thought you were merely teasing me." Turning toward Dorothea, I give her my full attention. "Tell me, dear friend, what is the difference?"

"Dear Elizabet, have you never wondered why it is that Emily is able to speak with Pastor Michael?" Dorothea's words carry a faint dusting of exasperation.

I respond with a shrug. I suppose I never gave it much thought. Pastor Michael has wandered in and out of the halls and sanctuary for the past thirty-two years, coming and going as he pleases. During those years, he has had much to talk about, not to mention preach about. The sound of his voice is familiar to me, so I didn't consider it unusual when he began speaking to Emily.

My cheeks redden with the awareness of such an oversight. I think of myself as an intelligent woman, but given this realization, I do wonder where my head has been. Under Dorothea's scrutinizing stare, I attempt to save face with a deflecting comment. "In all honesty, the man has become a fixture within these walls, similar to the pipe organ itself. I must have taken his presence for granted and not considered his movements too fervently."

Dorothea leans toward me. "Oh Elizabet, I am afraid you most certainly have spent far too much time in your own grief. Pastor Michael is a spirit, just as I am. We have chosen to return to the physical world for a time or a purpose." Dorothea's voice softens. "I am here for you, my dear friend. I am here for you."

"And Pastor Michael?" It is all I can do to utter these few words.

Dorothea stares blankly at me, evidently not concerned with any purpose outside of her own. "I imagine he is here for the girl, though I cannot be certain. I have never asked him."

Emily is leaning over the diary, engrossed in its words while my perception shifts around me. There must be something more beyond this, I consider. I open my mind a mere sliver to the plausibility of such an idea. If Dorothea and Pastor Michael have come from somewhere else, perhaps there is a reason to entertain the possibility. Dorothea's tardiness, her tendency to not be where she said she would be, all flutter across my memory, and the skeleton of an understanding takes shape in the dark corners of my mind.

Dorothea motions me over to Emily's side, pointing at the diary entry she is reading.

July 30, 1925

Dear Diary,

. . .

I am in awe. I am fascinated and overcome all at the same time. The novel Mrs Dalloway *by* Virginia Woolf *arrived two short days ago. The ladies and I are set to have tea and discuss the latest title next Tuesday, and an interesting discussion I expect it to be.*

What can I say? I have had my nose buried in the novel since the day it arrived, wrapped in brown paper and tied with a string. I barely rose to dine, let alone bathe or set foot out of doors, so engrossing the story was to me. I read and reread portions of it as I connected with the characters and their own personal plights.

I have been able to think of little else but Ms. Woolf's words. When a book strikes me so, I begin to wonder what experiences led the author to write something of such a nature. Was it their own experience or that of another? Did the author have an overly healthy imagination, or is there a thread of truth woven between the sentences?

I do wish I was in the position to write to Ms. Woolf and ask her these questions, but I've no idea where I would begin. So I will wait until my thoughts become clearer. What struck me most was how Clarissa Dalloway and Septimus Smith each had a break in reality, though from two very distinct experiences. Throughout the novel, they each venture back into their mind to relive that which delighted or haunted them most from their past.

I am all too aware of how closely this storyline resonates with my current situation. Before reading Mrs Dalloway, *though, I hadn't thought of my experience of reliving my life with Rupert as a break from reality. I must admit that I find this news to be more than a little unsettling. The realities of the Great War interrupting their reveries fell a little too close to my own front door. I have only begun to wonder where I go from here, knowing what I know now.*

I must console myself with the thought that I am more akin to Clarissa Dalloway than I am to Septimus Smith. Though I can appreciate his desire to end his life, I am pleased to say I have never given the perspective any more than a passing thought. However, I am slightly ruffled by the awareness that my life these past few years, since Rupert's death, has been rather melancholy. I am of two minds on the topic. I am grieving, and I know that grief can and will take its own time and its own path. But I am happiest when reliving my life with my beloved husband. The fact that I tend to think of those experiences as occurring in the present day is one I cannot come to terms with at this time.

I am keen to think most people in my situation would do the same. Virginia Woolf created Clarissa Dalloway from something or someone, after all. If I were the only one to ever stream her past consciousness in present time, Woolf would never have written anything of the sort. More thought and time on the subject is most certainly required, and since I am here and Rupert is not, I have the time and space to consider such things.

Emily looks up from the diary, and I move around the desk in an effort to read her expression. Tears glisten in her eyes and I realize she is sad. Not for herself this time, but for me. For the grieving widow I was. For the grieving widow I still am, I admit reluctantly. The girl has pointed out that which I have been avoiding, and she managed to do so through my very own words.

I look to Dorothea and find her watching me with a gentle expression. Moving forward is all she has talked about. I shudder at the thought of what it might mean to take this step. I am not without fear or worry, but I am also not without a friend who cares enough to see me through difficulties. I must at the very least consider the possibility of leaving the sanctuary that I love so dearly. My heart is heavy with the knowledge, but as I search Emily's expression and then Dorothea's, I know what I must do. Before a decision can be made one way or another, I must do everything I can to help both Emily and the sanctuary. Their futures must be secure before I can even begin to think of my own.

My attention is pulled back to the desk as Emily opens the

second diary, the one rich with entries of adoration and appreciation for the church and, more importantly, for the sanctuary. Several years after Rupert passed, I found myself living week to week, waiting in anticipation for Wednesday morning. In the sanctuary, I found solace and comfort. Within these walls, any guilt I might have felt over my inability to move past my grief dissolved completely. The sanctuary was the place where I felt most like myself.

The sanctuary, I have told myself all these years, is where I feel Rupert's presence the strongest. But as I read my own words over Emily's shoulder, I realize that it was myself whom I found each week, wrapped in the comfort of the sanctuary's round walls. It isn't Rupert I have been seeking to locate all these years. I miss Rupert every day, and dearly. This is true. But I understand now more than ever that it was not Rupert who was lost. It was me.

Emily closes the diary and quietly leaves the room. I don't have to follow to know she is headed for the sanctuary. I am certain of it. My words may not have been enough to encourage her to rally and fight to save the building, but in light of my new understanding, I believe they might be enough to nudge her toward a new life. She may be able to accomplish what I have been unable to thus far. Emily has the opportunity to move through her grief and find out who she is and what she wants from her life. Though I am more than a little sad at the thought of losing this beautiful building, which has seen me through a lifetime and more, I find myself content with the knowledge that the girl is on the right path.

CHAPTER 23

*W*ednesday, May 6, 2015
Emily

Standing silently at the open double door leading to the sanctuary, Emily glances around nervously before stepping forward. The stillness of the vast, peaceful space wraps around her as she takes a tentative step over the threshold. Surveying the room, she hopes she will find herself alone. The high dome at the center of the room gives the feeling of being outdoors. The light filters in like sunshine through a canopy of spring blossoms, casting its beams onto the polished wood panels near the altar.

Taking a seat in a row of pews near the center of the room, Emily sighs. She intends for the slow breath to settle her nerves. Her eyes search the rounded walls, noting the intricacies of the room's design that have gone unnoticed during her previous visits. She cannot deny the sheer beauty of this circular space, nor its comforting ease. Despite being the only one in the room, Emily is keenly aware she feels anything but alone.

As she sits in quiet contemplation, the truth appears. Gentle at first, as though aware that its presence might frighten her, the truth simply nudges her. A single tear rolls down Emily's cheek. "And there it is," she whispers to herself. "Pastor Michael is absolutely right. The sanctuary has stories to tell and weary hearts to console." Her chin drops to her chest as more tears gather in her eyes. "I suppose all one has to do is be open to hearing what the sanctuary has to say." Emily sniffles as she allows quiet tears to fall freely. Without mandating her thoughts or her response to them, she soaks up all that the sanctuary has to offer.

With her defenses lowered and Elizabet's written words in her memory, Emily allows herself to embrace her own connection to the church. She doesn't know whether the connection was formed by the knowledge of her parents' union here or the place's history, which has become deeply embedded in the fabric of her own experience. All she is certain of is that she loves this building. Seeing it destroyed is the last thing she wants. Rational or not, Emily cannot deny her true feelings any longer.

Embracing her past and her loss isn't quite as simple, but she understands now, more than ever, that the past is a part of her. Just like the church's history is a part of its future. Her parents, both their lives and their deaths, are part of her story. A hiccup of grief escapes from deep within her as she realizes that her story isn't over yet. She thought that losing her parents ten years ago was the end of everything, but that moment was merely the beginning of something different.

Understanding seeps into her consciousness. Her refusal to accept her new reality all these years has only held her hostage. Emily is startled to recognize her naivety. She's been intent on "moving forward," but her actions have only kept her stuck. All these years she has been frozen in a moment of time she has been unwilling to accept.

"How do you expect me to accept a reality I can't stand?" Emily's voice rises as her frustration mounts. "How am I supposed to say I am okay with losing them?" She shakes her head at the distasteful thought. "No matter how much I want to be tugged forward, I can't believe that having my parents ripped from my life was acceptable. I just can't."

Her head falls into her hands, her broken existence racked by emotion. Tears pour out of her like water through a ruptured dam. *Weary hearts to console.* Pastor Michael's words reverberate through her mind loud enough to convince her he is nearby. *You must only be brave for one moment at a time.*

Emily's tear-stained face searches the space for the man who has infiltrated her thoughts and her life in the most unexpected manner. His gentle smile and stories have given rise to Emily's new perspective on everything from the importance of saving the church to the value of allowing Ryan into the innermost part of her heart and mind.

Sitting in the quiet and serenity of the sacred space, memories of the past wash over her. One by one, images of her parents and their life together press against her. Buffeted by the imaginary movie reel playing across her mind's eye, Emily lets her guard down. She smiles, cries, and even laughs along with her remembrances. Several minutes pass as she embraces the powerful flashbacks.

With her emotions spent and a new calmness taking up residence within her, Emily takes a deep breath. She stands and whispers a quiet "thanks" to the vacant sanctuary. *Weary hearts to console*, she thinks to herself once more as a slightly amused expression stretches across her face.

Feeling more assured than she has in weeks, Emily moves

toward the exit. Knowing the archives are waiting for her drives her steps forward. She is already contemplating how she might be able to help save the church from demolition. As she steps into the long narrow hallway, Emily glances back at the sanctuary. The memories, it seems, will push their way into her heart one way or another. All she can do is step aside and allow them entrance.

CHAPTER 24

*M*onday, May 11, 2015
Emily

The following Monday, Emily stands in front of the desk, a file box before her. She thinks about the text message from Ryan that appeared on her phone late Sunday afternoon. A project, he said, has kept him busy these past several days. He's been working weekends and into the late hours each evening. He apologized for his schedule and promised they would sit down and talk soon. Emily is comforted by the knowledge that, according to Ryan, things aren't over. At least not yet anyway.

Returning her focus to the box, Emily peers inside, assessing the nature of the contents. Retrieving stacks of paper, some crumpled by years and haphazard packing, she places the disorganized papers onto the desk's large surface. With the box empty, she drops it to the concrete floor. She wheels her chair closer to the desk and tucks herself into its hard molded seat, her attention focused on the newfound mess.

Emily quickly separates five editions of the church's cookbook, which she assumes was created as a yearly fundraiser. Several days ago, she located several similar publications with varying years inked on their colored paper covers. Like a high school yearbook, the cookbooks offer a glimpse into another place in time. They contain a few photographs of the ladies of the church and popular recipes of the era, some of which Emily wrinkles her nose at. They would certainly not appeal to a modern-day crowd. Each cookbook closes with an extensive list of acknowledgements to both recipe contributors and cookbook organizers.

Carefully examining each cookbook cover, Emily puts aside for further investigation any editions published during the lifetime of Elizabet Thomas. So far, her search for another glimpse into Elizabet's life has not been fruitful, but Emily is not easily deterred. Since, she reasons, the files need to be archived anyway, she gives everything a thorough look through before recording and archiving the data.

Several hours later, Emily is tapping the box's lid in place. She has worked through lunch, given the lack of desk space upon which to eat. The black felt marker stands out against the white file box, displaying her accomplishment in stark contrast—as if, given the chance, it would shout out to the dark, gloomy room. The boxes are one step closer to being completely organized. Emily positions the archived box on the new metal shelving system, this one ordered by the church administrators and built by the janitor. She tucks the cookbooks, in chronological order, into the growing collection of First Church recipe books.

"More cookbooks, I see." Pastor Michael steps into the room as Emily turns to greet him with a warm smile. His frequent visits offer both entertaining stories and a breath of fresh air.

Emily laughs. "I am sensing a pattern. One a year, I imagine, though they seem scattered in almost as many boxes as there are years."

"You've done a wonderful job, Emily. Truly you have." Pastor Michael gestures to the shelving units and their contents.

"Thank you." Emily turns and gives the box an extra shove into place, buying her flushed cheeks an extra moment to return to their natural state.

Returning to the desk, Emily rifles through her bag. She pulls out her fabric lunch bag and thermos before reaching for a diary to read.

"What is next on today's agenda?" Pastor Michael strolls to the darkest corner of the room. The area is filled with odds and ends that have already been catalogued but are too large to fit in the shelving units.

He disappears into the shadows, leaving Emily feeling as if she is talking to herself. "I have my eye on that monstrosity." Emily inclines her head toward a heavily damaged, enormous box. It leans to one side, its contents pushing it apart from within. "I've been avoiding it for weeks. Perhaps because it is bigger than me." Emily pulls her sandwich from her lunch bag. "Seems the time has come for us to do battle though, as I can't reach anything behind it until it is out of the way." Emily shrugs. "I've got to go through it." The chorus to the children's camp song plays through her mind as the words exit her lips in a singsong manner.

"Going on a lion hunt?" Pastor Michael's voice reaches her from the darkness, and they both laugh out loud.

"Just what I was thinking." She giggles before taking a bite of her sandwich.

A commotion from outside the archives room door draws Emily's attention. Footsteps descend the stairs in short, hurried strides. Placing her sandwich onto its wrapper, Emily swivels her chair to face the door.

"Oh! Ms. Reed. I'm so glad you are here." Mrs. Peters shuffles into the room, her face flushed and perspiration beading across her upper lip, whether from the intensity of her movements or the words she is eager to share.

"I'm here." Emily stands to greet the stout church lady. "But, then again, I usually am."

"Yes. Yes, of course, dear. It is just—" Mrs. Peters pats her moist lip with the tips of her fingers. Pink pastel nails glimmer in the shadowy light. "We have been called together for the news, and I thought you would want to join us." Mrs. Peters' eyes roam the room. "Given all the effort you have put in to sort through all of this."

"Join you?" Emily asks, the question creasing lines in her forehead.

"Yes. Upstairs, dear." Mrs. Peters moves toward the door, beckoning Emily with one arm. "Please, do come. I am most certain you are as anxious as all of us to hear every detail." Unable to contain her excitement any longer, Mrs. Peters clasps her hands together, bending her knees a fraction as if she might jump for joy. "The verdict is in."

"The verdict is in," Emily repeats in a whisper. She hurries to wrap her sandwich, thrusting it into her messenger bag, along with her lunch bag and thermos. Grabbing her jacket, her bag, and the copy of Elizabet Thomas' diary, she decides she will hear the news before venturing outside to finish her lunch on the front steps of the church. She hopes the early sun from this morning remains in a clear blue sky.

Mrs. Peters is well on her way, huffing and puffing her plump body up the stairs as Emily steps over the threshold and pauses. Sticking her head back into the archives room, Emily cranes her neck toward the darkened corner. "Aren't you coming?"

"You go on ahead, Emily." Pastor Michael steps into the light, reassuring her with a nod and a smile.

Emily offers a brief wave before climbing the stairs two at a time, in a hurry to catch up with Mrs. Peters.

Gathered in the narthex, along with the twittering Mrs. Peters, are all twelve members of the church board. Also present are the ladies from the church offices located on the top floor of the building and a young minister Emily has never seen before, dressed in casual attire. They are all clustered, talking over one another in an animated fashion.

Mr. Holt, Emily's boss and the chief legal counsel for the church's decade-long legal battle, catches her eye before clearing his throat to quiet the group. "Thank you all for coming on such short notice." He takes a moment to meet the eyes of everyone in attendance, a tactic Emily is certain he would use on a jury if given the chance. "I have called you all here this afternoon because the Supreme Court of Washington has shown themselves to be both wise and compassionate and has ruled in favor of the First Church of Seattle on all counts."

A jubilant cheer goes up around her like Fourth of July fireworks, and Emily cringes, feeling the assault as if an earthquake has unmoored her once-steady legs from the ground. She watches in disbelief as hugs and high fives are exchanged. Shaking her head back and forth, her emotions run deep. She watches everything she hoped would not happen come true.

Emily takes a few steps back from the group as Mr. Holt continues. "Friends," he says in his deep baritone voice, "this is just the beginning."

"The beginning?" Emily's voice cracks with emotion, and all eyes turn toward her. "What about the past? This church's past? What about the building's right to exist? To have its history, its rich, beautiful, storied history appreciated and valued?" A river of unease runs through her, shaking her body, and her bag falls from her shoulder to the floor with a thud. "All these months I've spent knee-deep in the history of this place, your place." As her words gain momentum, tears well in Emily's eyes, threatening to spill. Emily holds up the diary in her hand. "Knowing what I know now, I can't imagine any of you want to see it destroyed. I can't fathom a Seattle without this building, this church, anchored in the heart of it." The narthex is as quiet as a congregation deep in prayer as they follow Emily's pleading eyes. "I understand more now than I ever have. The history matters. The past matters, and whether or not you want it to, it follows you, begging for acknowledgement. I don't know why you would want to let it go, let alone destroy it entirely with the swing of a wrecking ball." Emily bends down and picks up her bag, sliding it into place on her shoulder. "I'm sorry. I am not intending to be rude or unsupportive. I just don't understand how you can let it all go. I'm sorry." Emily bows her head, embarrassment rising within her at having spoken her truth. "Excuse me."

"Emily," Mr. Holt calls after her as she sprints for the door, his voice carrying more concern than anger.

Tears blur Emily's vision as she races down the steps. The sun is bright, blinding her with its direct gaze. She reaches the bottom step, her head down while her mind spins like an amusement park ride. With her eyes focused on her shoes, she doesn't see him until she runs right into him, the collision fueled by her intense desire to put distance between herself and the church, and those within it.

"Em!" Ryan whispers into her hair as he wraps his arms around her shoulders, squeezing her in a safe embrace.

Emily allows Ryan to hold her. She lets him stroke her hair, and probably to Ryan's amazement, she allows tears to fall with reckless abandon. Together, they stand on the wide sidewalk in front of the church, entwined in each other's arms.

Ryan leans his head back, meeting Emily's eyes. "Em, I am so sorry. I was hoping we could talk before they announced a verdict."

"So, you heard? You must think I'm overreacting. Crazy even." Emily takes a step back and digs in her bag for a package of tissues. "I just fell in love with the building and all of its stories."

"I know you did." Ryan uses his thumb to softly caress a tear away from her cheek. "And I don't think you are crazy." Ryan inclines his head and meets Emily's eyes. "Em, I was too hard on you. I am sorry. I should have listened." Ryan lets out a long, slow breath. "I've been talking to a guy at work. I may not understand completely, but I do get how you've become so attached to this place. I have been so focused on new buildings, innovation, green energy. I forgot the reason I fell in love with architecture to begin with."

Emily's eyes dart above Ryan's head, taking in the tall buildings at every angle as she contemplates her next words. "Ryan, you weren't altogether wrong. I'm not sure what I have to say yet, but I do want to share it with you. I want you to be the one person in my life who knows the truth, all the truths about me, even if I am still discovering them for myself."

A wide smile emerges on Ryan's face. "That is the best news I've heard in weeks." He glances behind Emily. "Are you done here for the day? We need some serious time together. I have few things I need to tell you myself."

Emily lifts the diary in her hand. "I should take this back, but—" Emily peers over her shoulder toward the oversized wooden doors of the church's front entrance. She shakes her head. "I don't think I can go back in there. Not now. Oh, Ryan, I think I may have just ruined my career." Emily's breaths quicken as anxiety bubbles up within her. "I said some things. Oh, I shouldn't have let my emotions get away from me. I should have—" Emily bends at the waist, beginning to hyperventilate.

"Em. Emily." Ryan's hands are on her biceps, lifting her to an upright position while pumping her arms to help circulate blood. "Trust me, you haven't done anything that can't be explained. It's not too late. I have news. Good news to share with you." Meeting her eyes again, Ryan's face softens. "Trust me, Em. Can you do that? Can you trust me?"

Emily nods, and together they walk down Fifth Avenue, away from the church. Ryan's arm is wrapped protectively around Emily's shoulder. "Let's get some food, and then we will go from there," he says.

"Okay." Emily leans her head against his shoulder. "Okay."

CHAPTER 25

M onday, May 11, 2015
Elizabet

I meet Dorothea in the corridor, both of us summoned by the commotion taking place outside the hall leading toward the sanctuary. We don't venture far before the announcement is made and elation erupts from the small crowd gathered in the narthex. The verdict is in favor of the church leaders. My heart sinks in despair for my sanctuary, the devastating blow delivered under the guise of a victorious win. The fate of the sanctuary has been sealed forever amidst a ream of legal jargon.

"Oh my." Dorothea follows me as we move stoically into the archives room. "That certainly did not go as I hoped."

Words are lodged in my throat, unable to decide whether to voice themselves or hide from the knowledge that now runs through them. I pace about the room, tugging at my suit jacket as it threatens to suffocate me. The arguments within my head mimic that of a spinning wheel. Like yarn growing wider on a spool, so too do my thoughts, crowding out the space where reason might exist.

"Did you hear Emily though?" Dorothea tries to garner my attention. "She spoke her peace. Her truth. I, for one, am very proud of her. That was because of you, Elizabet. Because of your words." Running her fingers distractedly through her long strand of pearls, Dorothea pushes on. "Of course, she did leave distraught and full of emotion, but credit must be afforded to her for speaking up. Don't you agree, Elizabet?"

"Dorothea, what are you rambling on about?" My words are clipped as agitation rises to the surface. "What a predicament we are in now. I can't help but think that all of our efforts have been for naught. We were delusional to think that Emily would be our voice, our guardian for the sanctuary. Don't you see? Our beloved sanctuary will be no more. Our home, our place of solace, wiped out entirely." A sob escapes my lips. "Before long, no one will remember the building existed at all. No one will remember us. Everything this building has been, everything we were will be lost, and Seattle will never be the same again. What, pray, will happen to us?" My words are shaky. Fear takes over what little stable ground I gained over the previous few days. This dreadful news has rocked my newly built foundation to the core.

"Elizabet, what are you saying?" Dorothea takes a cautious step toward me. "We move forward. Just as we discussed. Just as you promised me you would try to do. We move forward, together."

"How can you say such a thing? Our sanctuary needs us more now than it ever has. We cannot simply step aside and allow it to be destroyed. Seriously, Dorothea, if there was ever a time to remain in place, that time is now."

Dorothea is shaking her head at me. "We move forward,

Elizabet." Her voice is quiet, and her disappointment fills the space between us.

"Dorothea, Elizabet." Pastor Michael steps from the shadows, startling me and shocking my already frayed nerves with another jolt of adrenaline. "There is no need to panic. Things will work out how they are intended to." Strolling toward us, Pastor Michael's clear blue eyes seek my own. "All will be well, Elizabet. Not to worry. All will be well."

I turn away in an attempt to calm myself and hide the embarrassment at my outburst.

"Good things come from trying times." Pastor Michael's words reach Dorothea first. From the corner of my eye, I see her nod in agreement.

"You are both correct," Pastor Michael continues. "Elizabet's resolve to save the sanctuary is noble, however misguided by fear her reasons are."

I spin around as his words reach my ears. I am prepared to unleash my mind on him until his raised eyebrows and gentle smile come into view, stopping me from uttering anything but a fear-riddled sigh.

"We always have a choice, Elizabet. If you are so inclined, you may remain in fear, in anger, and in whatever becomes of the sanctuary. That is one of your choices." Pastor Michael inclines his head toward me. "However, I am not convinced that is actually what you wish for your existence going forward."

Turning toward Dorothea, Pastor Michael continues. "Dorothea is correct in her proposal to move forward." Dorothea smiles, eyeing me carefully from across the room. "We all, you, me, Emily, the congregation, must move on. There is only one direction in life that serves us well and continuously. That is the forward direction."

I bite my bottom lip, partly in defiance and partly in

reluctant agreement with Pastor Michael's words. His calm voice lulls me into submission, giving me reason to doubt my heated and irrational thoughts. Though I am far from ready to concede defeat, I step toward Dorothea, my pleading eyes begging her to forgive my harsh words.

My thoughts are spinning, and I attempt to find some solid ground beneath them. Pastor Michael glances my way, a knowing look upon his face, once again reminding me to allow myself time and grace.

CHAPTER 26

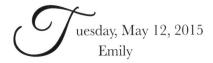 uesday, May 12, 2015
Emily

Emily wakes with the early morning light snaking through the living-room blinds. Ryan is snoring softly beside her, one hand laced within hers and the other flung over his head, dangling off the edge of the sofa. Emily inches toward the sofa's edge, and she braces herself with her hands on her knees before standing. Her neck is stiff, but any physical discomfort is of little consequence to Emily, given the gut-wrenchingly honest conversation she shared with Ryan last night.

After grabbing burgers, fries, and an indulgent milkshake to help her drown her sorrows, Ryan and Emily headed back to her apartment to sift through the type of conversation she would have previously avoided at all costs. Now, though, she is grateful. Puffy eyed from shedding so many tears but grateful that she has at last found a place to call home. Her home is with Ryan.

Taking Pastor Michael's advice to heart, Emily decided to be brave once more, long enough to start the conversation. So start she did. She told Ryan the details of her parents' accident. How they went out to dinner, just the two of them because she begged off, deciding her homework was more important than an evening with her family. Emily confided in him about the immense guilt she continues to feel for not having been with them that night. She told him of the last words she ever said to her mom, the last hug they exchanged. Through gritted teeth and with a solemn expression, Emily told him of the numbness that descended upon her the moment the police officers arrived at her door. The same numbness she has felt almost every day since.

Ryan sat across the table from her, his own tears falling. He held her hand, brought her yet another box of tissues from the cabinet beneath the bathroom sink, and took to heart every word she shared. He marveled at her ability to continue forward in life, yet in the same breath commented that he wasn't sure she had actually moved at all. Emily understood what he was trying to say, more aware than ever how little grieving she has done.

Stepping into the shower, Emily's thoughts turn back to the church. She thinks of the sanctuary and how it soothes her. She thinks about Elizabet and her grief. And about Pastor Michael and his whimsical messages and isms. Emily is certain that her work in the archives room has led to this very moment. Initially anxious about her past rushing up to greet her, she knows now that something more than her own experiences has played a hand. Coincidence or not, the archives have changed her. Mrs. Peters and her doting interest. Pastor Michael and his wisdom, always wrapped up in a story. Elizabet Thomas and her diaries. *I wonder if I would be where I am today if I hadn't read those diaries.*

Rinsing the shampoo from her hair, Emily thinks about Colin and the phone conversation she had with him last night. Through an emotional blundering of words, she thanked him and Veronica for stepping in and taking care of her after the accident. She babbled out an apology for being so difficult, promising him she wouldn't close the door on future conversations. Ryan had insisted she make the late-night phone call. "They only want to help, Em." He encouraged her. "This is where you start letting others in."

During their phone conversation, Colin confessed, albeit sheepishly, that he has been keeping tabs on her through his contacts at Emily's firm. He and Mr. Holt, both aware of Emily's emotional burden, had weekly check-ins regarding her state of mind as it pertained to the church. Colin acknowledged, though, that she was a tough nut to crack and said that neither of them had expected her outburst over the verdict. "Good thing you are both lawyers and not psychologists," Emily teased, the tension between them relaxing with each passing minute. Mr. Holt had telephoned Colin as soon as Emily departed from the church. Apparently, a text from Ryan to Colin was the only reason Colin hadn't shown up at her door in a panic.

Emily towels off, awareness dawning on her that she has never been alone in the loss of her parents. She has always felt alone, always. In reality and in hindsight, so many people love her. They have all been waiting in the wings, ready to catch her if she were ever brave enough to fall. *Being vulnerable is a difficult ask*, Emily thinks as she runs a comb through her wet hair. *But perhaps being vulnerable is simply part of the deal when loving one another.*

The steam from the shower escapes into the hallway of her apartment as Emily opens the bathroom door. In the kitchen, Ryan is tending a sizzling pan on the stovetop. The smell of bacon wafts up to greet her as she ties her housecoat around her waist and steps in to see if he needs help.

"Hey, beautiful." Ryan leans back to kiss her. "How are you feeling this morning?"

Emily's smile is shy. This unadulterated honesty between them is new, at least for her. "Emotionally drained but okay."

"Nothing some breakfast can't cure." Ryan moves to another burner and flips a large pancake. "Tea is on the table. Go ahead and sit down. Breakfast will be ready in a few."

Ryan turns back toward the stove as Emily sits at the table and reaches for the diary she brought home yesterday. Flipping to the bookmarked page, Emily sips from her teacup and continues reading Elizabet's words.

September 17, 1929

Dear Diary,

It seems another summer has passed. The weather is cooling. The flowers are beginning their descent in wilt, preparing for the winter ahead. Summer is my favored time of year. The warm air allows me plenty of time out of doors, enjoying the gardens and grounds.

The landslide took out much of the hill last spring when the heavy rains came, taking the carriage house, the chicken coop, and an additional six blocks of property. But I was still able to wander through the gardens this summer as the men worked to restore and preserve the rest of the hillside, which lies a few short feet from the house itself. All summer they have dug and installed thick beams, creating a step-like structure that adds an extra layer of stability to the hillside. I've been assured this measure will prevent the house from sliding off its foundation. If only Rupert were here, he would know precisely what to do and how to do it and worry, I would not, over the hefty cost of the restoration.

Once, a fully functioning, self-sufficient mansion, the landslide now makes us more reliant on the local butcher for our chicken and a neighboring farm for our eggs. Given the cost of the landscape repair, I miss my chickens more each time I pay someone else to feed those living under my roof. I must remind myself to be grateful for what I do have and not to dwell on that which I do not.

Emily turns the page and then the next. As she leafs through the pages, a black-and-white photograph slides from within the diary. Cradling it with care between her thumb and forefinger, Emily angles the photo so the reflection of the overhead light doesn't obscure the image. Through squinted eyes, Emily examines the photograph. Dressed in a high-necked blouse, large collared jacket, and straight skirt, a woman with severely pulled-back hair and an upturned lip stares at the camera with an otherwise serious expression.

Beside her stands another woman, much flashier in her style of dress. Even without the exposure of her collarbone or the double strand of pearls wrapped around her neck, her plentiful bosom would give her away. Though the image emits no color, one can assume the oversized hat and its large plume are as boldly colored as the woman's dark lips. The combination of the woman's attire, along with her confident and self-assured pose, confirms in Emily's mind that she must be none other than Dorothea Graham. That would make the rather stern-looking woman Elizabet.

Turning the photograph over, Emily reads the neatly penciled inscription, written in the familiar hand of Elizabet Thomas. *Elizabet and Dorothea, September 2, 1929.* Emily examines the image more closely, noticing the framed photograph hanging behind the two women's heads. A handsome dark-haired man, dressed in a three-piece suit, stands with one foot resting on a raised ledge. He has a pocket watch in one hand and a cane in the other, with a hat completing his formal attire. Emily doesn't have to guess; she is quite certain he is the only man who was ever important enough to be in Elizabet's life. This must be Rupert Thomas himself.

Ryan sets the pancakes, bacon, and eggs on the table and returns to the kitchen for plates and cutlery. "What have you got there?" Ryan asks as he takes his seat.

"Can you believe it?" Emily turns the photograph for Ryan to see. "I'd like you to meet Mrs. Elizabet Thomas and Miss Dorothea Graham, or as you might know her, Madame Lou."

"Madame Lou?" Ryan's mouth is open, ready for a bite of pancake. "As in the Madame of Seattle, Madam Lou?"

"The one and only." Emily nods, a Cheshire grin upon her face. "Didn't I tell you about her? She and Elizabet became friends after Rupert passed. But look here on the wall." Emily points to the detail in the photograph's background. "It's a photo inside a photo. I think that is Rupert Thomas."

"Interesting. I can see those journals have captured your attention." Ryan scoops scrambled eggs onto his fork and takes a gulp of tea.

Emily grabs her phone and takes a quick picture of the black-and-white photograph before tucking it back between the diary's pages. Setting the book aside, she spreads butter on her pancake and then drowns it in syrup. "So, you said last night you have a plan." Emily raises an eyebrow in Ryan's direction. "A plan you said you would share with me in the morning."

"Only because you were exhausted. It isn't like I am

keeping it from you." Ryan gestures toward Emily with his forkful of pancake.

"Yeah, yeah." Emily teases Ryan with a coy smile.

"Em, I am not kidding, you were out like a zombie after Halloween." Reaching for his bag from the chair beside him, Ryan pulls out a thick file folder. "Do you want the long story or the short story?"

"If you haven't noticed by now, I am a bit of a stickler for detail, so give me the long story." Emily holds her teacup in two hands and eyes Ryan across the rim.

"Long story. Okay, here we go." Ryan opens the folder, glancing at the first page. "After our argument at the diner, I went back to the office for a meeting."

Emily nods, slight embarrassment creeping up the back of her neck at the mention of their argument.

"Turns out, the meeting I had didn't go well. I was distracted. Anyway, after the meeting a colleague pulls me aside and asks me what's up. I tell him a few details. Don't worry." Ryan reassures Emily, her face already beginning to contort with worry. "I didn't tell him about us per se. I told him about the job you were doing and how you felt passionate about saving the building. Thing is, Em, he agreed with you. He went on and on about the importance of historic architecture in the city. He reminded me of where my love of architecture originally came from. We talked the rest of the afternoon about the old buildings we studied at school. About the sources of today's inspiration and how a building can become so many things to different people."

Ryan swallows his final few bites of pancake before pushing his plate to the side and moving the file folder in front of him. "So, this guy tells me about a company on the east coast he has been following. A development company that works with old architecture, but with a twist. They locate historic buildings and then work around them, remodeling them and bringing them up to code. They turn them into functioning buildings for today's needs while keeping intact all the historic charm and heritage."

"Interesting." Emily's mind is whirring.

"So, after we spoke about the church, we reached out to them and told them about the property and the never-ending court case. Turns out they've been following it all along. I didn't realize the story had become national news. They have been waiting in the wings, so to speak, as events unfolded."

"They are interested?" Emily is halfway out of her seat. "They want to save the building?"

"Nothing has been finalized yet. We will have to see where it goes, but it is better than nothing." Ryan pushes his chair back as Emily dashes around the table to tackle him with a hug. "Thank you. Thank you for caring about what I care about." She kisses Ryan all over his face before burying her face in his chest. Emily sighs. "There is hope at least."

"Well, if I'd known I would get this reaction, I would have told you last night, exhausted or not." Ryan's devilish smile meanders from his lips to his eyes. He pulls Emily to his lap and kisses her with intensity.

Tilting his head back and meeting her eyes, Ryan continues. "There is one more positive development coming from all this business with the church."

"There is more?" Emily asks, inclining her head.

"Remember the big project I told you I was in charge of?"

"The super-secret, can't-tell-Emily-anything-about-it project?" Emily teases him as she nods enthusiastically.

Ryan chuckles before continuing. "That would be the one. Well, it turns out that our discussion over the important nature of historic buildings spurred our project forward in a way we never imagined. We shifted gears and set about creating a new building plan. It has all the up-to-date technologies of a smart and energy-efficient building, but we also incorporated plans that will allow the building to serve the needs of many in downtown Seattle, just like a church might do."

"Innovation pulled from the past?" Emily beams at Ryan, her arms looped around his neck. "So, what happened?"

"Well," Ryan says, releasing a lungful of air, "the project's change of direction is the reason I've been working all these late nights and weekends, but it has paid off. They awarded our firm the contract to build a multi-use facility, which has downtown offices alongside family housing. I am told that we were awarded the contract because of the strong sense of community we incorporated into the building's design."

"Ryan, this is amazing news. Congratulations, I am so happy for you."

"Happy for us." Ryan corrects her. "Happy for us, Em. Things work out how they are supposed to work out in the end."

Emily leans in, giving him another hug. She thinks of how all that was has turned into all that can be.

CHAPTER 27

uesday, May 12, 2015
Elizabet

The sunlight peeking in the nooks and crannies of the sanctuary infuses a desire within me to watch the sunrise. I glide toward the choir loft and pause. I can almost conjure the music and the voices in my memory. Oh, the music that delighted us through the years. The church's award-winning choir traveled the globe, bestowing their angelic voices to thousands before returning home to grace us with their magic once more. Having spent a great deal of time in the church, with the Ladies Aid Society and other charity organizations, I was fortunate enough to enjoy the talent of the choir regularly. Even a simple rehearsal would bring a smile to my lips, pulling me into the sanctuary to listen and watch with rapt attention.

Even today, the pipe organ is an impressive feature, taking up the entire back wall of the domed alcove. The intricate designs and the fleur-de-lis etched onto each pipe are breathtaking and inspiring. My eyes gaze upward, passing over the rafters of the curved ceiling, before I slip past the secret door hidden in the panel and move up the steep stairs. The anomalous curve of the stairs never disappoints me, and I anticipate the view from above.

Out along the roofline that circles the dome, I am instantly at peace. I can see my city. My beloved city. The waterfront, the market in the near distance, and Pioneer Square to my left. Though the shiny new buildings block the view, they do little to barricade the aroma of Elliott Bay. I have always felt most at home when I could smell the sea. Rupert, thoughtful as ever, designed the sitting room of our bedroom to look over the grounds toward the water's edge. He had the bay alcove fitted with an opening window so I could catch the breeze, as he knew how the water's movement comforts me.

Taking in the surrounding view, my shoulders begin to relax. The stress of the past several months has taken a toll on me. I have been wound tight with worry over the church meeting its end, the demolition of this historic piece of Seattle. Only now do I realize how distraught I truly was. Not knowing what would become of me or my beloved sanctuary has been more than I could bear. And now, with news of yesterday's verdict, all that seems to be before me is the end.

I am becoming more and more aware that I alone am to blame for the predicament I find myself in. I turn my face toward the water and let the breeze blow through me. I created my existence in this world in between. Not only did I create it, but I fostered it so I would continue to live, or rather not live, in this way.

This, I understand now, is my doing. I was afraid to live once Rupert was no longer of this earth. I was paralyzed into believing I couldn't be happy, that I couldn't even find myself if he wasn't by my side. I did everything under my control to bring his memory to life, in an effort to ensure I never felt completely alone—until, of course, the time were to come for us to be reunited in death. My thinking on the topic has not worked out the way I expected. Any control I exerted over the situation was the illusion of a sad and desperate woman. There was never any control to be had. More than Rupert's existence after his death has been a figment of my imagination, it seems.

A gust of wind blows, and I watch the clouds shift. My thoughts turn to Emily. I see a kindred spirit in her. I suppose this is why I have a fondness for the girl. She is smart, not unlike I was at her age. I wonder how two smart women can be so bullheaded? So unaware of how their actions and choices contribute to the outcome of their life?

Emily seems to be working steadily at keeping control over her entire life. The news about the sanctuary is beyond her control and not at all to her liking. I worry for her, unsure as to how she will move forward with this knowledge. She is not so different from me, I think, especially in the early years after Rupert passed. Emily, though, doesn't appear to feel the grief that I did. She hasn't allowed her grief to become interwoven into her existence. Instead, she seems inclined to push it down inside of her. I am deeply concerned for what will become of her stomach should she continue to hide her pain with such vigor.

Then there is the matter of the boy. Ryan, I think he is called. Such a nice young man from what I can see. His love for Emily is apparent in his every movement, pouring out with each word he speaks to her. Clearly, the young man is smitten. Why, then, would she send him on his way? I may not understand modern-day courting, but something doesn't feel right. The heart always knows what it wants, and given her distress over the situation, I am not convinced Emily's heart is finished with Ryan just yet.

Perhaps if Emily were to allow her grief out. Let it breathe a little. Then she might be able to give up some of the exhausting and often thwarted efforts to control everything. I believe her unmanaged grief is holding the girl back. It is allowing Emily to create her own life in between. She is not living a real life, but a fractured one. I am embarrassed by my own revelation as the words float across my mind. Like I am one to talk. Not only was the second half of my life a fractured existence, but so far, the entirety of my death has been as well.

Though Emily's life is taking place among the living and mine is not, she is in just as much of a pickle as I am. We have each, in our own way, mastered the art of becoming stuck in our existence. This is our common thread. We may approach the predicament differently, but at the end of it all, we are both unabashedly stuck.

I cringe at the thought of Emily losing out on the rest of her life or, worse yet, being faced with a death such as mine. I do not know if something else awaits me on the other side. All I can reason out is that if I were where I am supposed to be, then so many others who passed would be present. And they simply are not. I must be doing something wrong, though I am not entirely certain I am yet ready to learn what.

Of course, Dorothea is here with me. Then again, something tells me Dorothea knows more than she is saying about what waits for us beyond this world in between. I have little hope she will share what she knows with me. If there is one thing Dorothea has mastered, it is keeping a secret. Her secret-keeping abilities must have been a key ingredient to the success of her brothel business, since I am quite certain her male clients were not at all keen to have their wives know of their whereabouts while visiting Dorothea's establishment.

I turn slowly, capturing each angle of the view in my heart and in my mind as if I were taking a photograph. I am unsure of what lies ahead, but I can't seem to shake the notion that this is the last time I will enjoy this view of my cherished city. I am so glad the sun shone today. Seattle is the most beautiful when the sun is shining. I lift my face to the sun once more and linger in its light before circling the perimeter of the dome.

I return to the sanctuary via the steep, curved staircase. I enter through the secret paneled door beneath the choir loft, only to find Pastor Michael at the pulpit, rehearsing yet again. Given that he will never deliver another sermon, I wonder if he simply never tires of practicing? With his back to me, I let myself out via the side entrance and return to the basement, my thoughts no less muddled than when I left.

I find Dorothea hovering about the desk, rereading my open diary. The page is open to my entry regarding *Mrs Dalloway*. She glances up at me as I enter, not even the slightest glint of guilt crossing her face.

"Haven't you read enough yet?" Though I attempt to deliver the words with a lighthearted touch, they come out stilted and bathed in anguish.

"Oh, hush now, Elizabet. You really do need to get over yourself." Hands on her hips, Dorothea watches me through narrowed eyes. "You know, if you didn't want anyone to read your private thoughts, perhaps you shouldn't have written them down in the first place."

I have little to say in response, given my inability to argue her logical yet smarting point.

"I was just noticing something curious is all." Dorothea bends her head toward the diary once more as she reads out loud. "What struck me most was how Clarissa Dalloway and Septimus Smith each had a break in reality, though from two very distinct experiences. Throughout the novel, they each venture back into their mind to relive that which delighted or haunted them most from their past."

I remain silent, raising only my eyebrows in question.

"Well, don't you see?" Dorothea moves around the desk, placing both hands on her wide hips. "If you can't see what I am talking about when it is in your own hand. Your own words, for crying out loud. Honestly, Elizabet, I have no idea how else to point out the obvious."

My eyes find the floor as my shoulders lift in a meager shrug. An inkling of Dorothea's meaning prickles around me, but I am reluctant to agree outright without first hearing her thoughts on the passage.

"Elizabet! Seriously now. You wrote it yourself. Don't you see? You and Emily are much like Clarissa Dalloway and Septimus Smith. Of course, hopefully not in the same way regarding poor Mr. Smith's demise, but alike still." Dorothea waves her hand to dismiss the unpleasantness of the image of Mr. Smith's ill-fated departure before moving closer to me again. "Two very distinct experiences. You and Emily have both suffered two very distinct yet defining experiences. Wouldn't you agree?"

"Yes. I will concede the point." I nod but offer nothing further.

"I am sorry to say, dear Elizabet, but I believe both you and Emily have had breaks in reality. Emily's break differs from yours in that she avoids what haunts her most. Wouldn't you agree?"

I nod once more.

Dorothea takes another step closer, lowering her voice to a mere octave above a whisper. "Your break differs from

Emily's, because instead of avoiding the grief of your loss, you do venture back to it. On purpose. Reliving both the happy memories and the grief. It is as if you decide each day to cut your hand with a knife and delight in the pleasure, the pain, and the release of the experience. Day after day you've done this, in life and in death." Dorothea pauses, studying my face. "Emily chooses not to feel anything and thus finds herself unable to move forward in life. You choose to live so intricately and completely with your grief that you are unable to move forward in death. I am sorry to say, Elizabet, unless you two make different choices, both of you will remain stuck where you are right now. Forever."

CHAPTER 28

 uesday, May 12, 2015
Emily

The Hickory Dickory Dock Clock near University and Third Avenue reads half past ten as Emily hurries by on her way toward the church. Dad used to take her to visit the clock on the way to Pike Street Market for their Sunday father-daughter breakfasts. He always pointed out the small brass mouse on the whimsical pendulum-style clock. By the time Emily arrives at the church doors, she is later than she has ever been to work. Sweat beads upon her temples. Awareness of how others may view her outburst and hasty departure yesterday afternoon stops her just short of pulling on the handle. Pivoting in place on the top step, Emily's eyes take in the thin tufts of clouds in the blue sky. "Seattle is prettiest when the sun is shining," she says to herself, her voice a low whisper.

The door behind her creaks and Emily turns toward the

sound. "Ms. Reed, I thought it might be you." Mrs. Peters gives her a kind smile before wrapping an arm firmly through the crook of Emily's elbow and nudging her through the door. "I felt a presence as I passed by the narthex just now and I said to myself, 'Beverly, don't you stop listening when God is speaking to you now. Go on and check that door.' And so I did, and here you are."

Emily stares at the woman, unsure of how to respond. "I'm sorry," Emily stammers, her eyes focused on the thick red carpet beneath her feet, "about yesterday. I am sorry. I was emotional and I . . . It wasn't my place to speak out like I did. I will finish the archiving, and I promise you, Mrs. Peters, I will do my best to archive everything with as much care as I possibly can."

Mrs. Peters pats Emily's arm. "Come now, dear, you can't think we are upset with you." Mrs. Peters guides Emily toward a bench positioned against the wall. "Heavens to Betsy, child, we have all mourned the loss of this beautiful building from time to time. We've mourned with every crack in the plaster over the years, even more so after the earthquake." Mrs. Peters' sigh is heavy. "And every single time the financial reality of having to part with our beloved church reared its head. It is not because of a lack of love, dear. We adore this building and all that it represents. As beautiful as the sanctuary is, it is beyond our ability to maintain its existence. And so we must move forward, while still holding the past and its memories deep within our hearts. I suspect we will continue to mourn the loss of this space in the future, but I hope we will reach a time when we can embrace without a tinge of regret all of the wonderful moments we were fortunate enough to share within these walls." Mrs. Peters dips her head while raising both eyes, along with her thin eyebrows. "You are not the first and you will most certainly not be the last to grieve the loss of something that holds a piece of you within it."

Emily nods, moisture rimming her eyes. Mrs. Peters' words hit closer to home than she imagines the church lady realizes.

"Moving forward is tricky business. A balance exists between the past and the present. You cannot appreciate one without the other, but you must not allow the past nor the present to do all the guiding. That creates imbalance, and imbalance simply won't do." Mrs. Peters nods with assuredness. "They must move together in unison. Learn from and appreciate the past while building those lessons into the present, always allowing your eyes to cast toward the future." Patting Emily's shoulder in a grandmotherly fashion, Mrs. Peters stands and tugs her skirt back into place. "All of life is a balancing act, Ms. Reed, but I do appreciate the sentiment and your attachment to the church."

Mrs. Peters' stout legs carry her toward the bank of dark-stained stairs leading to the church offices. "I won't keep you from your day, Ms. Reed. I only wanted to let you know that all is well." Mrs. Peters glances one last time over her shoulder, offering Emily a comforting smile.

A few minutes later, Emily is once again in the depths of the archives room. Among the dim shadowy light and the cool earthy air, Emily finds comfort among the archives. "Who would have thought?" She asks herself out loud as she tugs Elizabet's diary from her bag. "Who would have thought this place would bring me comfort?"

Emily places the row of chronologically organized diaries that she has already inspected into boxes for storing. Gathering the final five diaries of Elizabet Thomas' life, Emily takes in the covers, which were once deep red, blue, and green. She runs her fingers over the old leather binding before sitting at the desk to read the final editions of Elizabet's life.

Emily spends the rest of the morning perusing Elizabet's entries from 1930 to 1934 before taking a break to eat the ham sandwich Ryan insisted on packing for her.

After gathering her strength, she tackles the behemoth, disintegrating box that blocks her path to the last section of the basement. The remaining items yet to be archived are hiding behind the mountain of a box.

By three o'clock, Emily is damp with sweat from her efforts. She sits with a thud in the hard wooden chair that she claimed months ago. She swivels her chair to face the now-clear view of the room. Within the oversized box, she found items suitable for a typical 1960s office, including a heavy pastel blue typewriter, a desktop copier that was awkward and not remotely portable, and a lava lamp. An outdated filing system and a package of carbon paper rounded out the 1960s experience. Emily dragged the copy machine closer to the door, assuming the church administrators would wish to dispose of it, and placed the rest of the box's contents with the other artifacts that did not fit well on a shelf or in a file box.

With only one diary left to read, Emily uses her feet to pedal her chair back to the sturdy desk. Fingering the gold embossed lettering, she feels a pang of sadness. This is both the last diary and likely the last year of Elizabet's life. Until the day a fall fractured her hip, Elizabet maintained weekly visits to this church—in her mind, to sit with Rupert. She never let go of her earnest desire to be by Rupert's side. She clung to the hope of being reunited with him soon, and she wrote of it as if their reunion would take place on the same earth she herself was living on. At sixty years old, Elizabet was bedridden after her fall and further weakened by a lack of appetite. Her diary entries read more like the pleas of a desperate and lonely woman than the thoughtful contemplation of a life in motion, as they had before the fall.

The diary ends without warning, a scant quarter of the way into the lined pages. According to the newspaper clipping of her obituary, which someone tucked alongside her final entry, Elizabet succumbed to her injuries. Caught off guard by the sense of grief she feels for a woman she has never met, Emily lets her tears fall freely. As she rereads the pages, the source of Emily's grief pivots from the loss of a life to the fact that Elizabet's life was willfully wasted.

With crocodile tears and hiccupping breaths, Emily's sobs rattle her body. She realizes, somewhere in the depths of her grief for Elizabet, that more than Elizabet's last days were wasted. Every day she didn't live life to the fullest was a waste. The bleakness of the reality all but hits Emily over the head, ushering in a fresh wave of tears, along with an intense desire to do better for herself.

Taking a few minutes to gather herself, Emily gently tucks Elizabet's obituary back into the diary and places the final record of Elizabet's life into the box with the others. Labeling the box in thick black ink and securing the lid, Emily tells herself that archiving is her role in preserving the building's history. No matter the outcome for this church, she should be proud of her contribution to keeping history alive. Emily places the three boxes of Elizabet's diaries on the shelf in chronological order.

All that remains on Emily's to-do list waits for her in the corner that was previously blocked by the 1960s time capsule. The remaining boxes are overflowing with documents. Knowing this last section of archival work will take her another few months, Emily decides there is no time like the present and begins by hoisting a cardboard bank box toward a squat metal filing cabinet. As Emily nears the filing cabinet's dented but relatively level surface, the bottom of the box gives way, spilling papers and file folders. Emily's eyes grow wide as the contents of the box scatter across the smooth concrete floor like spiders fleeing a flood.

With a deep sigh, Emily kneels in resignation and begins gathering the papers into stacks. Smoothing out edges and newly formed folds, Emily sifts through the pages, attempting to group like documents together. She places birth certificates and death certificates into a semblance of rudimentary order. Stretching her right arm forward, Emily slides a bundle of documents closer, many of them more crumpled than what the fall would have caused.

Emily is attempting to smooth out a thick cream-colored piece of paper when the name, written in calligraphy with fine black ink, catches her attention. "Reed," Emily says her own surname out loud as if to confirm what she is seeing is real. Scanning the document, Emily reads first her mother's and then her father's first, middle, and last names. A swirl of gold at the top of the page seems to shout at her, *Certificate of Marriage*. With a flurry of immediacy mixed with tears pricking the corners of her eyes, Emily presses her hands flat against the certificate, pleading with it to conform into a pristine and flattened state.

Feeling the cold concrete floor beneath both her knees and her hands, Emily stands, moving the certificate to the desk's surface where she can examine it more closely under the light of the desk lamp. She fingers her parents' once-familiar signatures and it dawns on her that this would be the first time her mom ever signed her new last name. The date of June 18, 1983, brings a smile to Emily's lips as she remembers the wedding photograph with the date written on the back.

Starting at the top again, Emily reads the certificate in full, marveling at her good fortune for having spilled the box and also for having found a little piece of something to call her own. As her eyes near the bottom of the certificate, Emily's heart feels caught halfway up her throat. *Ceremony performed by Reverend Michael Reiley.* "Pastor Michael," Emily gasps, clutching the certificate with both hands, her knuckles turning white as her grip tightens at either edge of the page. "He knew them. Pastor Michael married my parents."

CHAPTER 29

uesday, May 12, 2015
Emily

Emily stands frozen in place in the middle of the cavernous room, the insufficient artificial light casting beams at strange angles, creating shadows of nooks and crannies that appear to lead to dark and mysterious places. Having searched almost every inch of the room, Emily is stunned by this newly discovered link between her parents and Pastor Michael.

Carefully placing the certificate on the desk, Emily rifles through her bag with both hands. The stern frown etched into her features softens when she feels the hard rubberized phone case. Emily lets out a sigh of relief as she flips the phone right side up, illuminating the time. "Four twenty. Mrs. Peters rarely leaves the building before five o'clock, so there is still time." Emily grabs the certificate and rushes to the door.

Climbing the steps two at a time, Emily is out of breath

when she reaches the main floor. Peeking down the long hall and into the sanctuary, Emily takes a quick look around before dashing toward the second set of intricately carved, dark wooden stairs that lead to the offices on the top floor.

"Ms. Reed, are you looking for me?" Mrs. Peters' voice and the sound of the closing front door spins Emily around on the landing.

"Mrs. Peters, there you are. Yes. Yes, I was looking for you." Emily jogs down the steps with ease, the sound of her footfalls muffled by the thick carpet. Stopping abruptly before Mrs. Peters, Emily catches her breath as the church administrator eyes her over a paper cup of steaming coffee.

"I just stepped out for a moment for a little boost of energy." Mrs. Peters lifts the cup slightly. "There is another meeting scheduled for later tonight, so I thought I could indulge in a little afternoon treat. Just a little something to keep me going until I can have a proper meal this evening." The church lady smiles with the innocence of a child, before taking another sip.

"I didn't mean to intrude on your break time."

"Not at all, dear. What can I help you with?"

Emily holds up the certificate. "I found this among a box of records." Emily pauses as she assesses the emotion rising in her throat, threatening to spill. Taking a deep breath, Emily cautions herself. If she isn't careful, the emotion will flow out, right along with her words.

Mrs. Peters leans forward, eyes squinting to take in the cursive writing on the certificate. "Yes?" Mrs. Peters inclines her head in question.

"It is a marriage certificate," Emily says. "My parents' marriage certificate."

"Oh my." Mrs. Peters steps closer, taking the certificate

into her free hand. "I am so sorry, dear. I do hope this didn't upset you.

Emily shakes her head, eager to move the conversation forward. "Do you know where Pastor Michael is?"

"Pastor Michael?" Mrs. Peters' eyes shift from the certificate back to Emily, the kindly church woman's face paling at the mention of his name.

"Yes, Pastor Michael. I haven't seen him since yesterday, and I was wondering if you knew where I might find him today?"

"We don't have a Pastor Michael, Ms. Reed." Mrs. Peters' eyebrows pinch together in what looks like concern. "Perhaps it is someone else you are looking for?"

"No," Emily says with assuredness. "It is Pastor Michael I am looking for." Emily points to the bottom of the certificate. "He performed the ceremony back in 1983." Emily smiles, hoping a friendly nudge will help Mrs. Peters' recollection.

Mrs. Peters places a plump hand on Emily's arm. "Yes, dear. I see that. It appears that Pastor Michael did indeed perform your parents' marriage ceremony in 1983, but—"

"I understand if he isn't available this afternoon, but I would like to speak with him." Emily's voice falters, fresh emotion woven with a hint of disappointment. She wants to discuss her discovery with the man whose company she has come to enjoy immensely. "He is a new link to my parents, and well, I would like to hear anything he can remember about them."

Mrs. Peters purses her lips before glancing toward the arched ceiling. "Ms. Reed, how long did you say you have been meeting with Pastor Michael?"

"Since the first day you showed me to the storage room. I assumed you had asked him to check in on me. To ensure I had everything I needed."

"I see." Mrs. Peters folds one arm nervously across her stomach, her index finger tapping her other forearm as she watches Emily's expression.

"Is there something I am missing, Mrs. Peters? I feel as though we are misunderstanding one another." Emily's anxiety rises in her chest and she squeezes her fists into tight balls, attempting to calm herself.

"Can you describe him? This Pastor Michael, that is." Mrs. Peters bites her lip.

"Sure. He wears a white clergy's collar and dark-colored pants, top, and jacket." Emily chuckles as the image of Pastor Michael flits across her mind's eye. "To be honest, he reminds me of a cross between Happy—you know, one of Snow White's seven dwarfs—and Mr. Cunningham from *Happy Days*." Emily laughs again. "He is a little on the shorter side of things. Does that help?"

"Ms. Reed, would you mind coming with me?" Mrs. Peters turns on her heel and motions for Emily to follow her.

Climbing two sets of stairs, Mrs. Peters guides Emily to the upper floor of church offices. She pauses at a closed door. "Ms. Reed, this is our clergy's office. I assume you have never been in this room before?"

"No ma'am, I haven't been down this hallway before."

Mrs. Peters nods once, then opens the door. It is a small but cozy room with dark glossy wood accents and furnishings. Mrs. Peters motions Emily inside. After scanning the room, with a tidy desk and a chair with a sweater draped across the back, Emily looks to Mrs. Peters for clarification.

Pointing to the wall above the wooden chair railing, Mrs. Peters directs Emily's attention to the framed photographs. They make almost a complete circle of the room. As Emily examines the photographs, she realizes they are portraits of former pastors.

Mrs. Peters walks to the far left wall and points to a photograph. "Ms. Reed, is this the Pastor Michael you are speaking of?"

Emily steps forward, relief flooding her as she recognizes the face. "Yes, that is him. Jovial-looking sort, isn't he?"

Mrs. Peters purses her lips again, and Emily takes another step closer, examining the photograph in more detail. She notices the small brass plate attached to the bottom of the frame. Leaning in even closer, Emily reads the words on the brass plate out loud. "Reverend Michael Reiley, 1916 to 1983."

"You see, Ms. Reed, Pastor Michael passed away in 1983," Mrs. Peters says, her voice soft. "He served the church for thirty-three years. Very well, he did. I adored his sermons, always crafted with such care and sincerity. How he loved this building too." Mrs. Peters' voice softens another octave as her hand runs along the top edge of the chair. "He did so much."

"I—I don't understand," Emily stammers. "He married my parents in 1983."

"Yes, this is true." Mrs. Peters agrees with a small nod. "He must have passed after their June wedding. It is the only thing that makes sense. Wouldn't you agree?"

Mrs. Peters' voice fades into the background. Emily doesn't hear anything more the older woman says. Nothing makes sense to her. A chill runs through her body. Turning out of instinct, Emily retreats from the room. Fleeing from the hallway, she runs as fast as she can toward the basement, hastily gathering her belongings before climbing the stairs once more, her eyes narrowed in on the front doors.

Feeling once again unmoored, Emily is staggering toward the door when something catches her attention. As if a rope were tied around her waist, she finds herself tugged past the pristine white, arched beams of the long narrow hall and into the sanctuary. Dropping her bag to the floor with a hefty dose of exasperation, Emily slides into a pew and bows her head.

Her mind swims with uncertainty. Did she imagine it all? Is she losing her mind? Did stress create this figment of her imagination? But no, how could it have? Until today, Emily had never seen a photograph of Pastor Michael. She couldn't possibly have conjured up a replica of a man she had never met.

It felt so real, their chats, his smile, even the way he counseled her with advice—not at all as if he had been out of practice, dead, for the past thirty-two years.

Sitting in the silence of the sanctuary, Emily is overwhelmed by how much has changed in the past three months. The last thirty-six hours, especially, have been a whirlwind of events. Emily never considered she would lend her attention to the thought of ghosts or spirits.

Emily stands, the uncertainty and anxiousness of her thoughts leading her down paths she is not comfortable navigating. With tentative steps, she moves toward the pulpit on the raised platform at the front of the church. Being far too pragmatic to have previously considered the possibility of ghosts, now she is forced to ask the question. Standing near the front row of pews, with her head bowed and her eyes closed, Emily whispers to herself, forcing her mind to consider the possibility. "Are my parents waiting for me too? Have they been waiting patiently all these years?" Before the idea has the chance to settle within her, Emily dismisses it with a shake of her head. Her eyes fly open and take in her surroundings, feeling uneasy as she gazes around the sanctuary. "If my parents were here somehow, I would have known. I would have felt them a long time ago. Wouldn't I?"

Finding a seat in the front row, in the center bank of pews,

Emily allows her eyes to wash over the view before her. She stares at the pipe organ, the choir loft, and the painted brass pulpit. She takes a deep breath, and her hands grip the front cushioned edge of the pew as she attempts to quiet her raging nerves. A single tear runs down her cheek as moments with her parents filter through her memory. Surprised by the vivid nature of the images, Emily inhales sharply before allowing her past to consume her.

Emily's overwrought emotions gather steam as her parents' smiling faces beam at her, exuding all the love they so effortlessly gave throughout her young life. She smiles, and the tears pour down her face like a waterfall in spring. The images, not at all chronological, span the years. Some are as recent as the night they died. Others are from Christmases, birthdays, dance recitals, and softball games when Emily was as young as five.

"I am sorry." Emily's voice is quiet and filled with sorrow. "I don't know where to begin."

Pastor Michael's words vibrate with clarity in Emily's mind, full of conviction, encouraging her forward. "When in doubt, start at the beginning, Emily." Snapping her head up, Emily searches the sanctuary for the man, whose few words are forever rich with meaning. "Pastor Michael?" She whispers to the empty sanctuary. Emily waits for several minutes, holding her breath, while her heart pounds in her chest.

Sneaking one final glance around the room, Emily closes her eyes again and clears her throat. "I am sorry it has taken me this long to pay you proper attention. I thought— I just thought that if I could avoid thinking about you, then losing you wouldn't hurt so much." A sob escapes her lips. "I didn't want to forget about you. I really didn't. I just didn't know how to live without you. I miss you both so much. Every day, in fact. Every single day, the moment I wake up each morning, you are in my thoughts." Emily's posture sinks. She rounds her shoulders in a deflated gesture. "And then I tuck it away so nobody else will see where I am wounded, where I still bleed."

Emily's chin drops to her chest, and her voice shakes. "I didn't want you to be disappointed in me. I've failed your memory at every turn. I understand this now." A strangled sound sneaks past her quivering lips. "My biggest fear all along was that I would fail." Emily's honesty sputters out of her in fits and starts, like an engine running out of gasoline. "At everything. I obsessed about failing at school, at university, and even now with my career, even though it's just starting out. All because I thought that if I could hold it together, make my life perfect somehow, then I wouldn't feel how much I have missed with you gone. But all I've done is fail. I should have done this years ago. I failed to grieve losing you. I didn't want to let you go. I reasoned that if I didn't grieve losing you, it would be like you hadn't left. I know this sounds crazy. Even I cringe a little saying it out loud."

Quiet in her own thoughts, she sniffles and tears run. Inhaling quickly in an effort to halt her runny nose, Emily captures the scent of vintage perfume in the air. Warily, she glances over her shoulder toward the sanctuary doors, a shiver taking over her body. "I should have honored your lives, not hidden myself away from them. I should be living each day instead of fearing it." Emily pauses as a hiccup induced by the onslaught of emotion beats its way out of her.

Her thoughts turn toward the words Elizabet wrote in the pages of her diaries. Those words bring a new level of clarity to Emily's grief as she recognizes how Elizabet did not actually live a single day after Rupert's passing. Feeling compelled to voice her understanding out loud, Emily continues, "I've learned a lot working in the archives these past few months, and I think I understand what I must do now. You see, a long time ago there was this woman. This incredibly strong and accomplished woman. Her name was Elizabet Thomas. Elizabet lived decades ago, and she was one of Seattle's greatest champions. She helped fundraise for hospitals, orphanages, and the homeless. Then she lost the love of her life, and she never recovered. Elizabet loved deeply, just as you two did. She made a difference in the world around her, like you did and like you taught me to do."

An anguished smile stretches across Emily's face as the happy memories collide with grief-filled images of devastation. Fresh tears cascade down both cheeks. "You see, Mom, Dad, Elizabet's grief and her unwillingness to embrace the present moments cost her most dearly. She lost out on every day of the rest of her life, simply because she was unwilling to move past her grief."

The perfume in the air seems heavier, and Emily shuffles farther along the pew in response to the scent. She scans the sanctuary from her new angle, expecting to see Mrs. Peters or another church lady lurking in one corner or another. Emily shivers again. The charge running up and down her spine feels as if some part of her has been plugged into an electrical outlet. Another sob erupts from her throat as she continues her one-sided conversation with her parents. "In order to hide from the pain, the past, and I suppose now that I've had some time to think about it, even my own future, I've been telling myself lies for ten years now. I have somehow convinced myself I can be strong and resilient, which aren't necessarily bad traits. But I didn't realize until recently that by telling myself to be strong and resilient, I meant that I should never grow attached to or depend on anyone or anything. Depending only on myself has become a key coping mechanism. Being strong has meant keeping it together, aiming for perfection, and never admitting defeat.

"This isn't a sane way to live. I know this now. I cannot sustain any of it, and if I am being honest, I have only been holding on by the tips of my fingernails for all these years." Emily looks up to the ceiling, praying the words will be forceful enough to fuel the burning inside of her and to help her move forward toward a different life. "But what I've come to understand is that Elizabet told herself lies too, and for far too many years. I can't imagine the weight of it all. She must have been exhausted." Emily pauses and examines her hands laced together in her lap. "I know I am."

Whether real or imagined, Emily hears a woman harrumph and glances to her right. Fearing she might be losing her mind for real, Emily squares her shoulders and pushes on, determined to say what she needs to say before scurrying from the building and all of its oddities. "If I could have told Elizabet anything to help her with her grief all those years ago, it would have been that we only ever have to be brave for one brief moment at a time. A friend of mine told me that recently." Emily smiles as she allows Pastor Michael's words to bring her comfort, while nudging to the back of her brain the uncertain and somewhat disturbing circumstance surrounding Pastor Michael. "Through her written words, Elizabet gave me the courage to be brave for this moment. So here I am, telling you how sorry I am for holding on and holding back in all the wrong ways. I'll do better from now on. I promise you I will."

Emily remains in the sanctuary, sitting in contemplative silence for a few minutes before rising to leave. Deciding a stroll along the water's edge will do her good, Emily grabs her bag and walks up the aisle of the sanctuary. She talks through her next steps in her head. *Like Elizabet, I need some time to think things through, to marinate in my grief. Like Pastor Michael told me time and time again, "Never hurry, Emily. Never worry. It will all work out in the end."*

CHAPTER 30

uesday, May 12, 2015
Elizabet

I am in complete shock. After an emotional evening spent in contemplative and worrisome thought, it takes me a moment to identify what is happening. In the quiet of the old building, we felt rather than heard the anguish being poured out in the sanctuary above us. Both of us, Dorothea and myself, rushed to be there. To be at Emily's side. The girl is finally grieving. I am most assuredly relieved, but I am also filled with immense sadness. I sit beside her as she mourns the loss of her parents. Her grief is raw and fresh despite the many years that have passed since her loss. Years passing mean little to the heart, I think as I hover a little closer, a mothering instinct to comfort the girl rising within me.

I desperately wish to place an arm about her shoulders, to offer her assistance and a shoulder to cry on. I understand all too well what she is finally allowing herself to experience. I sit closer than I've dared before, my desire to connect with Emily drawing me in.

I nod my head in understanding as Emily professes her sorrow and her desire to never forget her family. I understand more than the girl would realize, I imagine. I never wanted to forget my dear Rupert either. Perhaps my own break from reality, as Dorothea not so subtly mentioned only moments ago, was in part due to my desire to never forget him. A sob catches in my throat and I push it back down. I was most afraid I would forget him, that I would lose him via a fading memory by merely continuing to exist in this world. I worried that if I allowed life to go on without him, soon there would be no him left at all. Instead, I realize now, I lost myself in the process of clinging to Rupert.

Emily's words strike a chord within me, and I swivel my head to gaze at the heartbroken expression contorting her face. "I should have lived each day instead of fearing it." Did she really just say that? When the words left her lips, I was silently thinking the exact same thing. The pair of us are more alike than we are different. Dorothea was right after all. I glance toward Dorothea as she hovers on the opposite side of Emily, her face painted with anguish over watching the girl suffer.

I am lost in my own thoughts when Emily's words pierce the silence of the domed sanctuary. Her voice is shaky with grief and filled with tears. Wait! What? Did she just say my name? Lies? What lies? So many years. Whatever is she talking about? I look at Dorothea only to hear her harrumph with closed lips. What was that for, I wonder?

Dorothea is nodding her head slowly, as if in complete agreement with Emily's message. Between the two of them, the room is beginning to feel uncomfortably warm. I have the distinct impression I've been placed under a microscope, as they confirm what they already believe to be true about me. Emily is right about one thing. Even I cannot deny I am completely and utterly exhausted.

I distance myself from Emily while attempting to escape Dorothea's scrutinizing eyes. I move to the shadows of the sanctuary, seeking time and space to think over these recent events. It seems Emily has done just as I hoped she would do. She has found a way to move forward. She has become unstuck. Though I would not wish to see her in such agony as she is now, I am aware of the need for her to grieve her loss so she can look toward the rest of her life. She is choosing a different path through life than the one she was on when she first interrupted our world with billowing dust and the shuffling of boxes. I should be pleased by this news, yet I feel unsettled. As if Emily's abrupt change in direction is only the beginning.

I wait in the shadows until Emily finally rises from the pew and leaves the sanctuary. Dorothea hovers a moment before deciding to follow Emily, and relief floods through me. In the quiet of this sacred space, I allow myself to replay the events of the past few days. For a church that is soon to be vacated of its possessions and occupants, there has certainly been a plethora of activity within these walls as of late.

I am so very tired. Emily was right about that. Watching her grieve so openly, so bravely, I felt both proud of her and scared for her. Perhaps my own trepidations were sneaking in. I have known grief. That is for certain. But I wonder if I have known the right kind of grief. Is there such a thing even? I shake my head in disagreement with my own thoughts. There can't possibly be one right way to grieve. Each individual must grieve how they see fit. How they are guided to do so. Though I have no extensive knowledge on the subject, save for my own experience, I can't imagine there is a one-size-fits-all grieving process.

The words Pastor Michael delivered to his imaginary congregation only a few weeks ago feel as if they are embedded within the walls of the sanctuary. Instead of whispering their wisdom to me, the walls seem to shout at me from every direction. "Time gives us grace, and grace pushes us through time. If we persevere and walk the path before us, eventually we find ourselves on the other side, with our new companions, strength and resilience, walking right along beside us. The journey is yours to take. Free will isn't always easy, but it is always available to you."

I've had more than enough time, I think. Perhaps it is the grace aspect of the equation I am missing. I let the message settle over me once more. That overly joyful little man is as determined as Dorothea, with all her talk about choices and moving forward. I cringe a little at my own thoughts, knowing they both mean well. Just as I meant well for Emily and her journey.

"Emily." Her name slides off my lips. "She appeared so calm, so serene when she left here." I pace up and down the length of the aisle. "She seemed taller somehow. More self-assured." I take another lap up the aisle. "Unburdened. That is what it is. She has been released from the weight of hiding from her grief. The weight has hung around her neck like a noose all these years." I smile at the discovery, before the similarity of our situations glares back at me once more, wiping the smug smile from my lips.

Emily was brave for one moment. She stepped up in that moment, allowing grace to enter her heart and her life. As soon as grace got ahold of her, she was pushed through time, toward the path that had been waiting patiently for her all along. Or so I presume. It is so easy to see from the outside looking in. The lies Emily used to fool herself into avoidance are precisely what kept her at arm's length from the grace she needed.

I stop midway up the aisle. "Emily's lies are no different from my own." My hand moves toward my mouth, agape with my realization. "Different in context, yes. But not different in purpose. The lies were there to protect me from everything I feared. I really have been lying to myself. What a fool I've been. Oh, Rupert! Can you ever forgive me? The time I've wasted. I am so sorry, my dear."

My heart aches anew. The grief I've carried with me since Rupert's passing is balled up tightly and is pressing against my chest. My mind is reeling, and I feel as if I have come undone. Dorothea was right. All this time, my dear friend saw what I could not.

I move with haste toward the pulpit, toward the three-tiered railing, eager to be as close to love and forgiveness as I can be in this world in between. "This is all my fault." The words are halted by the same emotions that fuel them. "I've spent more than a lifetime in this beautiful building. The comfort of these walls. The familiarity of the dark wood and the pipe organ. The nooks and crannies that I know so well. The cupboard beneath the stairs where I used to hide in my early days here, when my emotions got the better of me." My voice trails off as I turn and take in the pews where I so often sat with Rupert, among a congregation of Seattleites all striving to make our little place on earth the best it could be.

Images of all I witnessed these past eighty years, through the veil of a ghost's vantage point, filter through my mind. Christmas pageants sparkle in my memory, each child growing and changing with every passing year. The choir's angelic voices fill the air around me. The desperate days of what they now call the Great Depression, though devastating, brought the congregation even closer together in service. Many overzealous and not entirely well-thought-out nuptials occurred as men were shipped off to battle during the Second World War.

Then, of course, there were the baptisms and the bake sales and the unending service of the Ladies' Aid Society. Despite being on the outside, I have been proud to be a part of all of it. This building has served as a cornerstone of the community's past and has been a crucial element in my own life, and in my death. It has given so much to so many, but now it is time for me to give it back. The church, this beautiful church, can no longer be my home. It can no longer be my sanctuary.

The grief washing over me is immense. But it is not, I realize, the same shape of the grief I experienced over losing Rupert. Instead, I am beginning to grieve the loss of the life I could have had and the death I should have allowed myself to experience. I understand now that I did this, all of this, to myself. For far too many years in a row, I was afraid to be brave for one tiny little moment at a time.

I love this building with all my heart. It is a true place of solitude, communion, peace, and dare I say it, grace. In hindsight, it does not surprise me that I chose to remain here, surrounded by all I am familiar with. By the many experiences that brought me so much joy and comfort throughout my life. I steady myself near the rail, staring despondently at the intricately sculpted pipes of the organ. A bundle of emotions bubbles furiously just under the surface of my existence as the complete understanding of what I have done registers within me. "My biggest mistake was allowing myself to become a prisoner in my beloved sanctuary."

CHAPTER 31

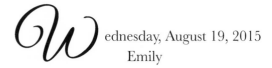

ednesday, August 19, 2015
Emily

Emily rolls over in bed, tossing the covers to the floor as she moves, agitated in sleep. The dream feels real, swapping out the cool early morning air from the open window for the chill of the archives room. The cold touches her skin, tugging her forward through the veil of her subconscious mind.

As she stands in the middle of the now-expansive archives room, Emily's eyes scan everything the less than sufficient light touches. She has searched every inch of this room. During the lifting and the sorting, any nerves Emily might have had about the eeriness of the dark, dank basement room vanished. Her mind has been occupied with busy tasks.

The makeshift bookshelves constructed from concrete blocks and wood planks now line the walls, holding boxes of church archives, directories, and photographs. The desk she claimed six months ago sits in the center of the room. An odd positioning, Pastor Michael has told her on more than one occasion. But she knows the placement ensures the best lighting with the least amount of shadow.

Shadows, Emily learned early on, work against both a productive researcher and a well-sighted one. She teased Pastor Michael once, in response, that her job was to shine a light on the subject matter, to eliminate the shadows so the truth could be viewed. Pastor Michael nodded thoughtfully at her comment, hands clasped behind his back in his contemplative manner. With a twinkling in his eye that was reminiscent of a vintage Santa Claus, he offered, "Light is the only thing that will drown out the darkness, my dear, just as love is the only thing that can remove that which comes from fear." Pastor Michael was full of isms. Whether they originated from the pages of his Bible or his own poetic view on life, he never shied away from sharing them with her.

She was about to counter his comment that day, certain he meant to say "hate" instead of "fear," but he changed the subject, moving on to a new topic with a deft hand.

Emily glances around the room at the tidy stacks. A sense of pride at a job well done fills her, while a sliver of sadness creeps in at the thought of the project coming to an end. A happy end, but an end all the same. When she entered this room for the first time, she was overwhelmed by the chaos and the dust, and now every item has been filed and catalogued. The boxes are ready for transport to a new building, once the church leaders decide what is next for the congregation.

The managing partners of Patterson and Holt told Emily that the church administrators are pleased with the result. All parties have done what they set out to do, and the concerned citizens of Seattle know the church's history will remain alive, no matter where the congregation worships. This knowledge may quieten the rumbling of concerns, or perhaps it will reignite the fight to save the building. Either way, the job is complete.

Stepping toward the desk, Emily places her bag on the old wooden office chair and begins to clear out the drawers. She places notepads, sticky notes, pens, and unused file folders into a banker's box.

"A place for everything, everything in its place." Pastor Michael stands in the open doorway, hands stuffed into his pants pockets.

Emily smiles. "I didn't think it possible in the beginning, but I will miss this dingy room." She bends to unplug the desk lamp from its extension cord.

The room falls deeper into shadows, the overhead lights struggling to stay on task. "How about you?" she says. "Are you ready for the next move?" Emily nestles the lamp into the box before tapping the lid into place.

"The place kind of stays with you, doesn't it?" Pastor Michael steps toward her, and for a moment, her eyes are unable to find him in a darkened section the light cannot reach.

Emily squints to focus her eyes. "It does, but then again, so do you. Thank you for all of your help. I'm not sure I could have done it without your guidance and insight. Whenever I wondered what my next step might be, there you were, guiding me all the way."

"I am happy to be of service, Emily."

Pastor Michael steps forward into a beam of shadowy light. Disturbed specks of dust linger about him, framing his smiling face. He reminds her of the dwarf named Happy from *Snow White and the Seven Dwarfs*. She is about to mention this, intending to tease the man into one of his sweet blushing episodes, when his voice rings through, soft but clear and direct. "You found what you were looking for, then?"

"Yes, I suppose I did. It will all work out in the end." She extends her arms in a sweeping gesture encompassing the room. "The church's archives are in order and ready to be relocated once they make a decision about a new building. If things work out with the developer, then the sanctuary will also be saved. I'd call that a win-win." Emily offers a quiet laugh and a smile for the kindly man. She will miss his presence in her life. Emily consoles herself by making a mental note to keep in touch with him, even after the congregation has moved.

"Ah, but that is where you are mistaken. It was not the sanctuary you were seeking salvation for, my dear."

Emily's brows knit together as she considers his words. "I think I understand." She hesitates, organizing her words in her head. "It was my job to prepare the historical records in the event of continued community unrest about the sale of the property. But I kind of fell in love with the place, and I didn't want to see it destroyed in the end. I guess you could say this project changed my mind on the value of remembering the past."

With a finger placed to the side of his nose and a slight nod of his head, Pastor Michael continues as if speaking of a secret shared between them. "You misunderstand me. You said it yourself. There is a great deal of importance to remembering the past, and to celebrating it, I might add. It was, however, not the sanctuary you were seeking salvation for. Your own salvation was at stake, Emily. I have said it before, my dear. These walls have stories to share, lessons to teach, prayers to hear, and weary hearts to console. You were the one they were intended for. It was all for you."

Emily finds herself at a loss for words as Pastor Michael

turns and walks toward the door, hands clasped behind his back. The sage advice he offered many months ago now dances about her head, tugging at her to understand its true meaning. The words quoted from her favorite childhood storybook, *Charlotte's Web*, echo in Emily's mind. "Never hurry, never worry." Before she can utter another word, Pastor Michael steps toward the threshold of the door, and whether it is the play of light and shadow or her own eyes blinking out of sync with his movements, he appears to vanish right before her.

Emily bolts upright in bed. A shiver runs through her as the cool breeze from the window caresses her sweat-beaded skin. Reaching for the strewn blankets on the floor, she snuggles herself into them before rolling onto her side. Taking deep breaths to slow her heart rate, Emily lets the images of the dream, still fresh in her memory, filter through her mind. She soothes herself with the reminder that it was only a dream.

Thirty minutes pass as Emily plays a game of hide-and-seek with the possibility of further sleep, her fully engaged brain races ahead of her like a preschooler impatient for an afternoon at the park. Giving in to the demands of the child within her, Emily grabs her housecoat from the closet and shuffles toward the kitchen to make coffee, already certain she will need more than one cup.

The water warms in the kettle as Emily busies herself with scooping instant coffee and sugar into her favorite blue mug. Today is the final day in the archives room, which is most likely the cause of the vivid dreams that kept her tossing and turning most of the night. She sighs deeply. Her mixed emotions over the uncertain outcome of the church and her brain's constant need to puzzle out all that transpired between her and Pastor Michael have made her weary.

Having kept the knowledge of Pastor Michael's appearance in the archives room between herself and Mrs. Peters, Emily's desire to unfold the mystery presses against her heart and her mind, consuming both in a constant and steady thread of contemplation. The summer months have flown by as Emily finished archiving the last remaining section of the basement room. Many of the remaining boxes were filled with church records and photo albums, and all of it required a precise and detailed written account for future reference.

Emily had planned to return to the church this morning, to gather a box of office supplies and for one final check that everything is in its place. Mrs. Peters, though, caught up with her as Emily was on her way home last night, indicating she had found a box in the back of her office closet, under a heap of old choir robes. "Would you mind including it in the archives as well?" the endearing church lady asked in a tone so sweet that Emily thought honey might very well appear in her mouth. "Of course," Emily replied. It was still her job, as well as an appreciative gesture for the woman who had been generous and understanding.

Pouring boiled water into her mug, Emily stirs her coffee, the smell alone giving her a boost from her sleepy state. Glancing at the clock, Emily reasons that an earlier start to her day might mean a free afternoon, so she sips her coffee and decides to tackle her morning tasks an hour earlier than originally planned.

CHAPTER 32

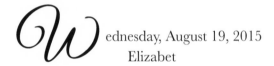ednesday, August 19, 2015
Elizabet

"Any historic building is only as rich as the memories it holds within its walls." Pastor Michael's voice catches me by surprise, and I turn toward the sound, seeing him in his dark blue suit and white collar. Talking to himself again, I muse. "These walls have stories to share, lessons to teach, prayers to hear, and weary hearts to console." I smile demurely in his direction, offering him a cordial nod as I cross his path.

After months of self-reflection, during which I've often been the recipient of Dorothea's silent treatment, and considerable time spent watching Emily transform from the devastated shell of a girl into a warm and loving young woman, my time has come. I move into the hall and head purposefully toward the basement stairs. I find Dorothea in what used to be the basement storage room. A quick glance around brings a smile to my lips. The room has transformed into a tidy, well-situated, and much friendlier space. Part of me wonders whether the room changed the girl, or the girl changed the room.

Dorothea hovers over Emily's left shoulder with a concentrated interest as the girl writes in her oversized archiving notebook. My heart warms as I watch my friend. She does not notice my presence at first, so I pause in an effort to collect myself before moving closer. The confession burning deep within me is desperate to be released, if only so that I can prevent myself from having the opportunity to take it back.

I gather my resolve and straighten my posture as much as my wool suit jacket will allow. Balling my lace-gloved hands into fists of determination at my sides, I usher the words out in a rush. "I no longer wish to be a prisoner." The words tumble forth like a boulder set free from the top of a steep hillside, gathering momentum as it rolls and taking with it anything in its path.

Dorothea's head, clad in her plumed hat, snaps up sharply. Her deep blue eyes narrow in attention. Lifting her chin with a slow, deliberate motion, she surveys me with a questioning expression upon her lips. I wait, wondering whether she will believe me or cast suspicion on my announcement.

Unable to stand the silence any longer, I burst forward, both in movement and in voice. "It is true. I swear it is true. I have been thinking it over and I realize the time has come." My propped-up bravado falters, resulting in a less than steady voice. I twist my hands nervously, squeezing them together in an effort to calm myself. With my eyes lowered toward the middle of my torso, I watch my fingers lace and unlace, fidgeting like a schoolgirl about to be reprimanded. "I—I have been a fool. All these years." My words trail off into a whisper. "I see how much of a fool now." My eyes flick up briefly, taking in Dorothea's expression. "Truly I do, Dorothea. Please allow me to make amends."

I move a little closer toward the desk, and from the corner of my eye, I notice Emily's back stiffen against the chair as she straightens her position. She places her pen on top of the desk as she examines her work. A slight shiver runs through her, causing the pen to roll slightly as it meets the solid surface.

"I am so very sorry, Dorothea. Truly, I never meant for any of this to happen. I should have listened to you sooner. You were right. I should have realized what a mistake I was making in insisting I remain here within these walls. Please forgive me, dear friend." I plead with my eyes. "You have been so patient and kind and I—I have been stubborn like a mule." It is difficult to disguise the overwhelming feeling of embarrassment that clings to my every word, like the bad smell of a frightened skunk. I may be a proud woman, seldom contorting myself toward the expectations of others, but my mother taught me years ago that a proud woman must also know when to apologize for actions unbecoming. If it is humble pie I must eat in this moment, so be it. A friendship, this friendship especially, is far more important than my wounded pride.

"Well, I dare say." Dorothea places her palms together in front of her ample bosom, as if she is about to kneel and say a prayer of gratitude. "It most certainly is about time, Elizabet Thomas."

My eyes sheepishly dart about the room as Dorothea watches me, beaming with delight. I dip my head in a single acknowledging nod and do my utmost best to hold my tongue. I allow her this moment of satisfaction, with both of us aware that she has been right all along.

The lightness of Dorothea's mood washes over me. Watching Emily work, I can't help but feel a small sense of pride myself. This girl, our Emily, has grown up right before our very eyes. My eyes pool with emotion, and I imagine this being precisely how a mother might feel about her very own daughter.

Dorothea dances about the room, taking advantage of every inch of exposed concrete. Emily leans back in the chair and stretches. Smiling at the notes she has written, she closes the large book and tucks it into her bag. A lighter mood has prevailed in Emily these past few months, helping to move her forward. She appears to be filled with a sense of ease, which perhaps has been encouraged by the reappearance of the boy.

Dorothea was beyond thrilled the afternoon Ryan appeared in the archives room. Hours after he and Emily departed, she continued to gush. Well into the wee hours of the morning, she went on about every word spoken between them. She provided a commentary on each of Emily's smiles, nods, and laughs. Convinced she was right to encourage their relationship, Dorothea strutted about like a proud peacock for many days after. How she presumed to be the cause of their reunion, I have no idea, but given her delight with such an idea, I decided I would not rain on her parade.

"Well then, I suppose . . ." I interrupt Dorothea's dancing with my words. "I suppose I should figure out what the next steps are to be." I pause as a trickle of fear attempts to surface from beneath my chest. "Wherever forward may be, I remain compelled to go there."

Dorothea's smile is as wide as her hips. "I knew you would come around eventually, Elizabet. I am so very proud of you."

"Just to be clear." My voice fills with a slight shrill of seriousness. "This in no way means I am not fearful of what is ahead. I must be honest with you, Dorothea. I am most fearful that I will never see Rupert again if I leave this place, this world in between." I spread my palms wide. "Can you understand? Do you have it in your heart to understand where I am coming from in this moment?"

Dorothea's voice softens as she moves around the desk. "Elizabet, he is not here. Surely, we would have bumped into him by now if he were. If Rupert is not here now, and he has not been here for the past eighty years, I think we can safely assume he won't ever be here."

"I suppose you are right." I begrudgingly agree, despite the murmurings at the edges of my mind.

We stand in silence for several minutes, waiting, watching, thinking our own private thoughts. Emily, too, sits in what I can only presume is quiet contemplation, staring blindly at the desk before her. These past few months have been deeply emotional and completely immersive. I wish I knew more about what is going on behind Emily's eyes. Perhaps she would be able to offer me a word or two of solace, something to take with me, wherever I am going.

This train of thought only leads me to wonder what actions I must take to move myself forward from this world in between. Does Dorothea really know the way, or does she only think she does? Perhaps she is too proud to admit she hasn't the faintest idea of what comes next. Though part of me would like to think I am correct on the subject, I am present enough within my own mind to recognize when my ego claims a right to something that doesn't belong to it.

Uncertain of how much time I have remaining in this building, I make a plan to revisit the sanctuary. I need to be certain Rupert is no longer there. I can't bear to risk missing him when I go. I will take my time along the way, poking my head into the nooks and crannies that have become so familiar and comforting to me over the years. I will force myself to say a proper goodbye. So often in life, we aren't afforded the opportunity for such a farewell. I promise myself I will take advantage of this opportunity in death.

After several minutes of quiet contemplation from all of us, Emily stands and retrieves a box from the opposite side of the desk. My eyes follow her movements as she lifts the lid. I move a little closer. This may very well be the final box in the entire room left to archive. No wonder the girl is deep in thought today. She will be leaving the sanctuary too. This awareness sends a quiver through me. For the first time, the thought dawns on me that I will be leaving not only the church, but also Emily. Dorothea catches my eye with a sad smile. She too understands these next few days are to be filled with goodbyes.

Emily reaches into the box, and I set my fragile emotions to the side as she extracts a brown leather-bound book. *History of Woman's Work* is embossed on the cover in thick, italicized gold letters. I catch Dorothea's eye and she shrugs, apparently having no knowledge of the book either. Emily positions herself in the chair once more and opens the book to the first page. Dorothea and I lean in, eager to discover, one last time, what Emily is about to uncover.

CHAPTER 33

*W*ednesday, August 19, 2015
Emily

Arriving in the archives room, Emily spots the box Mrs. Peters left for her on the desk. Setting her bag down, she examines all four sides of the cardboard box, looking for an indication of what might be inside. Placing the box on the floor beside the desk, she extracts the master binder from her bag, intent on first checking the room and its contents. Perusing the binder's pages, she runs her finger down the list of items within the hundreds of tidy boxes that line the walls.

Emily scans the room as she mentally ticks off the steps she has taken to ensure a consistent level of accuracy in her archiving. The binder is the key that unlocks the map to the church's history. Emily feels a rush of nostalgia and a burst of pride at having been the one fortunate enough to bear witness to the church's past. After several minutes spent in deep contemplation, Emily retrieves the last box from the floor beside the desk and lifts it onto the flat surface. Taking a lungful of air, Emily prepares herself for her final excursion into the history of the First United Methodist Church of Seattle.

Lifting the lid, Emily finds a thick brown book. The leather-bound book is heavy in her hands as she turns the large volume right side up to read the gold shimmering letters embossed onto the cover. *History of Woman's Work*. Emily places the book on the desk and opens the heavily padded cover to reveal the words *Volume One*. Between the pages, Emily presumes she will find a century's worth of documentation, financial records, meeting minutes, church service programs, special event menus, and stories of the ongoing and generous assistance provided by the Ladies Aid Society, beginning as early as 1853.

The book, compiled much like a scrapbook, is a treasure trove of historical accounts. Eager to archive the data, Emily pulls out the master records binder from her bag and notes the book as an important piece of the church's history. Flipping pages at random, Emily examines the photographs and delights in the varied menus of 1923 fundraising dinners. For pennies, one could enjoy ham rolls, salad, baked Boston beans, Boston brown bread, pumpkin pie, tea, and coffee. The generosity and dedication of the Ladies Aid Society is impressive. Good deeds and exceptional accomplishments fill the book's pages, reminding Emily of what is possible with a willing mind and a little hard work. Something her dad might have said, she thinks.

Emily continues reading, learning of the church's origins as far back as Seattle's first minister, Reverend David Blaine, and his wife, Catherine. Apparently, Catherine requested that women in the community save books, magazines, and newspapers so they could be donated to Dr. and Mrs. Maynard's hospital lean-to. The donation for the hospital, located against the Maynards' own log cabin, was one of the first noted acts of organized volunteerism. It is said that this donation of books and more to the young men receiving treatment at the hospital was the unofficial beginning of the Seattle YMCA.

As time went on, the women of the church took on the responsibility of paying the cost of the church's first mortgage, encouraging the establishment of the first Seattle Chamber of Commerce. The women sent clothing, medical supplies, and $273.79 to the city of San Francisco after the devastating earthquake and fire of 1906. In addition to these forward-thinking endeavors, the Ladies Aid Society set up a Red Cross unit at the church when war came calling in 1917. During the years to follow, the women continued to fight for the well-being of those less fortunate than themselves. They worked within the church and the community of Seattle and made positive impacts abroad through the Woman's Foreign Missionary Society.

As the needs of those around them changed, so did the organization. The Ladies Aid Society nurtured sectors that required more assistance while allowing successful operations to stand on their own, demonstrating a model of self-sustainability within the charitable organization. Emily is overcome with the pride of being a native Seattleite as she reads the many accounts of successful charitable work. Emily recognizes, somewhat in awe, that several of the Seattle charities listed in the notes and budgets are still in operation today.

When World War II impacted the daily lives of Seattleites,

the city was divided. With a robust sense of what was acceptable and what was not, the women of the church rose to the occasion. At the train station, they supported Japanese Americans who were being rounded up and transported to internment camps elsewhere in the state. The church went a step further, holding the deeds of many businesses owned by Japanese Americans until the deeds could be properly reinstated to them upon their return to Seattle after the war.

Emily's head bobs in agreement with what, at the time, must have been a controversial and somewhat unbecoming view of how an American woman should behave. "Good girls really don't make history, it seems." Emily's voice pierces the quiet of the basement. She turns pages at a steady rate, contemplating her own options should the plans Ryan spoke of for saving the church fall through. Leaning back in her chair, Emily is about to close the book entirely and move on with her day when a page captures her attention. It isn't the content of the page that catches her eye, but the way it is laying within the book, slightly lifted and at an angle. Emily examines the page more closely, realizing something is tucked within the book, almost hidden by the thick binding.

Tugging free the loose piece of paper, Emily unfolds it to reveal a copy of the first page of the last will and testament for a Dorothea Georgine Emile Ohben. "Dorothea?" Emily says the name out loud, her voice echoing about the room, bouncing off concrete floors and brick walls. Wondering if it is possible that this Dorothea is the same as Elizabet's Dorothea, Emily leans toward the paper and squints her eyes. A tiny handwritten note underneath Dorothea's typed name reads *AKA: Lou Graham.*

Reading Dorothea's will, Emily quickly ascertains that a large donation of almost her entire estate went to the Seattle school board. "Oh, Madame Dorothea," Emily teases, drawing out her name long and slow. "Well done, Dorothea. Well done, indeed." Emily lifts her head at the scent of vintage perfume about the room. Out of curiosity more than anything, she sniffs the legal document, discovering it is not the origin of the perfume, before folding it and tucking it within the pages of the large book. Emily closes the book's cover with a gentle hand. "The women of Seattle are certainly something." She stands to place the book back into the box, pleased that Mrs. Peters was thoughtful enough to bring her the historical record for archiving.

Peering into the box, Emily realizes the box is not yet emptied. Placing *History of Woman's Work* on the desk, Emily reaches for the remaining item, wrapped in plain white tissue paper. Turning the package over, she tugs at the edge of the delicate paper, careful not to tear it. Before she can extract what she presumes to be another book from the paper, a note falls out from beneath the tissue and floats to the floor. Emily bends over and reaches for the note, unfolding the paper as she stands upright once more.

Dear Ms. Reed,

    I believe Pastor Michael may have intended this for you.
    I wish you well in your future endeavors.

Yours sincerely,
    Mrs. Peters

Placing the note on the desk, a shiver rattles through Emily's body as if a freight train has plowed into her at top speed. She doesn't understand how Pastor Michael could have left her anything, since, well, he hasn't actually been alive for decades. This insight alone is still unresolved in Emily's mind. Mrs. Peters agreed the day after the realization occurred. "Mum's the word," the church lady said to Emily as she pretended to lock her lips with an imaginary key before tossing it over her shoulder.

Shaking her head in an effort to settle her rising nerves, Emily unwraps the rest of the tissue paper. A deep blue, leather-bound notebook is soft and smooth in her hands. A leather strap is wrapped several times around the body of the notebook, securing the pages from prying eyes. Emily unwraps the strap of leather, revealing the gold embossed front cover. *All the world is made of faith, and trust, and pixie dust. J.M. Barrie.* Emily's fingers caress the letters as she reads the quote from the beloved story of *Peter Pan.*

Holding the book tight to her chest, a tear snakes down her cheek. Faith, trust, and pixie dust may not always be visible to the human eye but believing in them is what makes them real. "Thank you for having faith in me. For showing me how to trust again, and for adding a bit of pixie dust to my life, Pastor Michael. I will remember you always." Emily's words are soft. Her heart is humbled by the gift, the message, the kindness offered to her within this building, within this sanctuary.

Once free of the leather strap, Emily opens the book fully. The glittering gold edges of each page add a luster and a fluidity to the otherwise plain lined paper. A delicate bronze ribbon is sewn in to mark the place of the writer or reader. The pages slide through Emily's fingers as she fans them cover to cover, and giddiness over what she might write within the pages bubbles up inside of her.

Feeling light, unburdened, and renewed, Emily places the

notebook on the desk and walks to the center of the basement. Spreading her arms wide, just as she would have done as a young girl, Emily spins. She spins and dances and moves about the room as if music is playing louder than she's ever heard it before.

She imagines them there with her, Elizabet and Dorothea, dancing around the room with joy, and hope, and happiness. Maybe even Pastor Michael is there, watching the three women from the corner. So much is ahead of Emily now, and all she had to do was be brave for one tiny little moment at a time.

Dizzy with glee from the childlike spinning, Emily halts her motion and leans into the desk for support. She runs her fingers through her brunette waves and considers her options. "I might be scared at times or frustrated, or even devastatingly sad and grief-stricken." Emily's voice catches in her throat as she whispers to herself. "But I promise, I will never, ever allow fear to control the direction of my life again."

Using both hands, Emily lifts *History of Woman's Work* into the waiting box before securing the lid in place. Labeling the box with the book's title, Emily places the box in the middle of the last shelf, with room to spare, and steps back to admire her work.

What began as a heaped pile of disorganized and neglected dusty records now resembles a history. A lifeline to the past, with a steady arm stretched out, still reaching into the future. *The story isn't over yet,* Emily thinks. *It has only just begun.*

Emily fills a box with office supplies she brought from the law firm before she scans the room one last time. Her eyes linger on the boxes, the shelves, and the friends she's never met but has come to know and love all the same. Scooping the box into one arm while swinging her bag over her opposite shoulder, Emily moves toward the door and stands ready to switch off the light. "Thank you." She pauses, a tremble in her voice. "Thank you for everything." She flips off the light switch, and the archives room descends into blackness as the door closes behind her with a soft thud.

CHAPTER 34

*W*ednesday, August 19, 2015
Elizabet

I am giddy with excitement as Emily turns off the light and closes the door. It had never occurred to me that I might wish to have the company of the living while in this world in between. Of course, after Rupert passed, I didn't wish for the company of the living when I was still alive myself. It is funny how one doesn't know what they do not know, until all of a sudden, they do. Then the knowledge is staring them in the eyes, often with a haughty little attitude that says, *I've been here all along. You were simply too stubborn to let yourself see me.*

I laugh at myself. Our shared dance with Emily lifted my spirits. Years may separate us, but hearts always find a way to connect people. I sneak a glance toward Dorothea as she continues to float about the room, slowly, gracefully, as if she were as light as a feather. I join her in a final spin around the room, twirling like a small child.

"Emily certainly is a doer, isn't she, Elizabet?" Dorothea has slowed her steps and now sways side to side in place, an indication that the fun and lightheartedness have had their time and she is about to become serious once more.

"She most certainly is. Right from the beginning, in fact." My hands clasp together as I remember Emily's first encounter with the basement space, now the archives room. "Remember how she took one look at the chaos and set straight to work? She impressed me even then. I knew there was something special about the girl in those first moments."

"I may not have said so before." Dorothea stops swaying entirely and straightens her skirt as she speaks. "But I am pleased we were here to see Emily. To be able to assist her and whatnot."

"What you are not saying, and graciously so, my dear Dorothea, is that you are pleased we were *still* here to see Emily." I sigh deeply. "You have been so very patient with me all these years. You are a true friend indeed."

"Does that mean you are ready, then? You are now comfortable saying farewell to the world in between?" Dorothea's eyebrows lift, testing and teasing me.

"Emily has made clear her planned course of action." I contemplate my next words. "I believe she will follow through and live a life with her heart wide open to the possibilities. She will have some challenging times ahead, for certain, but I trust that she has found the inner strength to sit with her repressed emotions and move forward from them."

"You do realize you have not yet answered my question?" Dorothea's hands move to her hips as she prepares to stand her ground.

"Yes, Dorothea." I sigh in mock frustration. "Though I may not be entirely comfortable with the notion, I am prepared to do whatever is required to move forward from this world in between." I nod my head with a firm and decisive motion.

"Good." Dorothea beams at me. "Because, quite frankly, I was running out of ways to coerce you so."

I laugh lightheartedly at her good-natured attitude before adding one more thing. "I do have one stipulation though." My gloved hand is raised, one finger lifted in hesitation.

"Oh, Elizabet. Seriously. What possibly could you need to stipulate now? Haven't you had more than enough time to sort yourself out? Or is eighty years not quite enough for you? You know, most people don't have nearly as long a run as you have had." Her words are direct, but a smile lives behind their delivery. "Whatever is it that you need, dear?"

My laugh springs forth at her put upon airs. "It is a meager request. I promise it is." I move toward Dorothea, my voice turning to the seriousness of the matter at hand. "I need to visit the sanctuary one last time. It might sound crazy to you, but I need to be sure Rupert isn't here. You must understand, dear friend. He was here for so many years after his passing. I know because I visited him often. The sanctuary is where I am certain I felt his presence most. It puzzles me still that he did not remain when I arrived." My eyes find my clasped hands, and I fidget with my fingers as my resolve quivers. "But—I need to be certain. I would never forgive myself if I weren't absolutely convinced that he is no longer here in the sanctuary."

Dorothea eyes me carefully. "You don't sound crazy, Elizabet. You sound sad. There is a difference, you know." Tapping a finger to her lips in contemplation, Dorothea keeps me waiting as she considers my request. "How about this? Why don't you spend the night in the sanctuary? Wait for him. Search for him. Pray for him. Then in the morning, I will come to collect you, and we will proceed."

I want desperately to ask what proceeding means. What does it look like? Will it cause us pain or joy or nothing at all? How does Dorothea know about proceeding? Was there a class taught in the Sunday school room that I missed? Does this have to do with her being a spirit and me being a lowly ghost? Do I need to prepare myself? How would I prepare for such a thing? My head is buzzing with thoughts, some rational, others fueled purely by fear.

Dorothea's voice breaks through my busy mind. "Do we agree?"

"Yes, yes," I stammer. "We agree. I will wait for you in the sanctuary tomorrow morning." I pause, wishing for Dorothea to elaborate on what tomorrow will bring, while contemplating whether I want to know at all. I take her silence as a cue. "Well then, I suppose I will see you in the morning." I turn toward the archives room door. A final glance over my shoulder confirms Dorothea's concerned eyes are on me. "Have a good evening."

"Have a good evening as well, Elizabet. I do hope you find the peace you are looking for. Truly, I do."

Me too, I think as I move with purposefully slow movements in the direction of the sanctuary.

I linger in the hallway of the church. The oversized wooden doors, which have welcomed countless souls into this inner sanctum, stand on guard tonight. I have taken them for granted all this time, and yet these doors are at the heart of everything that transpires both within and outside of these walls. The keeper of secrets and the teller of truths. As church bells rang, these doors have opened wide most Sunday mornings for the past one hundred and five years. They stood their ground and protected the building during storms caused by Mother Nature and human strife.

In celebration, these doors have flung open with gaiety,

announcing the happy unions of husbands and wives on more Saturday afternoons than I can remember. They have welcomed mourners and said farewell to loved ones as they passed over the threshold one final time. As it is said the eyes are the window to the human soul, perhaps these stately, beautifully carved wooden doors are the entry point to where the human soul comes to rest, recover, and relive memories.

I take my time moving down the corridor. The white, intricately designed ceiling accents contrast the red, plush hall carpeting that has always felt like a prelude to the main event of the sanctuary. Tonight, I want nothing more than to drink it all in. I take photographs with my mind, holding on to every snapped image as if I am seeing the place for the first time. I can feel the hush of the sanctuary before I turn toward the open doors.

A memory of my wedding day flashes across my mind. I think of the moment right before the doors were pulled open, revealing me standing arm in arm with my father. I strode toward a new life with Rupert as my husband. That blessed day was one of the happiest of my life, and I watched it unfold through a magical veil of white cloud-like tulle.

I move into the sanctuary, patience guiding my experience. The ethereal nature of the space captures my attention. The sanctuary can make even the most alive of humans feel as if they are floating through space. I am uncertain whether the effect is from the light, the dome, the stained glass, the sheer vastness, or the beauty of the pipe organ. No matter the reason, I remember the feeling well. I feel precisely the same today as I did the very first day I stepped into my beloved sanctuary and fell in love.

My mind turns back in time, and I remember with fondness the pageants and the bake sales. The fundraising dinners and the knitting circles. In the early years, with Rupert by my side and in support of whatever I set my mind to, I took part in many of the activities Emily noted while reading *History of Woman's Work*. Having never seen the book before, I stayed quiet while Emily read through the thick edition. But I was quite pleased to see my name listed among the women, many of whom were my friends. We worked toward a vibrant future for our Seattle.

The curved pews welcome me to the choir loft. I have always believed music to be both an effective and joyful manner in which to connect spiritually. Sadly, I was never much of a singer, but oh how I coveted a spot among the choir. I got lost in the hymns when the award-winning choir raised their voices to heaven. If I concentrate hard enough, I can still hear them.

I desperately long to sit on a red, cushioned pew. Instead, I hover near one, taking in the vantage point of a congregation member. The hymn books have all been removed from the shelves set into the backs of each pew. Even the flowers, which generally appear in time for Sunday service, are missing. The lack of colorful flowers lining the tiered platform leading up to the choir loft makes the platform seem slightly too large for the pulpit atop it. Despite not yet having a clear direction with regard to its future, the emptiness of the sanctuary ushers in a feeling of impermanence. "Everyone is readying for a move, it seems." My voice is as quiet as my thoughts are deep.

I too must prepare for the move ahead. I think back, beyond the eighty years I have spent in the sanctuary as a woman between worlds. I try to work out how I reached Rupert when I came to visit him after he passed. The memory is unclear, and I wonder if lack of practice or disappointment have tempered my enthusiasm.

I bow my head and wait for words to come to me. I sit in silence as remembrances of my life flit across my mind's eye. I search for Rupert's presence in each memory of our days and nights together. I call for him with my eyes squeezed shut and my heart open wide. I allow my mind to drift every which way, and I follow my scattered thoughts like a puppy follows its little girl.

CHAPTER 35

riday, August 21, 2015
Emily

Emily arrives at Murph's a good twenty minutes before she is scheduled to meet Ryan. She glances around the bar, searching for Allison.

"Hey, Emily." Allison pokes her head around the corner of the bar. "Why so shy? Your table is always ready. Come on in."

"Hi. Thanks, I will. I just— I was wondering if I could speak with you for a minute first." Emily's face flushes as she stumbles over her words.

"Sure thing. Give me a sec. I need to drop these off." Allison inclines her head toward the tray of drinks on the bar's sleek wooden surface. "Why don't you grab a seat in the restaurant, and I'll be right over."

The restaurant side of Murph's is still quiet this early on a

Friday evening, while the bar seems to have a continuous handful of patrons no matter the day or the hour. Tucking herself into a table for two at the back of the room, Emily decides the restaurant is a better atmosphere for dinner with Ryan. Planning to stay put, she removes her purse from her shoulder and hangs it on the corner of the chair.

"Sorry about that. Friday afternoon crowd. You know the type." Allison pulls out the chair across from Emily and sits down. "What's up? Everything okay with you?"

Emily nods. "It is. Actually, I believe everything will be fine from now on." Folding her hands in front of her, between an empty water glass and a white cloth napkin, Emily focuses on steadying the tremble that has taken up residence within her. Asking for help has never been her strong suit, but Emily knows that she must if she is serious about making lasting changes in her life. "I was hoping you could help me with something."

"Sure. How can I help?" Allison's ponytail sways back and forth as she nods her head with enthusiasm.

"I listened to what you said about grief, and I've been thinking about it for a while now." Emily pauses as she tries to read Allison's expression. "I have decided it is time for me to talk to someone. To get help. Professional help, I mean, and I was hoping we could meet up for coffee, if it is convenient for you. I—I don't want to take up too much of your time, but I thought you might be able to point me in the right direction. And I thought, well, we might have a lot in common. Do you think you could help me find someone?"

Allison's eyes fill with tears as she reaches for Emily's hands. "Emily, I am so pleased you asked me. I know this is not an easy step to take. To be honest, I have been sort of hoping you would confide in me. You have been coming in here every week for months now, and I could tell from the first day I met you that something was holding you back. I would be happy to have coffee with you. I know a few really great counselors in the city. I met them through my volunteer work over the years. We can sort out what kind of help you are looking for and then go from there. Emily, thank you for asking me. I would very much like to be your friend."

She squeezes Allison's hands, and tears fill Emily's eyes in response to Allison's kind words and generous nature. "I would like that too. More than you know."

They dab their eyes in unison, and giggles erupt as the tension of their shared emotional moment passes. Allison suggests a day and time to meet for coffee, then gives Emily a genuine hug before she returns to work on the bar side of Murph's.

Emily orders a bottle of wine before popping into the restroom to check her makeup in the mirror. She sends Ryan a text to let him know she has a table on the restaurant side. The wine and glasses have just arrived when Ryan walks through the door.

"Hey, Em." Ryan leans down and kisses her cheek.

"Hey, yourself." Emily says, beaming at him with a coy smile.

Ryan hangs his jacket over the back of his chair before pouring wine into both glasses. "An entire bottle?" His raised eyebrow meanders across the table, with a crooked smile not far behind. "You wouldn't be trying to take advantage of me, now would you, Ms. Reed?"

Emily pushes down a laugh and holds her serious expression. "I wouldn't dare think such a thing, sir."

Ryan laughs good-naturedly as the waitress approaches the table, pen in hand and ready to take their orders.

Feeling in the mood to celebrate, Emily orders Murph's famous onion rings, nestled beside an eight ounce tenderloin.

"We are celebrating, I see." Ryan nods in Emily's direction before returning his attention to the waitress. "I'll have the same but with bacon-wrapped scallops to start, please."

"So, did you speak with Allison?" Ryan asks as he places his napkin in his lap.

"I did. We have coffee planned for next week." Emily's eyes flick up to meet Ryan's. "Did you think I wouldn't?" Emily folds her hands on the table. "I told you I would start counseling, and I meant it."

Without missing a beat, Ryan lifts his glass. "To you, then, for finishing projects and moving forward."

Emily clinks her glass against his. "Thank you." She takes a sip as her mind spins in circles, still searching for a way to share three items of importance with him.

"Okay, Em, what is it? What is going on in that head of yours?" Ryan chuckles before setting his glass down. "I swear I can hear the gears turning."

Taking in a lungful of air, Emily reaches for Ryan's hands and gives them a quick squeeze. "I have been meaning to talk to you about something, and I, well, I don't want you to think I've lost my marbles. I'm not sure how to phrase it so it will make sense."

"Emily." Ryan's voice cuts through. "You can tell me. You can tell me anything."

Emily picks up her wineglass again. "Don't say I didn't warn you." Looking over the rim of the glass, she takes a gulp and presses on. "You remember me telling you about Pastor Michael?"

"Sure, the pastor from the church. He is the one who filled you in on some historical tidbits."

"Well, it turns out that Pastor Michael was actually the minister who married my parents." Emily lets the words hang between them.

"No way! What a coincidence, Em." Ryan's eyes light up as his whole face smiles. "Was he able to tell you anything about your parents?"

The bacon-wrapped scallops arrive, halting the conversation for a moment as the waitress places them in the center of the table. She pours more wine into both of their glasses before returning to the kitchen.

"Not exactly." Emily's lips release the words slowly.

Ryan has a scallop halfway to his lips. "What do you mean? I imagine he doesn't remember every detail, but surely he must remember something."

"Well." Emily draws out the word. "It seems Pastor Michael passed away in 1983."

"Wait. What?" Ryan's expression shifts from happy to puzzled in a matter of seconds. "How is that possible?"

"I'm not entirely sure." Emily leans over the table toward Ryan, glancing around the restaurant to ensure nobody is listening to their conversation before she whispers, "But I think he might be a ghost or something."

Always ready with a clever comment, Ryan says nothing. He stares at Emily, disbelief plastered across his face.

"I realize it sounds a little crazy." Emily twirls her finger beside her head. "But I've been over this in my mind a million times. There is no conceivable way I could have known what he looked like, what he talked like, what a kind and generous soul he was. And I knew all of that before I learned he had passed away thirty-two years ago."

"But how?" Ryan is struggling to put words together. "Did he actually marry your parents?"

Emily smiles. "Yes, he did. It might have been the last wedding he performed, come to think of it." Emily feels as if another puzzle piece is clicking into place. "Maybe that is why he appeared to me. Perhaps he showed up to take care of unfinished business."

"He is real, then? To you, he is real?" Ryan takes another mouthful of wine, regaining his composure.

"He was very real to me." Emily reaches for a scallop, placing it on her side plate. "He was real. I saw him several times every week for months. Up until I learned he had died, that is. After I learned of his death, I never saw him again." Emily's words are laced with sadness.

Ryan has recovered almost entirely. "You miss him, don't you?"

"Yes. Yes, I do." Emily shrugs as a tear slides from her eye.

"Then I believe you, Em. I can't begin to explain it, the how and the why of it, but I believe you." Ryan extends his hand toward her. "It would be impossible to miss someone you didn't know."

Emily half smiles, half cries as she takes Ryan's hand. "I have so many things I'd like to ask him now. He always had a sage bit of advice, and he talked like a greeting card, with little quips of wisdom. And he had, oh Ryan, he had the sweetest smile I've ever seen and these twinkling blue eyes."

"He sounds wonderful." Ryan caresses Emily's hand with his thumb.

"He was. He was wonderful."

Dinner arrives before they have eaten the scallops. With a slight shuffle of plates and glasses, they make enough room for the dinner plates.

They nibble at their meals, sipping wine until the bottle is almost empty. Emily tells Ryan how she learned of Pastor Michael's status, laughing at how she dashed out of the office, leaving poor Mrs. Peters to wonder about Emily's sanity. Emily shared how, the next day, she and Mrs. Peters discussed the situation. The kind woman admitted that it wasn't the first time someone in the church had mentioned unusual experiences. Mrs. Peters didn't elaborate, but Emily is inclined to believe that Mrs. Peters, like the sanctuary walls, knows more than she lets on.

Emily places her plate to the side, wiping grease from the onion rings off her fingers. "Then, on the last day of work at the church." Emily sips the rest of wine from her glass. "Mrs. Peters left me one last box to archive. She said she found it buried in her office closet." Emily reaches for her wineglass before realizing it is already empty. "I think we are going to need another bottle of wine."

Ryan looks up from stealing Emily's remaining onion rings. "There is more?"

"Oh yeah. There is more."

Ryan signals for the waitress and orders another bottle of wine. He scoops all of Emily's onion rings onto his plate and hands the waitress the empty plate. "I'm listening," he says as he dips another onion ring into sauce before popping it into his mouth.

"So." Emily leans in. "In the last box was this amazing book detailing women's work over a century. It is absolutely incredible. Anyway." Emily leans back and reaches into her purse, pulling out the blue leather-bound book. "This was also in the box, with a note from Mrs. Peters saying she felt the book had been left for me by Pastor Michael."

"What? How? Why?" Ryan's words echo Emily's own thoughts from the day she discovered the book.

"I have no idea, but that is what the note said." Emily places the notebook on the table and rests a protective hand on its cover.

The new bottle of wine arrives, and both of them decline dessert as the waitress pours the glasses. Clearing the remaining plates, she leaves, and the conversation continues.

"This leads me to my third and final announcement of the evening." Emily takes another large sip of wine before forging ahead. "I don't think I want to be a lawyer anymore." Emily pushes on, motivated by a fear of not saying what she must. The words spill from her lips like a racehorse rushing through the starting gate. "Aside from the research part of the job, I don't actually enjoy legal work. The hours aren't sustainable for a well-balanced life, and to be honest, I am not sure my heart can take the continual battering when the legal opinion doesn't coincide with my personal beliefs." She pauses a moment to gather her thoughts. "I guess I didn't really consider any other career as an option. It may have been a childlike delusion, but it was my way of paying tribute to my parents and the way they lived their lives. I wanted to be like them. And I suppose since I went from one household filled with lawyers to another when I moved in with Colin and Veronica, other career options didn't present themselves to me." Emily holds her breath, waiting for Ryan's reaction.

After a moment's pause, Ryan's face relaxes. "Oh good! I was worried it was something more serious. I wasn't sure how much more I could handle tonight, with or without wine." Ryan's relief is palpable as he raises his glass again. "Sorry." He ducks his head, mocking his potential misstep. "I should have started with, how come, Em? Why the change of heart?"

"What?" Emily is stunned by Ryan's nonchalant response. "You don't seem surprised."

"To be honest, Em, I haven't ever thought a career as a lawyer really suited you."

"You do realize I spent a lot of time and a ton of money getting my law degree? Right?" Emily should feel relief at his reaction, but Ryan's response leaves her wondering why it has taken her so long to reach the same conclusion.

"Life happens, Em." Ryan shrugs and tilts his head in an

easygoing, what-are-you-going-to-do-about-it kind of way. "Simply adjust your sails, and your path forward can be whatever you want it to be. It may be hard work, but then again, you've never shied away from a little hard work." Ryan squeezes her hand in the middle of the table. "We can figure it out together. Do you have any thoughts on what direction you would like to go? What will make you happy, Em?"

Picking up the notebook from the table, Emily holds it in her free hand, a sudden burst of enthusiasm fueling her words. "I want to write stories about historic buildings. You know how much I love the research, and I am good at it." Emily's gaze lowers, embarrassed at having spoken her new truth out loud. "Besides, somebody needs to pay proper respect to these buildings, especially before they are torn down. Pastor Michael once told me that the walls of the sanctuary had stories to share. I believe I am the one who is supposed to share them."

"A writer, huh?" Ryan nods and a wide smile spreads across his face. "I can see you as a writer."

Emily's smile matches Ryan's. "I made a few phone calls this week, and it turns out Historic Seattle needs some assistance." Emily's eyes twinkle in anticipation of her new adventure. "I will volunteer to start, but the opportunity will allow me to learn so much more about Seattle's historic sites and the preservation process. I have offered to write highlights for their quarterly newsletter, featuring historic buildings that are being preserved and those in need of saving. I've also offered to assist them with some pro bono legal work. I think it will help me learn a lot about the intricacies of working with historic architecture."

Ryan leans forward, his face mirroring Emily's in excitement. "Sounds promising."

"Then, perhaps after I get my feet wet, I might try my

hand at writing a book about the church." Emily's cheeks blush with her admission.

"I think you can do anything you put your mind to, Em." Ryan squeezes her hand. "I can't wait to see what you come up with."

CHAPTER 36

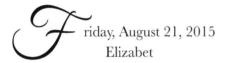riday, August 21, 2015
Elizabet

I remain in quiet contemplation, like a monk who's been hidden away in a cave at the top of a mountain. With little else to occupy my mind and no one to talk to, I am drawn deep into my consciousness. There is nowhere to hide in the quiet of my contemplative mind. My heart and soul lay bare as I filter through all I have come to understand.

I have sought to locate Rupert, but after many hours of thoughtful prayer, he has not materialized. When given the time to consider one's actions, it can be somewhat embarrassing to realize where one went wrong. After much concentrated thought on the subject, I have determined that I alone am to blame for the sorrow that has been so prevalent all these years.

I think on this outcome for as long as the sky is dark, wrangling with the question of whether I have learned something from Rupert's death. As the sky changes, lightening with the day's arrival, I still have no understanding of the reason for grief. A niggling suspicion is all I have to show for eighty years, plus a night spent in deep contemplation. I wonder, though, was my grief over what was lost supposed to teach me how to live again? Perhaps this is the reason why Rupert has yet to appear to me. I was the one who stopped living; he was merely the one who died.

Leave it to the living to muck things up for themselves, I muse. Pastor Michael pointed out in his sermon to a vacant congregation, "Free will may not always be easy, but it is always available to us." Free will might just be our biggest downfall, but it is also how we become completely ourselves in life, and apparently in death.

The sun is up, its beam filtering through the stained glass and onto the carpet of the sanctuary. Dorothea sweeps into the sanctuary like a fresh morning breeze, eagerness written all over her expression.

"How was your night, Elizabet?" Dorothea glides toward me, a confident smile upon her lips.

"Long and somewhat difficult." I do not wish to elaborate, fearing the muddled ideas mingling within my mind will not become any clearer should I set them free.

"No Rupert, I presume."

"No, you were quite correct in that department. Rupert is no longer in the sanctuary. I suppose he hasn't been for quite some time now, though I haven't allowed myself to believe it. I should have listened to you sooner."

"Come now, Elizabet. Don't be so hard on yourself. We did have some right jovial times here, did we not? Think of it. If you had listened to me sooner, we would never have met Emily. I do believe she was worth sticking around for. It was meant to be, after all. She needed us as much as we needed her in the end. Promise me you will never be sorry for paths taken. Pastor Michael always says that things work out how they are supposed to. We may not always know every inch of the plan, but we do know how to move forward. Moving forward is all we can expect of ourselves, don't you think?"

"Dorothea, dear, you are a gem. One of a kind, with a heart of gold."

"Oh, Elizabet. Stop now, you'll make me blush." Dorothea gives a deep curtsy and lifts her head. "Are we ready, then?"

"As ready as I ever expect to be, I suppose." My voice is weary, but my resolve is solid.

I take one more look around the sanctuary, trying desperately to memorize it for eternity. Dorothea is by my side, linking her arm in mine. Her confidence is contagious, and I can't help but smile back at her.

With a quick glance my way, Dorothea provides the only instructions needed, in a calm and confident voice. "Fill your heart with love, Elizabet. Love is all anyone ever needs to move forward."

The sunbeam expands, growing wider and more intense in brightness and warmth. We are engulfed within its light. I look around and find there is no place where the light does not touch. The vibrant and all-encompassing light drowns out the darkness and the fear. With a nudge from Dorothea, I step toward the center of the light, and the sanctuary disappears around us.

All that exists is light. Glorious, brilliant, loving light. I feel transported. The farther I venture from within the sanctuary walls, the more overcome I am by joy. The journey is both long and instantaneous, and at the end I see him. My Rupert is standing before me, a familiar smile upon his lips. Arms open wide, ready for my embrace. "What took you so long, my dear? I've been waiting for you all this time."

CHAPTER 37

 riday, August 21, 2015
Emily

"Well," Ryan says, air whooshing past his lips. "Now might be the best time for me to tell you my news."

Emily's eyes widen as Ryan delays by topping off their glasses of wine. Emily leans forward with anticipation and a touch of impatience.

"I didn't want to say anything until the deal was done." Ryan lets the words linger between them, teasing her with his boyish smile.

"Yes?" Emily traces the stem of her wineglass with one finger.

"As of this afternoon, they finalized a deal between the First United Methodist Church of Seattle and the development company I was telling you about." Ryan waits to let the news sink in.

"They are saving the church?" In response to Ryan's nodding head, Emily repeats herself enthusiastically. "They are saving the church!"

"Yes. They are saving the church." Ryan laughs as Emily erupts from her seat, rushing around the square table to wrap him in an exuberant hug.

Tears spring to Emily's eyes, and she dabs them with her napkin. "I am stunned. This is amazing," she says. "I am relieved and stunned."

Emily settles herself back into her chair. Even in the dim restaurant lighting, her expression mimics that of a child who has just learned she is getting a pony for her birthday.

Ryan fills in the details as Emily listens, a wide smile pasted on her lips. "My coworker—Rob is his name—called me into his office after I returned from a lunch meeting this afternoon. Our contact at the development company telephoned him as soon as the ink had dried on the contract. Rob said he had reached out to him a few weeks back to check in. He mentioned a personal connection regarding the church's outcome and asked for them to let him know if anything came to be.

"It will take some time," Ryan continues, "but in a nutshell, the deal includes the church getting a new, more suitable location within the city. The developer will design and build a new church building for them. And the developer gets the existing sanctuary building and all the surrounding property previously owned by the church."

"They will be thrilled, the church administrators and the congregation, I mean." Emily's fondness for the church and its people is evident in her delighted expression. "Did Rob say what they plan to do with the building?"

"I think they are planning to build a tower for offices

beside the sanctuary and then weave the old with the new for a hotel or something. I am sure the details will get sorted out soon. But the good news is that everyone wins this time around." Ryan, clearly pleased to be the bearer of such news, watches Emily as she relishes in the fortunate outcome for the church she loves so dearly.

Ryan lets a few moments pass before he lifts his glass. "So, Emily Reed, where do we go from here?"

Emily can barely contain herself as she raises her glass. She winks at Ryan as they toast. "We need a plan."

"We definitely need a plan," Ryan replies as they sip their wine, silly grins upon both of their faces.

"Well, for starters." Emily takes another sip before setting her glass down. "I was thinking I would remain at Patterson and Holt for another two years or so. I don't want to be rash or irresponsible and dive headfirst into a new career. Though deeply intriguing for me at the moment, it might not work out financially."

"Okay, so we are looking at a two-year plan." Ryan motions for the waitress and pulls his wallet from his back pocket.

"I think so. Two years should give me enough time to wrap my head around how Historic Seattle works and how I can be of service to the organization. I have the beginnings of a story rattling around in the back of my head, so I was thinking I could play with the idea for a while and see if I have enough for a book. I haven't decided whether to go straight down the nonfiction route or to weave in a fictional story. And I'm not entirely sure of how the actual writing will unfold. I've never done anything like this before, so I am certain there will be a steep learning curve, like as steep as Denny Hill before the regrade."

Ryan chuckles. The waitress approaches the table with the bill and the credit card machine. Emily makes small talk with her about the meal and the warm evening while Ryan pays the bill.

Emily slides the notebook back into her purse before placing the purse strap over her shoulder. "Shall we walk?" she asks Ryan as they stand, smiling at one another as they test out their wine-infused legs.

Ryan places a gentle hand on Emily's back and guides her toward the exit. With a quick wave to Allison, they are out the door. With the fresh air providing an extra burst of invigoration, Emily returns the conversation to the practical side of things. "Either way, I will probably need to spend some time at the library. The Seattle Room is a gold mine for historic records. I am sure I can find what I am looking for there."

"Well, you are in luck. I happen to love the Seattle Public Library. I have my own library card and everything. Want to see it? I have it right here in my wallet. It is that important to me." Ryan reaches for his wallet, his eyes laughing in jest. "Seriously, though, perhaps we can turn some of our weekend time together into a journey, uncovering the mysteries of Seattle's historic and might I add colorful past, especially if the past includes Madame Lou."

"I would like that very much." Emily wraps both arms around Ryan's waist as they stroll along the sidewalk. "There is a lot to do, isn't there?" Emily's voice sounds a little more subdued than she intended. With her plan making its way from the confines of her head into actual conversation, Emily feels a tingle of trepidation crawling up the back of her neck.

"Piece of cake, Em." Ryan squeezes his arm around her shoulders, pulling her closer in a supportive gesture. "One step at a time. Don't let the big picture scare you out of taking the small steps."

Emily has never spoken to Ryan about the money her parents left for her. She has never spoken to anyone about it at great length. She doesn't even think much about it herself. Whenever Colin wanted to discuss some aspect of the estate with her, she would simply wave her hand at him and tell him to do whatever he thought was right. Emily clears her throat and pulls away from Ryan's arm to meet his gaze. "My inheritance comes through when I turn twenty-nine. If things work out like I hope they will, I could use some of the money my mom and dad left me to help make the transition from lawyer to writer."

"The plot thickens." Ryan teases her, making theatrical sounds. "Buh buh buh bum . . . What else have you been keeping under wraps all this time?"

Emily thinks a moment before replying, "I will have the house too."

Ryan's eyes go wide. "You own a house? In Seattle? Why on earth are you living in that tiny apartment? But more importantly, why in the world are you paying rent on that tiny apartment?"

"Touché." Emily nods her head in his direction. "It's complicated."

Ryan guides her to a dark green bench overlooking Elliott Bay.

Taking a deep breath, Emily shares the details that she remembers about the estate. "I couldn't deal with selling my childhood home after my parents' accident. It was the one thing I had a complete and, if I remember correctly, more than slightly embarrassing fit about. The problem was I didn't have the financial resources necessary for the house's upkeep.

Colin was my parents' lawyer for the estate, so he went before the judge and arranged things so the house would be waiting for me when I received my inheritance, at twenty-nine."

Ryan shakes his head in disbelief.

Emily smiles with an innocent expression and raises her hands in an oops gesture. "It helped that my parents were beloved lawyers in the community with a straightforward will and an only child as their heir. They rolled the whole lot into my inheritance. Colin arranged for movers and renters. He was my dad's best friend, so he just sort of takes care of it for me. He collects the rent and ensures the house is being cared for."

"I can't believe you've never mentioned this before, Em."

"I guess I didn't think it was pertinent." Emily smiles sheepishly at Ryan. "But I'm telling you now." Emily swings her feet backward and forward, shuffling them across the top of the paved walkway. "Did I forget to mention how I've managed to sweep all of my emotions, my past, and my worst fears under a rug for ten years?" Emily laughs at herself. "I did everything I could to keep from thinking about this kind of stuff, Ryan. I wasn't keeping you in the dark for any reason other than the fact that I didn't want to deal with it myself."

"So, in April 2018, everything, the entire estate, reverts into your name?"

"Pretty much. I'm sure there will be papers to sign and other things to consider, but yeah, that about sums it up."

"Huh. Well that is something I never would have guessed about you, Em."

"I strive to be mysterious." Emily raises her eyebrows at him in jest before leaning against Ryan's chest.

"Mission accomplished," Ryan whispers as he holds her close, his chin on top of her head.

"What do you think?" Emily tilts her chin to meet his eyes in the moonlight. "Do you think we can make it?"

Ryan kisses her nose. "Piece of cake, Em. Piece of cake." Hand in hand, they continue their stroll toward Emily's apartment.

"Piece of cake," Emily murmurs, and she smiles.

CHAPTER 38

*S*aturday, December 31, 2017
Emily

Emily steps over the threshold, the wide wooden doors spread open like the arms of a welcoming great aunt, eager for a hug. The sensation of her black heels sinking into the luxurious red carpeting sends her back in time. She pauses, taking in the comfortable feeling of being inside the former church. Ryan steps from behind her, placing a protective hand at the small of Emily's back. "You okay, Em?"

She nods, looking into his concerned eyes. "Never better."

They make their way through the security line to the coat check, Ryan tucking the coat-check ticket into the breast pocket of his tux. Emily takes a deep breath and glances at her deep red lipstick in her miniature mirror. She slips the mirror back into her black evening bag before she steps into the hallway that leads to the sanctuary.

It has been a little less than two and half years since

Emily has stepped foot in this building, now aptly named The Event Center. Renovated and rebranded as Seattle's newest hot spot for special events, tonight is the gala opening where they will ring in the new year. Given Patterson and Holt's deep connection with the building's history, not to mention the firm's involvement in helping negotiate the deal between the church and the development company, all of the employees were invited to celebrate the building's reopening.

The guest list is impressive, including Denny family descendants and the mayor of Seattle. Press members are already positioned inside and outside of the venue, ready to capture key moments of the evening's festivities. Ryan squeezes Emily's hand as they shuffle toward the heart of the building, following a lengthy line of party guests.

Other than a fresh coat of paint, the elaborate hall, with its intricately curved and detailed archways, remains unchanged and as beautiful as ever. Emily lets out a breath. As the line moves forward, she decides her nerves are due to the possibility of the sanctuary being altered beyond recognition. Without missing a beat, Emily chastises herself for this foolish and unwarranted logic, given the great deal of effort and money invested to save the building. She argues with her overly emotional side. Of course the sanctuary will look different. But the sanctuary remains, and that is all that should matter.

The line moves slowly, allowing Emily to take in every detail. She tilts her head to examine the lighting, wracking her brain to remember whether the fixtures are original. Ryan stifles a chuckle. "It will be okay, Em. Piece of cake. Right?"

"Piece of cake," Emily replies with a steady nod and a slow exhale. After their celebratory dinner at Murph's back in August 2015, *piece of cake* became their new code phrase. The acknowledgment that, together, they have gone through tougher things and are stronger for them.

The line moves, and Emily and Ryan step into the vast and open space that used to be the sanctuary. Emily's breath hitches in her throat as the elegant, stunning room captures her full attention. Unsurprisingly, the pipe organ and church pews have been removed. What she notices most, though, is the feeling that washes over her. The hush of the sanctuary. The serenity within its walls. The secrets it keeps and the prayers it has witnessed all remain. Within the sanctuary, the heartbeat of the building lives on.

Tears prickle the corners of Emily's eyes as she pivots. Her floor-length, spaghetti-strapped black gown skims the new carpet featuring a swirling design. She takes in each section of the round room. Emily's eyes drift toward the upper balcony, where a neon halo keeps watch over the room below. She suppresses a giggle at the lighthearted reference to the building's origins. Now, one can grab a drink from the Halo Bar.

Ryan's eyes meet hers. "So, what do you think?"

"Different but the same." Emily smiles up at him, her fingers lacing within his. "It would be a great venue."

Ryan's face lights up, following her train of thought with rapid speed. "I like the way you think, Emily Reed. I will put in a call next week and see what they have available for June. We decided on a June wedding, didn't we?"

"Yes, June. Or whenever they have available." Emily nods, her eyes still roaming around the space. "I want us to be a part of this history too." She squeezes Ryan's hand. "I'd marry you on a Wednesday if that is the only day they have available."

"A Wednesday it is, then," Ryan teases before pulling her close and brushing her lips with his. "Shall I fetch us a drink from the Halo Bar?"

"Yes." Emily smiles, hiding a laugh behind her fingertips. "That will be a little odd, but lovely all the same."

As Ryan heads toward the stairs, Emily moves to the back of the room, seeking a better vantage point to take in the room.

"Ah, Emily. There you are." Richard Holt, partner at Patterson and Holt and Emily's soon-to-be former boss, approaches her from across the room.

"Mr. Holt. How are you? Did you have a good Christmas?"

"I think we can stop with this 'Mr. Holt' nonsense now that you won't be under our employ, don't you think? 'Richard' is fine, Emily." He wraps her into a hug fit for a daughter. "We are sad to see you go."

"Thank you." Emily stumbles before adding, "Richard." Her cheeks flush with the change in status between them.

"You are always welcome back. I want to be sure you know how much we have valued your work these past few years. Though I do not expect it to be the case, if life as a part-time member of the Historic Seattle legal team and a budding author does not suit you, it would thrill us to work with you again."

"I appreciate the sentiment." Emily's eyes roam, and she catches sight of a familiar face in the crowd.

"I have no doubt, Emily, you will leave your own mark on the history of Seattle." Richard leans in and lowers his voice an octave. "However, we may call on your research expertise from time to time, if it isn't too much of a bother."

"Anytime. It would be my pleasure. Anything you need."

Richard opens his arms as a woman approaches. "Well, Mrs. Peters. It is so lovely to see you. How is the new church?"

"Oh, Mr. Holt. It is just wonderful. The new church, though not as grand as this, is warm and welcoming. It has an airiness that reminds me of this beautiful old building. They have done a masterful job of recreating the spirit of our congregation."

Mrs. Peters directs her attention toward Emily, placing a hand on her bare arm. "Ms. Reed, I am delighted to find you so well, dear."

"It is very nice to see you, Mrs. Peters. I have thought of you often over the past two years." Not long after Emily left the church for the last time, she began to unravel the story of her experiences within its walls. On more than one occasion she has wondered what secrets Mrs. Peters really holds. No matter which way she spins it, Emily can't imagine that the trusted church administrator did not know about the goings on within the building.

"I understand you put that little blue notebook to good use." The twinkle in her eye gives away her secret, if only for a fleeting moment.

It is impossible for Emily not to smile at the mention of Pastor Michael's notebook. "I did. I hope you will be pleased with the result."

"I have every confidence that it will be just as it needs to be, dear. I do look forward to reading your novel though. When will it be available?"

"This coming April." Emily spots Ryan maneuvering through the crowd with two tall glasses of champagne. "I will pop by the new church with a finished copy for you as soon as I have one available."

"That would be lovely, dear. I am so looking forward to reading it. I see your young man, Ms. Reed. Things worked out well for you." Mrs. Peters winks and nudges the diamond sparkling on Emily's left hand. "I will let you young ones enjoy the party. I look forward to seeing you in April, Ms. Reed. Mr. Holt, always nice to see you, but so much nicer when a lawsuit is not in the works, I must say. Enjoy the evening."

Mrs. Peters shuffles away to join a conversation among other church members, and Emily's eyes lock on Ryan.

Before he reaches her, a slender, dark-haired woman approaches. The woman is wearing a formal green evening gown that sets her eyes aglow. "Pardon me, Ms. Reed? Hello. My name is Amanda. I work with the *Seattle Times* book review team. Your publisher said you would be attending tonight's event. I hope this isn't too much of an intrusion."

"Not at all. Amanda, is it?" Emily accepts a crystal glass from Ryan. He shakes hands with Richard, and the two of them exchange pleasantries.

"I received an advanced copy of your book," Amanda says, "and I was hoping to get a quick photo with you." She pulls an advanced hardback copy of *If These Walls Could Talk* from her bag. "I have to tell you how much I enjoyed your story. The history felt almost magical."

"Thank you for your kind words. I am happy to hear you enjoyed it." Emily places her glass of champagne on a high table and joins Amanda. They pivot themselves to place the crowded room in the background.

Summoning a photographer for the photo, Amanda holds up her copy of the book and they smile on cue. Before parting ways, Emily pulls her phone from her evening bag, and they take an informal selfie for Emily's social media feed. Thanking Amanda for her interest in the book, Emily tells her she will make herself available for an interview in the coming months.

With her phone in hand, Emily returns to Ryan's side. A wide smile spreads across her face.

"I see I will have to fight off the press." Ryan's arm slips around her waist, and she leans in to him with a delighted giggle.

Holding her phone up to eye level, Emily taps the screen to show Ryan the selfie. Emily's eyes go wide at first before narrowing into a squint. "Is that . . .?" Ryan peers over her shoulder and reaches around her, trying to steady Emily's shaking hand. "Do you see them too?"

They both swivel rapidly, their eyes scanning the upper balcony. Though crowded with partygoers dressed in tuxes and evening gowns, the balcony is vacant of the three people Emily most desires to see. She searches the space where the choir loft and pipe organ used to live. Emily's eyes dart around the room before she stops abruptly to calm herself, demanding she take a moment to think rationally.

Remembering the photo she took of the black-and-white photograph, the one with Elizabet and Dorothea posing together in Elizabet's mansion, Emily swipes at her phone with hurried movements. She flips back and forth between the old photo and the selfie with Amanda, showing Ryan the comparison. The recent photo shows only three faint silhouettes, two female and one male, far behind Emily's and Amanda's smiling faces. However, the outline of a feather catches her breath. "Dorothea's plume," Emily whispers.

Emily is quick to doubt her discovery. But as she does, the familiar scent of vintage perfume fills the air. She closes her eyes and inhales. As she sniffs the air, a warm sensation runs the length of Emily's spine. A warm and loving feeling wraps around her body, and a single tear slips from beneath Emily's closed eyelids.

The words are upon her, lingering as if floating atop a breeze. "These walls have stories to share, lessons to teach, prayers to hear, and weary hearts to console. You were the one they were intended for, Emily. It was all for you."

Emily's eyes fly open. She hears his voice as clear as if he were standing right before her. And there he is, a few feet away from her, tucked among the well-dressed and jubilant crowd. Dressed in his dark blue suit and white collar, Pastor Michael gives her an impish smile. His eyes twinkle in the light as he places a finger alongside his nose, a secret shared between them once more.

"Thank you," Emily whispers. "Thank you for showing me the importance of all that was, and all that is meant to be."

With a kind smile and a wink of his eye, Pastor Michael dips his head in a final nod. With his hands clasped behind his back, he strolls away, disappearing into the filtered light of the sanctuary.

AUTHOR NOTES

~

While researching the historical aspects of my books I usually come across some historical tidbits that are simply too good not to share. Those familiar with Seattle's history will already be acquainted with Lou Graham. Dorothea is the only character featured in the story who existed in real life. That being said, she did not actually live during the time period where the story takes place. Instead, Dorothea Georgine Emile Ohben, simply known as Madame Lou, was born in Germany around 1857. During her lifetime she traveled to Seattle where she opened and operated a highly successful brothel before moving to San Francisco where she passed away in 1905 at the age of 48. Further inquiry into Dorothea as a character was inspired by Amanda Robb, an underground tour of Seattle, and a handful of books written by Seattle authors. Since her name kept popping up at every turn, she managed to nudge her way into the narrative with a deft hand. I have fictionalized her in many ways, but it seems to be well accepted line of thinking that back in the day, more business was indeed transacted at Madame Lou's than ever was completed at city hall.

The other area where the story detoured from historical fact was with regards to the legal battle between the First Church of Seattle and the Landmarks Board. The court case took place over many years and the timeline of events have been altered and repositioned for the sake of the fictional story. A decades long legal battle is a tad dry for a work of fiction, but it is important to note that the Supreme Court of Washington's final decision was precedent setting and the court ruled that churches in Washington state could not be designated as landmark sites without the approval and consent of their congregations.

For simplicity sake, I have referred to the entire area of the church's inner sanctum as the sanctuary. Many churches today use similar terminology but to be historically accurate, the specific area where the congregation sits in a United Methodist church is called the nave. The sanctuary is considered the holiest of spaces within the worship area and is where the Eucharistic sacrifice is offered and where the clergy perform the service from. The sanctuary is often located behind an altar rail and in some cases a screen.

When it comes to the narthex, I actually wrote the entire novel using the word "lobby". It wasn't until beloved fellow historical fiction author and beta reader Kelsey Gietl questioned me on the terminology. After several hours spent researching terminology, I was pretty close to throwing in the towel and leaving the gathering space just inside the church doors as the "lobby" when I stumbled across the reason a church does not call the space a lobby. The word lobby has a political heritage referring to where lobbyists would gather with the intent to influence the lawmakers. With this in mind, I decided the change to narthex was both important and warranted.

I am delighted to share with you that the story about the Fresh Air Cottage, the children's orthopedic hospital, is a factual mention, though the framed dime from within the story's pages is entirely fictional to my knowledge. Spoiler alert! The Fresh Air Cottage was only the beginning. These women truly did exceptional things.

Though Dorothea is the only true to life character in the story, many of the historical details were inspired by real people and events. For example, Alberta H. Reynolds was inspired by the very real Mother Ryther. I retained the same middle initial of "H" as a nod to the woman who may have been responsible for establishing Seattle's first orphanage, official or not.

You will be pleased to know as well that the church building on the corner of Fifth and Marion does exist, and it is as beautiful as you might imagine it to be. The building has been dutifully restored, keeping the history alive, though the exact agreement, transactions, business purposes and use of the building are unconfirmed to me and thus cannot be taken as fact.

The radio station KDKA was likely not represented over the Seattle airways during the presidential election and talking boxes, aka radios, did not have wide distribution throughout the US during the timeframe mentioned.

I have used aspects of the Leary mansion, now the Diocesan House, as inspiration for the home that my fictional character Elizabet resided in on Capitol Hill. In addition, I was inspired by tales told to me during a tour of the mansion, though I have woven them among a great deal of fiction. One story in particular stood out to me and I was compelled to include the idea of Eliza Leary's horse drawn carriage rides into downtown Seattle. Apparently, Mrs. Leary did indeed travel by horse drawn carriage whenever she visited the downtown core and she did so all the way up until her final years in 1935. To me, the tale was another nugget demonstrating once again the tenacity of the women of Seattle.

The History of Woman's Work is a very real, very large book impressively created by the women of the First United Methodist Church of Seattle. I am indebted to both the church and Claire Gebben, church archivist, for sharing details about the building and the church community, while inspiring me with flourishes of color to the fictional aspect of the story itself. You can view the church's history on their website at www.firstchurchseattle.org and if you find yourself in Seattle, consider popping by for a Sunday service. They are truly a welcoming bunch and the sanctuary in their most recent location on Denny Way is stunning in its own right.

If you would like to know more about my inspiration and research, along with the truths and tales of All That Was, please subscribe to my newsletter where you will receive an eBook copy of At the Corner of Fiction & History, Facts and Follies that Inspire the Stories. This newsletter exclusive eBook dives into each of my novels as I take you behind the scenes and into the past that helps to shape the stories you have read.

Thank you again for reading All That Was. I hope you enjoyed the novel. I would love for you to leave a review at your favorite online book retailer as well as other book loving community sites such as BookBub and Goodreads. Reviews not only allow a book to become known by other readers, they are like a "hug" to an author. A simple line or two telling other readers what you enjoyed about the story is all it takes. Thank you for supporting authors by reading their books.

ACKNOWLEDGMENTS

∽

As always, I am humbled by the opportunity to be inspired by history while at the same time enjoying the luxury artistic license allows to fill in the blank spaces with fiction. My journey into Seattle's past was guided by the passion of others and I am indebted to many for their generosity of time and historical insights that helped shape the story of All That Was.

This story would not exist had it not been for my husband who suggested we check out an old building in downtown Seattle while visiting the city for a Red Sox game. From that moment on, my love for the historic First Church building and the city of Seattle brought to life a thousand questions that I eagerly wanted answers to and thus began my search for more information.

Libraries are a constant source of inspiration and knowledge and I am grateful to the many librarians who assisted my search. Thanks to The New York Public Library, The University of British Columbia Koerner Library, Drew University, The University of Washington Library, and the Seattle Public Library with a special note of thanks to Joseph Bopp and the research gem that is The Seattle Room. Thanks also to Laura Edmonston at the Washington State Law Library for her quick reply with a bit of information I was desperately seeking while in the middle of an editorial deadline.

When I reached out to the librarians at the University of Washington, I found kindred spirits in Matthew Parsons (maps librarian), Jessica Albano (news librarian), and Amanda Robb (student librarian assistant) and I am full of gratitude for their knowledge, guidance, and interest in my novel. It was Amanda who commented on how interesting it would be to include Madame Lou in the novel and with my interest piqued, I set about to learn more about Seattle's famous Madame.

My perception of life as a young lawyer was influenced by three special people who freely gave of their time and knowledge over cocktails, dinner, and tea. Thank you to Laurence Scott, Emily Raven, and Clara Yoo. Your insights were responsible for creating Emily's character. Cheers!

To Diane Wells and Sherry Garman of The Episcopal Diocese of Olympia, I cannot thank you enough for your time and assistance. Sherry, the tour of the Leary mansion deeply altered the direction of the novel and for that I am thrilled to have had the honor of getting to know both you and Mrs. Leary through the history of her home. Perhaps another novel will be born out of our conversation and with it another trip to visit the beautiful home on the hill.

I am beyond grateful to church archivist Claire Gebben and the First United Methodist Church of Seattle for their willingness to share with me, their time, the church's history, photographs, archives, and an absolutely impressive collection of stories and accomplishments since its inception in 1853. The First Church of Seattle remains today at a new location at 180 Denny Way in a beautiful building that encompasses both the magic of the former 1910 church building and the beauty of the pacific northwest.

To my editor, Victoria Griffin, you never fail to call me out on what I leave off the page. I still don't know how you do it, but the story is what it needed to be because of your insight and encouragement. Your wisdom shines through and am grateful that you are first and foremost in the corner of the story that is waiting to be told. The greatest lesson I have learned from you, aside from the fact that my characters all too often nod their heads and shrug their shoulders, is to trust my own instincts. I will take that with me into the next project and beyond.

My cover artist is not only brilliantly talented, she is kind, generous, and thoughtful too. Ana Grigoriu you are a pleasure to work with and your care for the art and the people you work with shines through. Thank you for another stunning cover!

On a personal note, I have a multitude of people to thank for helping me get to the finish line with this novel. Huge hugs and a heartfelt thank you to Kari Wojak for her continual, unwavering support. It takes a special person to read and reread, and then read again every draft from a subpar attempt to a finished product. When you weren't rereading something

I wrote, you were there with a listening ear, offering up wise words of advice at every speedbump along the way and because of you, I never felt like I was alone in the process.

I am blessed to be surrounded by people who support me. Kelsey Gietl, your honesty and feedback are always appreciated. Your friendship, along with the novels you write, brighten my world. To, Kari, Kelsey, Tammy, Stefanie, Donna, Irene, Ginny, Kelly, Tanya, Janice, and Glen, you all make my world a better place. Thank you also to Carla Young for inspiring weekly check ins and for pushing me forward when my stubborn brain was getting in the way. I wish I could tell the world about your novels, so hurry up and finish them please!

My advanced reader team, simply put… you rock! Thank you for giving so much of your time and attention to my stories. I love sharing them with you. To the bookstagram community near and far, you restored my faith in human connections via social media. Thank you for sharing my stories with your own communities. The best friends are indeed book friends! Thanks so much to Suzanne Leopold for her love and support of both books and authors. A huge thank you to Samantha Pitsch for putting this author's mind at ease.

To my family, you are many but you all know who you are, thank you for your support and willingness to listen to me ramble about all things book related. To Dave and Justin, without you, this story would never have seen the light of day. Thank you for continuing to listen, encourage, nudge, and for pouring the Friday night wine. You two are the best research assistants I have ever had, and I am grateful every day for you. XOXO.

My dear readers, as Pastor Michael says, "to be of any value at all, a story requires two participants," thank you for being my plus one by reading the stories I write. It is a dream come true for me to be a writer and it wouldn't have been possible without you.

Xo,
Tanya

ABOUT THE AUTHOR

A writer from a young age, Tanya E Williams loves to help a reader get lost in another time, another place through the magic of books. History continues to inspire her stories and her insightful view into the human condition deepens her character's experiences and propels them on their journey. Ms. Williams' favorite tales, speak to the reader's heart, making them smile, laugh, cry, and think. *All That Was* is Tanya's fourth book of fiction.

facebook.com/authortanyawilliams

twitter.com/tanya_breathes

instagram.com/tanyaewilliams_author

ALSO BY TANYA E WILLIAMS

Becoming Mrs. Smith

Stealing Mr. Smith

A Man Called Smith

Breathe

Made in the USA
Columbia, SC
18 September 2020

21113199R00193